W WE DIED IN DEADWOOD.

DATE DUE

WHEN THE GOLD DUST DIED IN DEADWOOD

A TUCKER ASHLEY WESTERN
ADVENTURE

WHEN THE GOLD DUST
DIED IN DEADWOOD

C. M. WENDELBOE

FIVE STAR
A part of Gale, a Cengage Company

GALE
A Cengage Company

Farmington Hills, Mich • San Francisco • New York • Waterville, Maine
Meriden, Conn • Mason, Ohio • Chicago

LIBRARY OF CONGRESS CATALOGING-IN-PUBLICATION DATA

Names: Wendelboe, C. M., author.
Title: When the gold dust died in Deadwood / C. M. Wendelboe.
Description: First edition. | Waterville, Maine : Five Star, a part of Gale, a Cengage Company, [2019] | Series: A Tucker Ashley western adventure | Identifiers: LCCN 2019018319 (print) | ISBN 9781432866006 (hardcover : acid-free paper)
Subjects: | GSAFD: Western stories.
Classification: LCC PS3623.E53 W48 2019 (print) | DDC 813/.6—dc23
LC record available at https://lccn.loc.gov/2019018319

First Edition. First Printing: November 2019
Find us on Facebook—https://www.facebook.com/FiveStarCengage
Visit our website—http://www.gale.cengage.com/fivestar/
Contact Five Star Publishing at FiveStar@cengage.com

Printed in Mexico
1 2 3 4 5 6 7 23 22 21 20 19

ACKNOWLEDGEMENTS

I would like to thank the South Dakota Historical Society for much of the information contained herein, and Mike Runge of the Deadwood Historical Society for maps and information pertaining to the Deadwood area of the Black Hills. To my wife, Heather, my thanks for her support and keen eye for details.

This novel is for my wife, Heather, who continues being supportive and being a task master as she critiques and improves my books.

CHAPTER 1

Tucker Ashley stepped gingerly down from the freight wagon that had jarred his kidneys ever since leaving Cheyenne. He arched his back and stretched the kinks out. Riding the ox-drawn wagon these last weeks from Cheyenne to Custer City left him only slightly less sore than the cramped prison cell he'd occupied during the last two years. Both designed—he was certain—to cripple even a strong man. Which Tucker was certain he no longer was.

He counted the other freight wagons that stood waiting to be off-loaded at stores along Custer City's main street—eleven in a row. His wagon had hauled bolts of gingham and muslin, shoes and dresses of every fashion Montgomery Ward had to offer. Others, like the wagon in front of his, had hauled sugar and flour. A stiff wind caught a busted-open hundred-pound sack, and flour washed over Tucker like a miniature blizzard. The bullwhacker tilted his head back and laughed as Tucker brushed flour off his face. In another time—before his prison sentence—Tucker would shut the man's pie hole with a hard fist. But now all Tucker wanted to do was be left alone and start to live again. Like he'd been broken by the prison screws.

"Don't you go wandering off now," the bullwhacker said from his perch on the wagon seat. Where most ox men walked beside their oxen, this man was too fat and too lazy to climb off the wagon seat. He'd only offered the name of *Jacque* when they pulled out of Cheyenne, but that was all right—Tucker felt like being alone with his own thoughts, not talking to some crude bullwhacker.

The driver looped the lines around the hand brake and pointed to the row of stores. "We'll need to get these goods unloaded." As if to punctuate his order, Jacque reared back and spat a string of tobacco juice only slightly milder than the string of cuss words he heaped upon his brace of oxen. "Then we got to get these critters some hay."

Tucker stepped aside, and the tobacco missed him by inches. He had become pretty good at avoiding Jacque's spitting, though he couldn't avoid everything about the man. Short and fat and obnoxious, Tucker wondered how the man had lived to his fifties. Crude and water shy, he had declined dips in the creeks they crossed. "I worked too hard to get this smelly," Jacque would say, smiling, when Tucker offered to let him use his cake of soap.

"Now climb up back there and start off-loading."

"The prison paid you for my fare," Tucker said. "And nothing else. You want me to help, it'll cost you a quarter-eagle."

"Whoa!" Jacque said. "That's . . . robbery. Just like those road agents been hitting the stages."

"Unload the wagon yourself," Tucker said. "It might just work down that belly of yours. Besides"—Tucker looked around at the men waiting beside their wagons, to those riding their horses precariously in the deep mud of spring, to drunks knee deep in gumbo staggering toward the saloons—"I got a pard'ner coming in from Deadwood to meet me."

Jacque spat out his chaw of tobacco. He cut off the corner of another from the plug and stuffed it in his cheek. "You ain't fixin' to try your hand in the gold fields, now are you? 'Cause if you are, I heard all the claims have been snapped up."

An ox in the front wagon let loose with its own yellow stream, and Tucker backed away. Spray caught him in the cheek and mouth, and he swiped a hand across his lips. "My pard's got a claim registered. All we got to do is work it."

"Work it? Hell, son, all you got to do is hang onto it," Jacque said. "Deadwood's infested with men with bad intentions. Like claim jumpers. Men who will kill you for the price of a stiff drink." He nodded to Tucker's waist. "And you ain't even packing."

Tucker shrugged. It was all he *could* do. When the army had taken him into custody for assaulting a sergeant, the captain had taken his guns. His mule. Even his saddle and bridle. And when he was released from the new territorial prison in Wyoming, the screws had no idea where his possessions were.

"Wouldn't be the first time for that," one of the turnkeys said as he issued Tucker his five-dollar gold piece and chit to ride the freight wagon to Custer City. "Just be glad you still have your life after being in here."

Tucker wondered what it would feel like to be armed again. Before he was sent up, guns had been an extension of him, had defined who he was and how men respected him. Now he wasn't sure if, after two years, he would even know what to do with a gun.

"That your friend?" Jacque said, chin-pointing to the north.

Jack Worman rode his paint pony, dodging oxen and horses being led across the street to the livery. He spotted Tucker and dug spurs into his horse, kicking up mud and horse and ox crap. Jack took off his hat and stood in the stirrups, waving wildly, an excited *whoop* coming from his lips. He narrowly avoided a team of mules being led down the street, and a drunk that staggered out of Jack's way just in time.

Jack reined his pony hard, and he leapt off before it even set itself. Jack's hat fell into the mud as he ran to Tucker and threw his arms around him. Tucker gently pushed Jack away and looked at him at arm's length. "No offense, pard'ner, but I've been a little too close to men these last couple years."

Jack picked up his hat and slapped mud off. He stepped away from Tucker and looked him over, from his shabby trousers to the shirt with one torn arm. "My God, what did they do to you in prison?"

"Nothing that I couldn't handle," Tucker answered. "Why?"

Jack pointed to Tucker's worn trousers. "Those denims are falling off you. And that shirt's just hanging on your shoulders."

Tucker hadn't accepted that he had wilted while he was in prison—nothing he could do about it at the time. But Jack was right—Tucker had lost weight, and he forced a smile. "If all you get is a piece of hot bread and coffee for breakfast until your bowl of wormy gruel or stew at suppertime you're bound to thin out a mite."

"A mite!" Jack said. "You musta' lost twenty pounds."

"More like thirty."

"And what's this?" Jack tapped Tucker's cheek. Tucker knew it showed the fading remnants of a bruise even through a week-old growth of stubble. "Looks like a horse kicked you."

Tucker shook his head, for a moment reliving the fight between himself and another inmate while the turnkeys watched from outside the mess hall. "A horse named John Jackson. Jumped me for my bowl of slop once too often. As bad as it looks, I can say Jackson looked far worse the day they let me out."

"By the looks of you, it wasn't the only fight you had inside."

"I'm afraid my reputation preceded me when I got there. Prisoners wanted a piece of me, seeing as I wasn't armed." He laughed. "Guess no one figured out I could fight with my fists as well as I could if I had a gun."

Jack motioned to a makeshift café set up in a tent next to a dilapidated log building fronting as a feed store. "We'd better get you something to put some weight on before you have to fight some of those rowdy Deadwood miners."

"I don't plan on fighting *anyone*." Tucker hitched up his trousers, falling south due to one of his galluses straps breaking. He had tied the two ends together, and still he had to pull his trousers up. "Toss me my bundle," he said to Jacque.

Jacque reached under the wagon seat and handed Tucker his change of tattered clothes, the only things he had left of his former life. "Good luck in the gold fields, kid."

"All I want to do is pan enough gold dust to leave the territory in one piece. Someplace quiet."

Jack looked sideways at Tucker as they started for the meal tent. "That didn't sound like you at all."

"That's the Tucker you'll have to put up with if you want a gold-digging partner."

Jack bent to the reins in the mud and gathered them. He led his pony as they headed to the tent, and Jack slapped Tucker on the back. "I'll take you in any condition. 'Cept now we better chow down."

Jack and Tucker walked the two blocks down to an army tent with rough tables and planks for sitting. They were early in the day, the cook said, and he was happy to have the company, though Tucker wasn't. While the man cooked, he talked. Incessantly. "Custer City used to be prime country for a man catering to gold miners," he said, salting a piece of frying meat Tucker suspected was ox. "That was until they found a lot more color up in Deadwood Gulch. Then it was Katie-bar-the-door for the stampede of men hightailing it up thataway to stake a claim." He wiped his nose with his shirtsleeve as he turned the steaks over. "Now all I get is a traveler passing through on his way north, and teamsters and drivers staying just long enough to drop their load and get back to Sydney or Cheyenne."

The cook slapped steaks on plates and set them on the plank

used as a table. Tucker's first bite confirmed his suspicions—it *was* ox. But it tasted better than anything he'd eaten in prison.

"You boys are too late if you figure on panning. All the claims have been staked."

"I already got mine registered," Jack said as he sawed off a piece of ox with his knife. "Been showing a lot of color, too." To emphasize his point, Jack pulled out a pouch and pinched gold dust into the cook's scale sitting on the table.

The cook weighed the gold between wiping his nose some more. "It appears I owe you."

Jack waved his hand in the air. "I figure by the time my friend wolfs down another steak, we'll be about even." Jack nudged Tucker. "You will be able to eat another steak, won't you?"

Tucker gnawed at a chunk of ox. "As long as my teeth hold up."

After Tucker had eaten his second steak and potatoes with enough coffee to float the Merrimac, they started on the road to Deadwood. It felt odd, riding double on Jack's pinto, a small Indian pony Jack had traded from a Crow a year before Tucker went to prison. That's how Tucker had begun to think of his life—time before prison and now. Before, he had always preferred mules, those sometimes-obstinate critters who could go for days on what little short grass could be found, or ride through the Badlands miles between water holes and never complain. He thought fondly of his last mule and thought he would begin saving the twelve or thirteen dollars mules cost nowadays. Whenever he and Jack started panning together.

"This is as good a place as any to camp for the night," Jack said and halted at the edge of a small clearing. "We got a good view on three sides if any Indians try to put the sneak on us."

"Always the Indians." Tucker dismounted. "Can't blame them—this is still their Black Hills."

"It is," Jack said. "I'll gather firewood if you want to undress Daisy."

"Daisy?"

"My pony," Jack said, and Tucker grinned. "So she reminds me of an old flame I used to spark," Jack said, and a dreamy look overcame him. "Sort of flashy like, she were. Just like my pony."

Jack began picking up branches suitable for a campfire while Tucker tied Daisy to an aspen and stripped the saddle off. As Tucker looked around, he suddenly felt so vulnerable. Indians *had* been picking off miners and travelers invading their Black Hills this last year, if he believed the turnkeys in prison. With only Jack's rifle and one handgun between them, they wouldn't last long fending off a Lakota war party.

Tucker pulled loose a clump of buffalo grass and started rubbing down the pony's chest, her withers, feeling the twitch of coiled strength ready to erupt at Jack's command. "I see you haven't forgotten some things."

Tucker stopped rubbing Daisy and looked over the back of the horse. "Not that I don't remember *how* to do some things, it's just that I don't *want* to do much of anything anymore. Most of the things I used to do every day have got . . . stale with me. That make sense?"

"I think it does." Jack dropped the branches and twigs in a pile and dug for a lucifer. "Even I get to forgetting things now and again."

"Like how to spark a lady besides your Daisy here?"

"It'll all come back to me soon," Jack said, blushing, "when we save up enough to buy us some land. Maybe a few cows, like we always talked about. I might even send for one of those catalog women. I hear they're lining up in Chicago and St. Louis to come west."

"Sure, Jack. A mail-order bride would do you just fine."

Tucker bent and arranged rocks in a crude circle before setting the twigs and branches crosswise over the stones. Jack struck a match, and the kindling sputtered before flaring to life.

"Get used to it," Jack said as he added more branches. "We had a nasty blizzard this spring, and only now things are thawing out. Most wood we light up will be damp like that." He grabbed a coffee pot and cups from his saddlebags and squatted by the fire. "I bought us some airtights," he said and handed Tucker a can of beans and a can of oysters.

Tucker looked at them for long moments when Jack handed him a knife. "Sorry, Jack. I don't even own one of those."

"We'll get you one," Jack said.

Tucker pried open the cans as he watched the smoke drift lazily upward and dissipate among the trees. Indians even close would have a hard time seeing the smoke, and Tucker figured he remembered *some* things from his *before* time.

After he spread the beans onto a metal pan looking suspiciously like a gold pan, he set it on the fire and stood. Stretching. Always stretching, it seemed, ever since he was forced to live in a cage altogether too small for him with other men who were also too big for it. And when it got overcrowded later in his sentence, the prisoners had to take turns sleeping in shifts, always with one eye cracked, always assuming one of their cellmates would kill them for their blanket or piece of bread they'd hoarded since breakfast.

Jack handed Tucker his bedroll. "Only have this one blanket, but you take it."

Tucker handed it back. "Many nights the screws took our blankets for some perceived punishment just to see if we'd make it through the night."

"It gets mighty cold here in the mountains when the sun sets. As you can feel."

"Go ahead," Tucker said. "I'm used to it."

"Sure?"

Tucker nodded.

"Then at least wear my coat." Jack handed Tucker a sour-dough coat, canvas lined with some type of flannel. Even after the weight he'd lost, the coat was too tight to put on, and Tucker handed it back. "It'll be all right."

Jack had tossed out his bedroll beside the fire when the ears of his pony pricked up. Tucker followed where the horse looked. Jack saw it, too. He poured coffee over the flames and reached for his rifle. He handed Tucker his Colt and motioned to crawl into the trees.

Four Sioux rode the periphery of the clearing, not making themselves targets for any miner or trapper, keeping to the trees for cover. "Will Daisy keep quiet?" Tucker whispered.

"She's a calm one, that girl."

They watched the Indians ride the far side of the clearing, when the lead warrior stopped. He tested the air like a dog test-ing the scent of a coon. Tucker felt the heft of Jack's pistol as he eyed the Indians forty yards across the clearing. Before prison— when he shot his guns daily, either in practice or to save his scalp—he could hit a man at twice this distance. Now, he wasn't sure he could even hit someone half this far away.

After many long, tense moments, the Indians rode on, and Jack sighed deeply. "Better gather more kindling."

"That wise with Sioux around?"

"They're riding on," Jack said. "Unless you forgot, Indians are pretty smart—they don't want to freeze their butts off any more than we do. As we speak, I'm almost sure they are well away from us by now, looking for their own camp to hole up for the night."

"Almost sure?"

"Close as I can come with Indians," Jack said. "I'll go find water for coffee."

C. M. Wendelboe

By the time they had a fire going again and coffee heated, Tucker figured the Indians were camped someplace themselves fighting to keep warm. But then, he could never really be sure what Sioux would do.

Jack kept watching the clearing as he handed Tucker the plate of beans and filled their cups. Steam rose from Jack's cup, clouding his face, and he waved it away. "You know I tried to find you. But by the time I made it back to Ft. Pierre, Lorna said you were gone. She never said the army took you."

Tucker scooped up a smoked oyster and let it slide down his throat. *Slowly.* It had been so long since he'd had food this good, even if it was over a campfire. "Don't matter any now. I figured you tried your best to find me." Tucker hadn't heard from Jack until a month before Tucker was released from prison.

Jack had learned Tucker was in prison and sent him a letter. "Join me in the gold fields," Jack had written. "Within a year that small spread and a few cows can be ours."

"How is Lorna doing these days?" Tucker asked of the only woman he'd ever come close to marrying.

"That nimrod she hooked up with has had his horns clipped. Lorna tells him what to do in that mercantile, and how to do it. Her way. That could have been you."

Tucker walked off a few feet and dug into the ground, rubbing dirt over the pan to clean it. When he was done, he cleaned Jack's pan and sat cross-legged in front of the fire, sitting close, letting the heat wash over him. Except for the blistering heat three months out of the year, there never was enough heat in the prison to keep a man warm, and the prisoners had all been perpetually chilled to the bone marrow. "Lorna's father had something to do with me being transferred to the Wyoming Territorial Prison," Tucker said. "The army jockeyed me around to various jails until I mysteriously landed there."

"She ever come to visit?"

18

Tucker frowned. "None of us *ever* had visitors."

Jack slapped Tucker on the back. "She'll soon be regretting letting Tucker Ashley go after we make the big strike."

The only stories filtering from the gold fields into prison were less than positive, of men failing as miners, of claims lost. Of men quitting. Perhaps the grim nature of the men inside the prison colored how they interpreted news from outside. "I know your letter said you were pulling good color at your claim. But do you really think we can make a go of it?"

The light flickering off Jack's grinning face gave him an eerie appearance. He reached inside his vest and withdrew his poke. He untied the leather thong and handed Tucker the pouch. "It's a bull penis—"

"I know what it is, but why use *that* to keep your gold in?"

"Only thing tight enough a man can get that won't allow the dust to fall through. We're not picking up nuggets off the ground like Custer claimed when he came through here." Tucker hefted the pouch. "I've been pulling in five dollars a day out of my claim," Jack said. "Consistently. Don't sound like much, but if we don't spend it on women and drink like most of the other miners, we'll have enough saved to make something of ourselves. With two of us working the claim, we'll be in fat city by the end of summer."

Tucker fingered the two half-eagles the prison had issued him upon leaving, the only money he had to his name. "When do we get to your claim?"

"*Our* claim," Jack said. "Couple days, depending on how many other hunting parties we run into. But first on the agenda is getting you some clothes."

"I only have ten dollars."

Jack laid another branch on the fire before wrapping himself in his blanket. "There's more than enough in that pouch to buy you new clothes. Now get some sleep."

Tucker lay close to the fire, feeling the warmth engulf him. As he lay with his eyes open, he half expected some brutal prison guard to come by and crack him on the bottom of the feet. Just for entertainment.

CHAPTER 2

Tucker and Jack awoke to a heavy snow that lingered over their bodies a moment too long before melting. Tucker brushed off his arms and chest and placed branches on the dying embers of their campfire. He blew on them, and the fire flared up. "Who the hell ever said it was supposed to snow in June?"

"Welcome to the Black Hills," Jack said. He gathered his blanket tighter around his shaking shoulders and scooted closer to the fire.

They warmed themselves at the campfire just long enough to melt snow for coffee. Tucker wrapped his hand around the tin cup as he walked around the clearing, stretching the kinks out. He looked at the far end of the meadow, where he spotted grama grass bent at an odd angle and walked to it. He hadn't read a track since being sent away—not much use for man-tracking in prison—but it was the one thing, it seemed, that had never left him.

He walked around to where the tracks were between him and the sun, shadows appearing, telling him the story of what had bent the grass in such a fashion. Unshod ponies—six or seven— had ridden into the clearing. The Indians had stopped and looked around the trees . . . searching for a campfire? They may have smelled the wood smoke. They may have heard Jack's horse snort or whinny. But in the end, they had ridden off, and Tucker thanked Jack's wise decision to build camp back into the trees.

"They musta' come around early this morning," Jack said.

He had walked to where the grass was beaten down and ran his hand over the tracks. "If they had come sooner—before the fire died down—they might have spotted the flames and caught us flat-footed." He looked around the forest. "Keep your eyes peeled."

Jack rolled his blanket up and tied it behind his saddle before swinging atop Daisy. He grabbed Tucker's hand to help him into the saddle, and the two headed toward the gold fields.

Close to noon they scared up a covey of quail, and Jack shot one before the rest flew away to safety. "Not much meat, splitting this bird."

"More than I'm used to," Tucker said and began gathering firewood.

Jack plucked the bird while Tucker rigged a suitable skewer for it. They sat close to the campfire, the heat of the day filtering through the trees, melting what snow remained. "How's come you snagged a gold claim, when it sounds like there are none left?" Tucker asked as he sucked marrow out of a wing bone.

"Couple months after you left town—"

"Funny way to say I was arrested—"

"I didn't know it at the time. Anyways, I heard the army was hiring scouts again, and I drifted up to Fort Abe Lincoln. Signed on with Custer's expedition into the Black Hills as a line scout. We seen some pretty country, we did, even though there was enough troopers and wagons to scare what game there was away. During that expedition a couple archeologists from back east did some testing and found gold. Not so's a body could pick it up right from the ground, like the good colonel claimed. But enough so's the word spread there was gold up around Custer City. After we returned to Fort Abe Lincoln, my contract was up, and I hightailed it back to Custer. Panned for a few months until some feller found color along Deadwood Gulch. A *lot* of color. So I packed up and headed to Deadwood to stake a claim before the rush."

As Jack's pony plodded on with two men atop her back, she stumbled now and again, not used to the weight, throwing off the horse's stride. The burden might have broken a lesser critter's spirit, much like Tucker's spirit the prison had shattered. But then, that's what prisons were designed for—to break a man's will and leave him just enough strength that he could find a hole to crawl to and just die.

Tucker had counted the days when he would be free of the confines of his cramped cell. Free from fighting to keep the wormy and rancid food he ate every day from some other prisoner's thieving hands. Free from fighting over a blanket in the middle of a frigid night. Or just fighting when the guards wanted to be entertained.

As they continued toward their destiny in the gulch, Tucker thought how much more Jack believed in Tucker than he did himself.

By the time they arrived at the point of the road where they could look down on Deadwood, the snow had let up. Tucker slapped powder off his hat as Jack reined his pony beside a huge granite boulder. "What 'cha think?"

Tucker climbed down from Daisy and stretched, looking out over the vast expanse—a long, narrow valley packed with more people than Tucker had ever seen outside St. Louis. Freight wagons—some pulled by plodding oxen, others by contentious mule teams—struggled to move in the mud gumbo mixed with animal manure that sank wagons up to the axles, the stench thick when the wind shifted.

Men walked—their arms outstretched to their sides like tightrope walkers—on planks precariously placed atop the muck, connecting one business to another, risking sinking into the slop at any moment. Other men put their backs to wagons in efforts to free them from the mud. Somewhere in the depths of one of the saloons, a calliope played a brash, gala tune. A gunshot caused a horse tied to the post in front to rear on its hind legs and fall over backwards onto a man unfortunate enough to be close. Two drunks glanced at the injured man and walked past him into the saloon.

Jack led Tucker down the hill the remaining hundred yards and tied Daisy to a hitching post. "Try to stay on the walkway," he told Tucker. "Last week a drunk slipped and fell face-down in this slop and suffocated. Folks said he was dead, but still people stepped around him for two days before someone got tired of him stinking and dragged him away. This way," Jack said.

"Where we headed?"

"Gun shop," Jack answered. "It just don't seem right, Tucker Ashley without a gun."

They navigated the makeshift walkway. A horse pawed the muck and mud, and crap splashed onto Tucker's cheek. He swiped his hand across and brushed it onto his trousers. He followed Jack to a corner building and entered. There was no sign on the door, no shingle to tell folks what business occupied the tiny shop. Only the outline of a pistol painted crudely on the split-log door.

Bells overhead tinkled when they entered the shop. A blanket-covered long board spanned the front of the shop where rows of pistols had been lined up by caliber: .36 Navy Colts beside Smith and Wesson .44 Russians and Colt .45 Peacemakers. "I don't have enough money to buy a gun."

Jack waved the air. "I have more than enough in my poke to pay for it."

"I don't accept charity."

"Is that what you think this is? Charity?" Jack stood with his hands on his hips as if scolding Tucker like his mother used to do. "I hope the hell you don't think being half owner in a gold claim is charity, 'cause you'll earn every ounce of dust we pan outta' there."

"But I can't pay you back—"

"Let us just say I'll take it out of the first ounce we pan together. Look, I need someone to watch my backside. Someone good with a gun. There's a passel of bad customers hereabouts."

"But I don't know if I'll *ever* be any good with a gun anymore." Tucker looked down at his hands, broken and scarred and stiff from dozens of prison fights, and being beaten by turnkeys. "Jack, except when you gave me yours last night, it's been two years since I had a gun in my hand. And thank God I didn't have to use it, 'cause I don't think I could have hit anything."

"Handling a gun is like sex," Jack said. "You never forget about how to do that, either."

"What's sex?"

"Hopefully, something you haven't engaged in for the last two years."

"Shut that damn pneumonia hole!" someone called from behind a counter. "Don't you know it's cold outside?"

Tucker had to search among the piles of ammunition boxes and kegs of powder and bullet molds before he spotted where the voice originated from. An old man stood, his leather apron stained with oil and gunpowder. He looked up at Jack and squinted. "You want something or just wasting my time again?"

"We're paying, Pop," Jack answered.

The gunsmith set a pistol down on the table and wiped his greasy hands on his apron. "Paying for what?"

"A Colt," Jack said. ".45, if you have it."

Pop laughed. "That's about *all* I got." The man separated four pistols on the tabletop, and Tucker picked one up. It had slight holster wear along the side of the barrel and cylinder but just didn't heft right. "Let me see that long-barreled gun." He pointed.

"Suit yourself," Pop said. "But most gunnies want the shorter barrel."

"I am no gunny," Tucker said. The gun showed more holster wear than the others, and Tucker popped the cylinder out of the frame. He stuck his thumb where the cylinder had been and held it to the light as he looked down the barrel.

"It's got a clean, tight bore," Pop said, "even though it looks a mite rough."

Tucker thumbed the hammer back and pressed the trigger. *Sweet.* "You work on this?"

"I did," Pop answered. He filled a pipe with tobacco from a cedar humidor and lit it. "A soldier out of Fort Meade came in to sell it." He put his hands up. "But I can't say for sure he stole it from the army."

"It *is* army issue," Tucker said. He pulled the hammer and once more pulled the trigger. Pop had done a good job of working the roughness out of the Colt. And it had a long barrel, like his pistol the army had taken from him. Besides, he was no longer a gunny of any kind.

"Twenty dollars," Pop blurted out.

"Twenty dollars?" Jack said. "We can buy a new Colt for that price. And one that's not stolen from the army."

"Not one that's been smoothed out like that one," Pop said.

Tucker handed Jack the pistol, and he felt the trigger. "Here's the deal—twenty dollars and you throw in a holster."

"You're no better than a road agent. But all right."

"And three boxes of ammunition," Jack said.

"What!"

"And no one needs to tell the army you sold us one of their guns," Jack added.

Pop hung his head. "If I wanted to get robbed, I'd leave the door unlocked at night. But you got a deal." He squatted under the table and came up with three holsters. Tucker squeezed all three and took the stiffest one.

"And the ammunition?" Jack pressed.

Pop reached behind him and took three boxes of ammunition from a shelf and plopped them on the table.

Jack took out his pouch and handed it to Pop. He trickled dust out onto a scale until it started moving, then pinched a little more before he grabbed his blower. "Not too hard," Jack said. "Wouldn't want any gold dust blowing off, now would we?"

Pop glared at Jack, but he gently *puffed* the air until all the dirt and sand had been blown away, leaving only gold dust. "Ounce and a quarter."

"You can keep the extra if you throw in that Bowie over there." Jack pointed to a knife on a shelf along with twenty others.

"Fair enough," Pop said as he grabbed the knife and laid it on the table. "Not like I can sell any of those things."

Jack slipped his poke back into his vest pocket before he handed Tucker the knife to go with his pistol. "Nice doing business with you."

"Road agents," Pop said under his breath as Tucker and Jack left the shop.

When they stepped outside, Jack motioned to Tucker to step away from the gun shop. "We made a good deal back there. Now you can help us keep our claim from jumpers."

Tucker tested the heft of the gun once more. Shooting was something a man never forgot, if Jack was correct. Yet two years was so long to go without practice, Tucker doubted he could *ever* shoot straight again. Or even if he wanted to.

Jack led Tucker down a back street to Lou's Meal Tent,

advertising a steak with all the trimmings for two bits. "Trimmings being what wild parsnips and onions Lou's wife digs up around the hills," Jack laughed. "But he does serve the finest horse meat in town. When he can get it."

But it didn't even bother Tucker he was eating someone's horse they rode yesterday. He was just too hungry to worry what the critter's name had been in life.

Feeling full and satisfied, and with the sun already setting—it never seemed to shine more than ten hours a day, Jack said, as it was constantly fighting to shine through the steep sides of Deadwood Gulch. They entered a livery, and Jack called to the owner. "Guess Olaf's not here," Jack said and turned Daisy into a stall. He called for Olaf again before giving his pony a spot of hay.

They walked along the side street until they reached a single-story house that had been partitioned into sleeping rooms for miners. "We can't afford a room just for us yet," Jack said as they entered the house. "We'll be sharing with other miners."

A heavyset woman, looking as if she'd be more at home on the farm than operating a rooming house, waddled toward them. "This is the lovely Lucille," Jack said.

She smiled wide, and all four of her teeth smiled back. "That'll be one dollar. Each."

"For sleeping on the floor?" Tucker said.

"You want to sleep out in the mud?" Lucille's smile faded. "If not, cough up some dust."

Jack once again took his pouch out and pinched four times onto Lucille's scale. She used her puffer, and Tucker thought she was overly aggressive in puffing air across the gold dust. Some dust drifted to the carpeting under the scale. "Another half a pinch."

Tucker started to speak when Jack held up his hand. "We'll

make up for it tomorrow in the gulch."

And that night as Tucker lay on the floor next to a smelly miner who was as water-shy as Jacque, and near another man who gurgled like he was going to die any moment, Tucker didn't even mind. He was free and didn't have to worry about someone robbing his blanket or beating him in the middle of a sound sleep. Even if it did cost a dollar a night.

CHAPTER 3

Tucker and Jack made their way north along what Deadwood affectionately called a "road," knocking thick gumbo off their boots that reeked of animal manure and urine.

"Get used to it," Jack said. "Until it stops raining, this mud will never dry up." Jack told how he had been caught in the gulch that winter when the blizzard hit, and he barely made it back to town before all travel was shut down by eight-foot drifts. "I was one of the lucky ones. Some miners weren't smart enough to get to shelter and never made it back to town."

"This smells like where I've been living these last few years," Tucker said, taking the shovel off his shoulder and scraping his boots. Mud had soaked through the holes in the soles, even though Tucker had lined them inside with fresh paperboard. "Heading to our claim—and smelling the mountain air of freedom among this slop—is all right by me."

The morning sun had risen and cooked off mist that hung over the high hills like a prairie fire gone stagnant. As they walked along Deadwood Gulch, they passed miners already working their claims. Tents dotted the creek, and the sounds of shovels and pickaxes hitting hard rock and silted sand echoed along the bank. Jack leaned over the edge of the bank and called to a miner: "Hey, Tell, how're you looking this morning?"

A man in knee-deep water working the business end of a shovel stopped long enough to stand and arch his back. He dropped his shovel of sand and water into a sluice box where another man rocked the wooden contraption back and forth. "Making color," Tell said. He put his hands on the small of his back and winced. "Just wish there was an easier way to make money—"

"You could go back to punching cows at thirty dollars a month—"

"Not on your life." Tell dug into his pocket and came away with a pipe and tobacco pouch. "Who's your friend?"

"Tucker Ashley."

Tell tamped his tobacco down with a twig and lit it. "Heard about some gunny around Pierre named Ashley who was hell on wheels with a hogleg couple years ago."

"Different feller," Tucker said. "I just drifted in from Wyoming."

Tell blew smoke rings that dissipated in the easy breeze coming down the canyon, and he turned to Jack. "You've been gone a little while."

"Week and a few days. Had to hang around Custer City until Tucker came in on a freight wagon."

"Then hitch up your britches," Tell said, " 'Cause the mining district hired a couple . . . thugs to enforce their cockamamie rules."

"What's that got to do with me?" Jack said. "I just work my claim and don't bother anyone."

"Just a warning." Tell knocked burnt tobacco on the sole of his boot and pocketed his pipe. "Got to get back to making money," he said and sank his shovel into the sandy bottom of Whitewood Creek

"What's Tell talking about, some thug enforcing mining rules?" Tucker asked when they had gone another hundred yards upstream. He sat on a rock and scraped mud off his boots. Again. " 'Cause I don't want any trouble."

"There's always trouble in a mining camp," Jack said, using

the shovel to scrape his own boots. "But that don't apply to us. The mining district Deadwood established a few months ago came up with rules we all need to follow. I suppose some rules are in order when you get a couple thousand men all mining their three-hundred-foot claims next to one another; spats are bound to happen. We needed some order. But that don't pertain to us—all we'll be doing is minding our own business and working our claim."

They'd walked another quarter mile on the bank above the gulch, looking over the edge now and again at miners shoveling sand into sluice boxes—long wooden boxes set at gradually reducing heights meant to separate the gold from the sediment. "Over there," Jack said as he grabbed onto an overhanging pine bough to prevent slipping down the muddy bank, "is our ticket to that ranch we wanted." He took his pickaxe off his shoulder, and they half-slid down to the flowing creek fed by fresh snowmelt coming down the hills, making it perfect to pan for gold.

"What the hell?" Jack said. Other men stood in the creek working Jack's claim. One man bent over a pickaxe, while another waited beside a rocker used to separate gold dust.

"Who the hell are you guys?" Jack yelled, but the men ignored him. He dropped his pickaxe and gold pan and slid down the bank. Tucker followed, his shovel coming off his shoulder. Tucker sensed trouble—a skill he'd honed his last few years in stir. "Hey!" Jack hollered to one man in the creek shoveling sand into another man's pan. "What the hell you doing? This is my claim."

A big man—shorter than Tucker but filled out in the arms and shoulders—dropped his shovel and met Jack halfway up the bank. "This ain't your claim anymore."

"What do you mean, it's not my claim—"

"You abandoned it."

The man working the rocker waded out of the water and stood next to the other—an exact copy, except this one had a scar running down the side of his red head. He stepped closer to Jack and stood nose to nose. "You were gone more 'n a week. By right of abandonment, we've taken it over."

"What kind of stupid rule is this?"

The first twin smiled. "Rules of the mining district."

"Sounds like claim jumping to me, rules or no," Tucker said.

The man with the scar stepped around and squinted at Tucker. "Well if it ain't Tucker Ashley." He exaggerated looking Tucker up and down. "Looks like you fell on hard times."

"You know this peckerwood?" Jack asked.

"Unfortunately. He's Mick Flynn." Tucker chin-pointed to the other man inching closer. "And his twin brother, Red. Real sweethearts. What's the matter, Mick, no drunks to roll?"

Tucker turned to Jack and talked as if the Flynns were not there. "These two darlings worked as crimps in San Francisco, Shanghaiing drunks along the water for whatever ship's captain paid the most blood money."

"You asshole—"

"Now, Mick, I don't 'spect you've grown any *cojones* since the last time we met. My advice is: stay where you are, or hurt's coming your way."

Mick paused mid-stride, but Red started working his way around toward Tucker's back. "And when these brave souls were in New York during the war, they took three hundred dollars to take the place of wealthy men who had been drafted. Then they promptly deserted."

"Best keep quiet," Mick said. "I see you're not packing a gun."

"Neither are you."

"Then I'm going to beat your ass."

"Like you did last time?" Tucker kept Red, working his way

in back of Tucker as he spoke directly to Jack, in his peripheral vision. "This fool thought he'd best me a couple years ago when they stowed away on a riverboat that docked at Bismarck." He snapped his fingers. "I guess it was your brother's head I laid open and gave him that nice scar." He winked at Mick. "It didn't turn out so well for you either, did it?"

Mick's hand went to his nose that hadn't been set straight the last time Tucker broke it.

Out of the corner of his eye, Tucker watched Red circling around, now within grabbing distance. All he had to do was lunge, and he'd have Tucker in his grasp, with Mick sure to jump in as well. Although Tucker was taller than the Flynns, they had him by thirty hard pounds. Tucker had survived prison, where he fought nearly every day over some perceived injustice, and it had just worn him out. If there was a way to avoid a fight . . . "Why don't you boys just vacate Jack's claim. Mining district rules or not, he was the one who first staked it . . ."

Red took that last step, and his arms flailed the air, clawing at Tucker. Tucker caught the movement in time and turned into him as Red threw a hard right. Tucker held up his shovel, and Red's hand hit it. He howled in pain, blood dripping from broken knuckles and a split hand.

Tucker turned to meet Mick's charge, but he was too slow, and the Irishman hit him on the chin. Tucker dropped into the mud, and Mick had cocked his leg to kick Tucker when Jack jumped on his back. He grabbed Mick around the throat, arm-choking him, and Mick's legs buckled. He dropped to a knee, and Jack sailed off into the creek.

Tucker ignored Red's screaming and cocked his shovel over his shoulder as he stood above Mick. "You want your head flattened, or are you gonna' vacate Jack's claim?"

Mick rolled on the ground, taking in great gulps of air, his hand rubbing his throat.

Tucker lifted the shovel higher. "Last time I'll ask nicely."

Mick held up his hand. "Okay. Okay, me and Red are pulling out. Just don't hit us with that damn shovel."

"Help your brother hobble the hell out of here," Tucker ordered. "And leave your own shovel and pan. Let us say that's the price for stealing another man's claim."

Tucker shouldered the shovel again. He eyed Mick wrapping a bandana round Red's bloody hand before they made their way up the slippery bank. When they disappeared over the top, Tucker relaxed. He extended his hand and helped Jack stand. "You all right?"

"I'll live," Jack said. He bent to the creek and scooped water into his hand to wash the mud off his coat. He shook his head, and creek water flew in all directions. "Damn, that man's strong." He scooped more water. "They'll be back." Jack said. "Armed next time."

"I wouldn't worry about gunplay with those fools," Tucker said. "They'd rather beat a man to death as shoot him."

"Either way, they'll be around," Jack said. He motioned to the adjoining claim downstream from his. "That's their stake. Been working the creek this last month, though I never talked to them until today. They filed on the claim next to theirs— some army deserter named Miller—after he was found dead and scalped up the hills a couple weeks ago."

"Why didn't *you* file on the soldier's claim if he was dead?"

"The Flynns beat me to it."

"If they'd take your claim, that would give them three together. Seems like they aim to own all the claims in this part of the creek," Tucker said and picked up his shovel. "But we're no worse for wear. Let's get to panning so's we can afford a hot meal tonight."

The sound of splashing upstream caused Tucker to jump, and he swung around. A man sloshed toward them, his overalls telling Tucker he was another miner barely off the farm. The thin young man held out his hand to Tucker. "Good to see someone stand up to those bastards."

"Lowell Tornquist." Jack introduced him. "Working a couple claims up the creek."

"And I aim to keep it." Lowell motioned to where the Flynns hobbled off to. "Those two are bound to have the gulch sewed up halfway up the creek. Buying up claims. Kicking folks off when they won't sell." Lowell grinned. "Except you boys don't run off so easily. That's a good thing."

Tucker patted Jack's vest, and he handed him his bible. Tucker rolled a smoke and handed the pouch and papers back to Jack. "Where'd the Flynns get the money to buy up claims? I never knew them to be more than petty thugs."

Lowell shrugged. "Can't say. All I know is *I* ain't selling out."

Jack and Tucker worked the creek throughout the day until the sun began setting and it was hard to distinguish gold flakes from sand in the bottom of the rusty gold pan. Tucker's back ached from the day's work, and Jack had offered to swap duties. Tucker tried his hand at working the gold pan, but there was a certain knack to it that he didn't have, and Jack did. So they worked the day—Tucker shoveling sand and water into Jack's pan, Jack sloshing the silt around until faint specks of gold appeared in the bottom that Jack picked out and put into his bull-penis poke, tossing the rest of the sand aside and accepting a new shovelful.

"Getting dark." Jack knocked sand from his pan and motioned for Tucker to come out of the creek. "By the time we get back to town, it'll be dark."

Tucker accepted Jack's hand, and he picked his way up the bank.

"We did good today," Jack said. "With both of us working,

I'm thinking we did a ten-dollar day. Maybe twelve."

Tucker ran his bandana around the inside of his hat band. Despite the cold, his bandana soaked up sweat. "Then next year at this time we ought to have enough to run a few cows around the Missouri."

Jack slapped Tucker on the back. "And we won't have the likes of the Flynns to worry about."

CHAPTER 4

Rain throughout the night dripped from the roof onto Tucker's blanket and *dripped, dripped, dripped* onto his head. He moved several times during the night, but the leak seemed to follow him like past memories he could never shake. His thoughts returned—as they often did when he could not sleep—to Lorna, and to the betrayal he felt when he'd returned to her mercantile. Yet she still occupied his mind; he still thought of them being together. But only for a brief time, until his common sense emerged, and he realized Lorna *never* would be by his side.

As he wrapped himself in the blanket, the cold in the rooming house helped none. It reminded Tucker of the walls of the prison that always wept a cold, muscle-numbing moisture. He sat up and checked Jack's pocket watch lying beside his boots. "Time to get to making money."

"Already?" Jack said. "I could sleep for another day."

"You ought to be the shovel end of our team if you think *you're* sore."

They sat for a moment eating a few strips of dried ox jerky Lou had given them when they ate at his meal tent yesterday. "Tough as boiled whale shit, it is," Lou proclaimed. "But it'll put something in your gullet besides my greasy-assed corn dodgers."

Lucille sat warming herself beside a Franklin stove in the common area when Jack and Tucker came out of their dingy room. She motioned to cups hanging on the wall. "Be a muddy bitch today," Lucille said and poured them coffee. "My guess is that this will be the last warm thing you boys will be having all day."

Lucille was right. The overnight rains had thickened the mud, and Jack decided to saddle Daisy and ride to the claim. They entered Olaf's Livery to find the big Norwegian bending over a forge, hammering small pieces of metal. "Making hinges for dat new undertaker coming in." Olaf laughed. "And he had better set up shop before everyone in Deadwood is dead."

Jack followed Olaf into his office and pinched enough dust for another day's boarding for Daisy. "I wish you luck," Olaf said. "Those Flynn boys haf been bragging how dey vill throw you off your claim."

Jack patted Olaf on his broad back. "I think Tucker here was more than enough for them yesterday. We'll be fine."

They rode double again and arrived at the creek to the sounds of men splashing in the water. Shovels and curses bounced off the walls of Deadwood Gulch, mixed with shouts now and again when a man found a particularly big flake. Jack tied the pony up to a birch tree and had started toward his claim when he stopped short. "Not again!"

The two Irishmen worked Jack's claim—Mick on shovel, Red on rocker, sloshing water around with his good hand, the other bandaged where it had broken on Tucker's shovel. They had dragged their sluice box from their own claim to Jack's, and it sat waiting for the two to assemble it.

Tucker climbed down the hill and started toward the two Flynns, his shovel clutched tightly, ready to administer justice. Mick was the first to see Tucker, and he nudged Red. Mick held his own shovel menacingly over his shoulder as he and Red met Tucker halfway. They stood defiantly in front of Jack's claim marker.

"Maybe you two peckerwoods didn't get the message

yesterday," Tucker said, cocking his shovel over his shoulder. " 'Cause we can go for round two if you want."

"We've filed a grievance with the mining district," Mick said. "Perry ruled it was our right to work this claim until he could set up a hearing."

"Who the hell's Perry?" Tucker asked.

"Mining district representative," Jack said. "He carries the weight of the territorial governor."

"Well, he's not here now." Tucker stepped toward the Flynns, and they looked around for a place to flee.

"Perry's not here, but we are."

Tucker turned toward the voice behind him. Even if he wasn't sitting a bay gelding sixteen hands tall, the man would appear big. Taller than Tucker and forty pounds heavier, his shoulders were uncommonly broad beneath his sheepskin coat. He stroked a gray beard caked with this morning's breakfast and glared at Tucker.

Beside the big man sat a younger—and much smaller—version of the bearded one. He took his hat off, and the wind whipped flowing blond hair across his face. His features—the slender nose, the wide eyes—that of the other. "We're employed by the mining district to enforce rules here—"

"Thought that's what the law was for?" Tucker said.

The kid stepped carefully down from his horse. He stood rubbing a leg, grimacing, before he squared up to Tucker. The kid wore his cut-down holster low, like he was used to pulling it. A leather piggin' string hung from his belt, but Tucker doubted he ever used it to tie up calves or steers. Jinglebobs tinkled on large Spanish rowels as he stepped toward Tucker. "Perry said to make sure you two fellers don't come around here and make trouble. Until the hearing, this ain't Jack Worman's claim anymore."

"Maybe we'll go and hunt up this Perry feller," Tucker said, sizing the kid up. He had seen his kind a hundred times, coming into prison with the attitude that they'd whip the world, only to be whipped into submission themselves and never recovering. Tucker wondered when this young blowhard would get his comeuppance.

The kid shoved his duster aside to expose his gun. "Maybe you need ventilating—"

"Trait!" the big man said. "Stand down." He got down from his horse and stood between the kid and Tucker. "My boy here gets a little peeved when folks don't obey him. But you're new, so I'll explain it." He stepped closer. Even if Tucker hadn't gone to prison, even if he was beefed up like he used to be, he would have a hard time handling this man. Raw boned, his face held tales of a dozen brutal fights, and his ring finger was missing. Not that anyone would be marrying him any time soon.

"You'll have to excuse my son," he said. "I am Zell McGinty. And Trait here speaks the truth—we are the law here for all practical purposes until the territory deems it necessary to send a lawman out. Understood?"

"I understand you and your boy like to push your weight around."

Zell slapped Trait's back. "Maybe *I* do, but you can see that Trait hasn't enough meat on his bones to push anyone round." His smile faded. "But I know *about* you. When Mick and Red said Tucker Ashley was in Deadwood, I was skeptical."

"I don't know you."

"No reason to. But I saw you in Yankton . . . four years ago, seems like. Some fool goaded you into a duel, and they ended up planting him." Zell looked Tucker over. "You seem a mite worse for wear, son. Where you been?"

"Vacation."

Trait stumbled as he stepped around Zell and stood five paces from Tucker. The kid's hand hovered just above his gun butt.

Jack stepped between them, but the kid shoved him aside. "Stay out of this, Worman, or you'll be the first I drill."

He turned his attention back to Tucker. "You're about the fastest man in the territory, from what some folks say. I looked for you for months until I gave up." He stroked his curly locks. "No one's seen you for so long, everyone figured the Indians got you or your horse fell off one of those nasty Badlands cliffs."

"Obviously not," Tucker said. "But why you looking for me if'n I don't know you?"

"Best reason I can think of." Trait smiled. "I think I'm faster than you."

"Can't say," Tucker said, but he doubted he could even draw the Colt Jack bought for him without dropping it into the mud.

"I say you're not. Now drop that shovel and draw."

Tucker pulled back the canvas coat. "I'm not heeled."

"That's wise," Trait said. " 'Cause if you intend sticking around Deadwood, you might see just how much faster I am." Trait had turned as if to leave when he pivoted on his heel and drew his Colt before Tucker caught the movement. Trait stood with his gun leveled at Tucker's chest for a long moment before he tilted his head back and laughed. "Ain't that something— Tucker Ashley right in front of me, and I didn't plug him." He nudged his father, and his grin left him. "But being unarmed only goes so far," he said and holstered. "One of these times I'll catch you armed, and we'll see just how fast you are."

"You've had your fun for the day," Zell said and faced Tucker. "No harm done."

"No harm done," Tucker agreed, but his quaking knees told him otherwise a moment before he felt his face flush and the old fire rekindle in him. That SOB needed a lesson taught.

Jack must have recognized Tucker's growing anger because he tugged at his arm. "We're out of here for today. We'll visit the mining office and arrange for a hearing tomorrow." He motioned to the Irishmen. "Then you fools better be off our claim."

CHAPTER 5

Jack unsaddled Daisy and turned her out into a stall at Olaf's Livery. "Give her some oats, will you, Olaf?"

The big man squatted in a stall at the far end of the livery and poked his head around the gate. "Shore," Olaf said. "Soon's this filly here foals."

"That wise?" Tucker said to Jack. "We don't hardly have money to spare for oats. Hay's expensive enough."

"I got enough in my poke to last a week. Besides, after our hearing with Perry Dowd, we'll be back working the claim."

The one thing Tucker had developed in prison was his ability to suspect bad things coming his way. And right now, that feeling surfaced in spades. The McGintys wouldn't let Jack and Tucker back onto the claim unless forced, Perry Dowd's ruling or not. "I got the feeling the Flynns want that whole section of the creek for their mining."

"Won't matter in a minute," Jack said. "Let's hunt up Perry."

They walked the two blocks to the mining office, but Perry wasn't there. A note on the door said he had left for the day, and a pad hung on the door for folks to leave a message. Jack wet the pencil stub on his tongue and jotted that he needed a hearing on a claim dispute and slid it through the slot in the door. "We'll check back," Jack said. "Let's grab something to eat—I'm starved. How about you?"

"I can take it or leave it," Tucker answered. "Another thing I learned in prison—don't expect a meal, but if it comes your

44

way be damned grateful."

"You're not in prison anymore," Jack said and led Tucker toward Lou's Meal Tent. They walked planks laid on the muddy street, careful to stay well away from freight wagons that had been brave—or foolish—enough to fight the rain and the mud, waiting for hours to get into line to off-load their supplies.

Over the din of saloon rowdies fighting, a gunshot from somewhere in back of one saloon interrupted the noise of the mule skinners and bullwhackers cursing at their teams, snaking whips over heads of animals bogged down in the gumbo. Another gunshot had an air of finality a moment before the music and laughter blared up again.

But it was an eight-mule-teamed wagon that caught Tucker's attention. It had stalled—like so many others in the line of wagons waiting to be off-loaded in the slop. A mule skinner jerked one of his leader's traces before sloshing back to stand beside a swing mule. He grabbed his whip by the handle and hit the mule on the head with the hard leather. "Get your lazy ass to pulling!" he barked and hit the mule again. The mule shook his head and strained to nip at the mule skinner, but the man wisely moved out of reach.

When he reared his hand back to strike the mule again, Tucker stepped off the walkway. He sank to his knees in slop as he grabbed the man's arm and twisted the whip away.

"What the hell you doin'?"

Tucker cocked the whip over his shoulder. The mule skinner cringed and backed away. He fell into the mud, thrashing for his footing before he took hold of the wagon and struggled to stand.

"How's about I beat you with this thing?" Tucker said.

The man spit a string of tobacco that sailed over the heads of his team. "What's your game, mister?"

"My game," Tucker said as he stepped closer and shoved the

mule skinner back into the mud, "is I don't like to see animals beaten. Especially mules."

"He had it coming."

"How so?"

"He's been a lazy one ever since leaving Fort Pierre," the freighter said. "While the others pull their weight, he won't. Been trying to teach him manners, but he won't listen."

Tucker stepped to the mule, who ignored him as he ran his hand over open sores the trace leather had rubbed against. "You damn fool. He's big enough you should have traced him in the wheeler position. These sores are what's causing him to buck up on you."

The mule skinner regained his footing and held on to the side of the wagon. "I'm plumb done with this one. He won't listen to nothing. Only thing left for me is to shoot him."

"How about I buy him from you?"

The freighter looked sideways at Tucker. "Now who would want some damn animal that won't even pull his weight?"

"Someone as dumb as him," Tucker answered. "Your price?"

The mule skinner stepped closer to the mule but kept out of range of those snapping teeth. "This here's a big, strong mule. Bigger and heavier than the others, as you can see. He's almighty healthy—"

"A minute ago you were going to put him down. Your price?"

"What's he worth to you?"

Tucker dug into his pocket and handed the man one of his five-dollar gold pieces.

The mule skinner thought it over for a moment before taking the money. "But you gotta' unhitch him from the traces."

Jack tugged on Tucker's arm. "You sure about this?"

"I'll have to scare up some tack, but I can't let him beat this mule anymore."

Jack nodded. "All right. I'll run down to Olaf's and borrow a hackamore, so you can lead him to the livery. I figure that's where you're going to board him."

"Until our money runs out," Tucker said and started unbuckling the traces.

With every step, it seemed the mule craned its neck around to snap at Tucker. It had nearly nipped him that first time, and Tucker was careful to stay away from his powerful jaws and even more powerful legs. But he didn't blame the mule—if Tucker'd had to put up with that mule skinner all the way from Ft. Pierre, he'd be a little testy, too. Tucker would work on winning the animal's trust once the mule's sores healed.

Tucker led the mule into Olaf's stable. The big Norwegian was bent over his large forge, hammering a horseshoe, when he spotted Tucker. Olaf doused the hot metal shoe in a bucket of water and set it on the anvil. He stepped toward the mule as he shook his head. "Jack said you bought a mule for five dollars. I think you got took."

"How so?"

Olaf put his hands on his hips and walked around the animal. "That critter has a jughead. Joost look at him—almost too big to ride. And he does not like you."

"I figure he don't like *anyone* after that mule skinner ruined him. Can I board him? I'll pay you when I get back on my feet—"

Olaf waved the suggestion away. "Maybe I need help around here some time. Cleaning up, or unloading the hay vagon ven it come in. Turn him into the stall beside Jack's pony."

Jack opened the gate, and Tucker slipped the hackamore off the mule's head. He stayed well away from its hooves and released him into the stall. "One other thing—I understand you're pretty good doctorin' critters. He has some sores—"

"I saw how raw his back vas," Olaf said. "I vas planning on

rubbing some salve on them. No charge."

Tucker and Jack left the livery on their way to Lou's Meal Tent. The sun had nearly set, but still freighters braved the mud to deliver their goods before more rain came. The wagon where the freighter had sold his mule sat stuck in the muck, and they walked past it.

They entered the large army squad tent with the faded CSA still visible from when the Confederacy still owned it. They sat on a long plank and read from the menu hanging from the cookstove at the front of the tent. Lou spotted them and slipped off his muslin apron before walking over with a coffee pot. "From what I hear, you two could use a hot cup of coffee after the McGintys ran you off."

Tucker wrapped his hands around the tin cup to warm them. Much like the tin cup he had banged on prison bars. "You heard about that?"

"The Flynns were in bragging how you lost your claim."

"We did," Jack said, "for now. So I think we deserve a nice venison steak."

"Don't mean you're going to get it," the old Greek said. "I have no venison."

"But the menu says—"

"The menu is a week old. I ran out of what venison I had, and this"—he held up a small bird—"is the last of my scrawny prairie chickens. As of now, I'm meatless."

Tucker groaned. "What *do* you have?"

"I got potatoes," Lou said. "And bread and corn dodgers coming out my ears. If you hear anyone hunting deer, you send them to me. I'll pay top dollar for all they kill. Birds, too."

Tucker sipped his coffee and looked at the other miners eating bread and potatoes and complaining—wanting a steak so badly. At least Lou'd made up for his lack of meat with his coffee—hot and strong Arbuckle's. The kind that made Tucker think. Turning to Jack, he said, "How much ammunition you have for that Winchester of yours?"

"Box," Jack answered. "Maybe box and a half. Why?"

"If I can borrow your rifle and your pony—only until Soreback's ready for a saddle—"

"Who?"

"Soreback," Tucker said. "I figure the name says it all with that mule with those sores the mule skinner ignored all the way from Ft. Pierre. If I can borrow that rifle and your pony, I can find enough deer to keep us in meals. And livery fees."

"But we're miners," Jack said. "We ought'n be out hunting!"

"And just how much gold did we pan today?"

CHAPTER 6

Tucker worked Jack's pony slowly up the rising hillside to the west of town, heading for a stand of pine high away from the sound of the miners a mile down the gulch. He had picked up a game trail heavy with the hoofprints of deer. He dismounted and studied the ground. Deer came through regularly, and recently, their cloven impressions sharp in the damp ground.

He swung back into the saddle, rode Daisy a hundred yards away from the game trail, and tied her to an aspen. "You be nice and quiet," Tucker whispered to the horse, "and I just might make enough to give you and Soreback extra oats tonight."

He slipped Jack's .44-40 from its scabbard and walked downwind of the game trail, settling behind scrub juniper fifty yards from the trail. The sun was setting—at least for the gulch, with its high hills that shut out light much of the day. He warmed his hands with his hot breath as he brought the rifle to his shoulder, sighting down the barrel. Would he even be able to hit a deer after two years of not firing a gun? He knew he had better, or he and Jack would be eating Lou's potatoes and bread every day.

As he sat waiting and watching, he thought of his friend's predicament. Jack had been generous enough to offer Tucker a partnership in his gold claim, only to have it stolen by the Flynns when they bribed some bureaucrat at the mining district to say Jack had abandoned it. After these last couple years, Tucker had

50

few illusions about life, little hope that his would take a turn for the better. Jack's offer of a partnership had boosted those hopes, only to have them dashed against granita rock in Deadwood Gulch. Now all Tucker hoped for was to continue breathing the air of freedom.

But Jack was different. The letter he sent Tucker in prison was so full of optimism. They had talked many times about buying some cows and building a herd they could be proud of. That had been mere campfire talk—Tucker knew—talk among men with little chance to alter their status in life.

But the gold fields changed all that. At least for Jack. He was so certain his claim would give them the start they'd always talked about. Except now his hopes had been pulled out from under him. Under *them,* and Tucker's anger rose, thinking about it. He took deep, calming breaths. The last thing he wanted was to do something rash like take this rifle he held in his hand and nullify the thugs enforcing mining-district rules.

The snap of a twig a hundred yards below on the trail sounded loud in the cool mountain air, and Tucker caught a fleeting glimpse of a deer's rump as it passed behind birch trees. He blew warmth into his hand as he waited for the deer to work its way higher, and he thought about Jack. He hoped his friend had luck finding Perry Dowd today and knew he *had* to rule in Jack's favor. Tucker had no knowledge of mining laws, but common sense told him a man who had been away from his claim little more than a week was still entitled to it upon returning. If this Perry feller could set up a hearing, Tucker was certain he and Jack would be back in the mining business. And he wouldn't have to hunt deer to feed the two of them.

But when Tucker thought more about losing the claim, he knew he was right where he'd rather be—up among the deer and the cougar in air so crisp and sharp, it caused a man to suck in the breath of sweet freedom. Not down below among the squalor and the commotion mining a claim they couldn't even hold onto.

The Indians who had settled in this land long before the white man invaded popped into his thoughts. The notion of a Sioux hunting party in this area caused Tucker to look about, searching for danger, for he'd have little chance if a band of warriors crossed his path. He remembered what Jack had told him about the two soldiers he had met during the Custer expedition, the soldiers who had returned to the Black Hills to mine for gold. They had deserted, Jack was certain, though a man didn't ask about another man's business unless offered. And one of the soldiers—some private named Miller—had been killed and scalped by Indians, his partner never heard from again and presumed dead, leaving the Flynns to file a claim with the district office and take it over.

Another twig snapped, this one closer along the game trail. Tucker eased the hammer of the rifle back as he kept his head still, scanning with his eyes. A two-point buck, its white tail flicking from side to side like a snake's tongue testing the air, watched the trees as he led his harem of six doe up the steep trail. Tucker estimated they'd pass within thirty yards of him, and he silently held the rifle tight against his shoulder. He would leave the buck alone—his does needed him to fight off predators. And they would need this buck to lead them up the trail another day when Tucker went hunting.

The buck stopped suddenly, his head looking toward the trees where Tucker crouched. The deer's head tilted back, testing the air, nostrils flared. The buck knew danger lurked somewhere close. He just wasn't experienced enough to know where or what. That would come with age and experience. If he lived long enough.

After several minutes, the young buck continued up the trail, his ladies following close behind. Tucker pulled the stock tighter against his shoulder and took a deep, calming breath before letting it out. He concentrated on the leaf sight and fired at the last doe.

The rifle slammed hard against his shoulder from the recoil.

And he missed.

The herd bolted, and Tucker fumbled with the Winchester's lever to jack another round into the chamber. Just before the deer disappeared over the rim of the hill, Tucker snapped another shot. The last doe dropped, letting out a squeal not unlike a child in pain. He ran toward the fallen deer. His bullet had shattered her spine, and her legs flailed the air in an effort to get away from her tormentor. He had aimed for the lungs, always the lungs, but his shot had been off. Sickening squeals bounced off the trees until Tucker dropped beside her. He drew his Bowie and stuck the wounded animal through her ribcage and into her heart. In a moment, she was dead.

"That was damned impressive," he said aloud as he gutted the deer and let the entrails roll over the hill. *At least I still know how to field dress a deer, even if I don't remember how to shoot straight.* Two short years ago, Tucker's skills with *any* gun were the stuff of legends, things men talked about in whispers over campfires at night—so much so that the army had sent six men to arrest him at the mercantile. Now he was fortunate to have killed this doe with *two* shots.

He left the deer and walked to Jack's pony. He led her to the deer and lashed the doe over the saddle before tying Daisy to a tree.

He reached into the saddlebags and grabbed his Colt and box of ammunition. He strapped the holster on and set the pistol in it. It didn't feel right, as if the two years had been twenty years. Tucker had a cell mate—George Hanes—who had planned his escape from the prison. George had showed Tucker a knife he had made from a hacksaw blade with boot strings wrapped around it for a handle. "This is going to be my ticket out of here," George said.

"To get you by until you lift a gun from one of these guards or a rifle if you can snatch one from the armory?"

George shook his head. "Not me. I've been in jails and prisons for eighteen years. I do not trust myself to be able to pick up a gun and shoot it accurately. That would just get *me* killed."

When Tucker scoffed at him, George laid his hand on Tucker's shoulder. "Son, shooting is a perishable skill. A man's got to practice, and often, if he wants to maintain his proficiency."

"Except men like me." Tucker shrugged his hand off. "I'm a natural shot."

George had laughed heartily. "Ain't no such thing, son. I've never met a man who could pick up a gun after being away from it for very long and hit a damned thing with it."

When George made his escape, he had gotten himself shot anyway, but his words stayed with Tucker. Until just now, he wasn't certain the old man was right. Missing the deer showed Tucker George *was* right, and Tucker wondered if he was as rusty with a handgun as well.

He set the box of cartridges on a rock. He'd load them later, he thought, and he squared up to a tree stump twenty feet away. He drew and fumbled, cocking the hammer before holstering, and trying it again. He drew and dry fired the gun ten times before he loaded the Colt and eased the gun in the holster.

He drew and fired, hitting the tree stump a foot to one side. He holstered again. The gun felt . . . alien to him, as if he'd never picked one up before. But he had once been a gunny others feared. Before prison, he'd had a lifetime of using guns. He just had to remember how he'd done it.

He unloaded the pistol and faced the tree stump. He closed

his eyes, envisioning what he *knew* he had to do to hit it. *Grab. Draw. Cock the hammer before the muzzle gets on target. Press the trigger lightly.* He did as his memory told him, eight, ten times, thinking of the sequence each time before dropping the hammer.

He fished six cartridges out of the box and loaded the Colt. He gently holstered, noting where he would have to cut the leather away, thinking how some bear fat inside would help his draw.

He faced the rock as if it were a mortal enemy and drew and fired in one smooth motion. *Smooth is fast,* he told himself, drawing smoother and faster each time, splintering the stump. By the sixth round he was certain that he could almost clear leather before Trait McGinty drilled him through the heart. For that was who Tucker was practicing for; he had known all along, Trait's angry words imprinted clearly on Tucker's mind: "You come around wearing a gun, you'd better be prepared to use it against me."

Tucker didn't intend to run into the killer without a whole lot more practice.

Tucker reined Daisy in back of Lou's and stepped through a flap in the back of the tent. He got the fat Greek's attention and motioned him over. "I'm busy with these parsnips," he told Tucker. "I used to feed potatoes and bread. Now all the freight wagon brought is parsnips or what my woman can gather in the hills, so now I serve them instead."

"You want meat?"

"Meat!" Lou dropped his spoon in the boiling water and wiped his hands on his apron. "Does a fat baby want a sugar tit? Of course, I want meat. What kind?"

"Venison," Tucker said. "Nice, dry doe."

A broad smile crossed Lou's face, and he followed Tucker

outside. He patted the deer strapped to the back of Jack's pony. "What you need for her?"

"Whatever you think is fair," Tucker said.

"You know how to butcher."

Unlike shooting, that was one skill Tucker figured he still had.

"Okay, butcher her and bring in a hindquarter. Store the rest in my meat cooler out back, not that I've used it much lately. Then come inside, and I'll fry you up a thick venison steak." He looked over his shoulder before he took out two eagles from his pocket and handed them to Tucker.

Tucker stared at the coins for a moment before accepting them. "Twenty dollars gold?"

"What, you think the deer's worth more? What could you make if you broke your back panning today? Four, maybe five dollars? If you don't want it—"

Tucker closed his hand around the coins. "Seems like a lot just for meat."

Lou nodded to the tent. "When you go in there you'll see why this venison is a bargain for me. Bring me all the meat you can. When men hear I serve meat again, I'll have to hire help."

"I'll go out hunting again tomorrow," Tucker said.

"Good, because this will be gone once word spreads tonight."

"I'll butcher her," Tucker said and stopped Lou before he went back inside. "Have you seen Jack Worman?"

Lou jerked his thumb over his shoulder. "He's been waiting inside for you for two hours. He's my charity case for today— seems like he lost his whole poke."

"Lost his gold how?"

"He better tell you," Lou said. "I'll get the skillet ready for that hindquarter."

"Tell Jack to wait for me."

It took Tucker little over an hour to skin and cut up the doe.

As instructed, he put all but one hindquarter in Lou's cold locker four feet underground in back of the tent. By the time Tucker had given Lou the hindquarter and washed his hands in the basin in front of the tent, word had spread that Lou had meat again. Most places in the tent were taken, fifty men stuffed in a twenty-man tent. Tucker spotted Jack warming one corner of a row of planks, and he ran the gauntlet of hungry miners to sit next to him.

When Jack looked up, he stared back at Tucker through a swollen eye, one cheek red and bulging. He dipped a bandana in water and dabbed at a split lip. "I'd like to say you ought to see the other guy." Jack winced when he spoke. "But I didn't even *see* the other guy."

Tucker turned Jack's face to the light. "Whoever did a job on you did it right. Let's hear it."

Jack carefully sipped coffee from one side of his mouth. "I went to the mining district office to find Perry Dowd, but he was out again. At least that's what the note on his door said. I figured I had nothing else to do and decided to camp out there until he returned. I was damned sure gonna' file a complaint today. About the time it got dark I knew he wasn't coming back, and I went to leave. That's when somebody waylaid me. I went out like a light and didn't come to for another hour. When I did, I was like this." He ran his hand gingerly over his face. "Tucker, whoever jumped me stole my poke. I don't even have enough to buy us coffee. Lou had to give me this," he held up his chipped porcelain cup.

"It'll be all right for now," Tucker said. "Lou's going to fry us up a venison steak, and we got enough for the rooming house for another few nights." Tucker looked around, but none of the miners were paying him any attention as his hand came away from his coat pocket with his gold pieces.

"Where—?"

"Lou," Tucker said "This is for *one* doe. I'm going out hunting again tomorrow—unless we get a hearing at the mining office."

Jack tapped Tucker's holster. "I see you're packing again. I told you it'd come back."

"Jack, it took me two shots to hit that dear, and it was close enough I could have knocked it out with a tree limb. And this"—Tucker ran his hand over his holster—"is going to take more practice than ever. I figure if I shoot a little every day when I go out hunting, I might just get comfortable with it again."

"I hope," Jack said, "because Trait McGinty's been flapping his gums that it's just a matter of time before he gets you in front of his sights."

"That worries me," Tucker said. "Even in my prime—with the shooting every day that I did—Trait's faster than I *ever* was."

Jack dabbed at his split lip and put the bandana away. "You be careful, hear? I didn't send for you so you could get yourself killed by some gunny wanting a reputation."

"Believe me," Tucker said, "I'm taking off soon's we finish eating."

CHAPTER 7

Tucker walked beside Jack as he led his pony to the livery. Olaf sat in the chair in the corner of the barn he called his office, his snoring reverberating off the walls. "Glad I don't sleep close to him," Jack said.

Tucker grinned. "Not like I didn't hear snoring like that these last few years."

"At least I don't snore."

Tucker shook his head. "Wanna bet?"

As Jack stripped the saddle off Daisy, Tucker draped his arms over the stall where Soreback looked at Tucker, the whites of his eyes like those of many broncs Tucker had ridden. The mule's tail flicked back and forth, and Tucker kept watch that Soreback didn't decide to use those snapping jaws on him.

Tucker reached into his pocket and came out with a parsnip. Soreback sniffed the air and came over to where Tucker held his hand out. The mule sniffed it before taking it. While the mule munched on the tuber, Tucker reached over the stall and felt the mule's back. Whatever concoction Olaf had smeared on his back was working—the nasty sore where the traces had rubbed was nearly healed, and he didn't flinch when Tucker touched him.

"I still think he looks like some kind of jughead," Jack said. He closed the gate behind his pony and stepped up onto the stall slats. "Big-assed, raw-boned mule used to the traces is all he is. You sure you want to try hanging a saddle on him?"

Tucker motioned to Olaf, still sleeping, unaware anyone was in his livery stables. "He's got a McClellan saddle and britching someone left that he'll give me. And he's got a bridle he'll sell for two dollars. When I go out hunting in the morning I'm taking Soreback. I spotted a place where I can break him that won't kill me if he gets froggy."

"If?" Jack said. "Tucker, that critter's got hisself a real hatred for people."

"We're making progress, him and me," Tucker said and reached out his hand with another parsnip. "I'll be all right. Let's get us a drink—we deserve it."

"Soon as you take that pistol off," Jack said. "Last thing we need now is trouble when some gunny recognizes you. Or worse—Trait McGinty."

"Good point," Tucker said and looked around the livery. He grabbed a gunny sack hanging from a stall and wrapped his Colt in it before they headed for the saloon.

They left Olaf sleeping in his chair and walked out into the street. Though it was dark, freighters lined the street, cussing and coaxing their mules and oxen, trudging through the mud slower than a man walks, struggling to where they could unload their wagons.

Two drunks burst out of a saloon, swinging, tripping over one another as they fell into the mud. Others poured out to watch the fight, egging the combatants on. One man wearing a torn sourdough coat leapt on the other's head and forced him into the mud. Soon, the unfortunate miner who had tasted mud and crap stopped moving, and the crowd roared their approval. They patted the victor on the back as they ushered him into the saloon, leaving the loser in the slop.

"Let's make it to the Pony," Jack said, "before someone jumps us. At least it's somewhat civilized."

The Pretty Pony, run by Lady Madame Marcie—whom Jack

said was neither French nor a lady—nonetheless kept her clientele in check, as well as she could in a place like Deadwood. She stood off to one side of the bar as she eyed Jack and Tucker enter. The air inside was so thick with cigar and cigarette smoke, it was difficult to find a spot to sit. "Over there," Jack said and led Tucker through the maze of drunks teetering on wobbly legs, past the faro table surrounded by drunk miners who might as well have just handed over their poke to the house. Two tables in their path had hot poker games going, with the house taking in most of the bets, and they finally made it to the table in the corner.

Madame Marcie—Tucker's age, though it was hard to tell with the thick layer of makeup she'd pasted on her face—sauntered to their table. Tucker had more luck aging animal tracks than aging the woman.

A drunk stepped in her way and put his hand around her bustle. He leaned into her low top, announcing her other assets, and puckered up for a kiss. She kneed the man in the groin and he bent over, holding his crotch as she motioned to a man sitting on a high chair in one corner of the saloon. He set his shotgun aside and jumped to the floor. He elbowed past drunks and grabbed the man, giving him the bum's rush out the door.

Madame Marcie lit a cigarette and stuck it in a silver holder before she continued to Tucker and Jack's table. "Who's your handsome friend, Jackie?"

Tucker blushed as Jack introduced him. "He's working my claim with me."

Madame Marcie sat on a chair and scooted close to Tucker, her cologne as strong as the horse liniment Olaf used. "I have heard about you. Recently." She laid her hand on Tucker's. "Rumor is the Flynns have put you in your place." She batted her eyes at Jack. "And that they have kicked you off your claim."

Jack's face flushed. "Not for long. Soon as we arrange for a hearing in front of Perry Dowd, we'll be back in business."

She leaned over and gently ran her fingers over Jack's swollen face. "I would hate for a good customer to have another unfortunate run-in with Perry's men."

"You know it was Perry's men did this?" Jack asked.

Madame Marcie shrugged. "People tell me things. All sorts of things."

"Just give me names."

Madame Marcie waved the air, her cigarette smoke adding to the thick haze permeating the saloon." I stay in business because I keep my mouth shut." She leaned closer and lowered her voice. "Old Beggar Jim hears even more than I. Ask him."

She stood and patted Tucker's cheek. "Don't be a stranger. Either of you."

Tucker looked after Madame Marcie sashaying through the crowd, her tight bustle cutting the air in the right places.

"Don't even think about it," Jack said. "Rumor is, she was run out of Denver when she knifed her last two lovers. I'd hate you to be number three."

The bar dog came to their table carrying mugs of beer. "You'll have to pay for this round."

"Sure," Tucker said.

"Two dollars," the bartender said.

Tucker handed the man the eagle.

"You don't have dust?"

"It's all we got," Jack blurted out.

The man frowned and returned to the bar.

"Monty has a habit of blowing a little too much dust onto that piece of gingham under his scales," Jack said. "Even if I had dust, I wouldn't *ever* pay him with it if I could help it." Tucker blew foam off his beer, which left him with half a glass of warm liquid. "It looks like we won't have gold dust any time soon anyway, unless we corral Perry Dowd and demand a hearing. Who is this Beggar Jim Madame Marcie mentioned?"

"Old war vet. Sits around the street begging." Jack took a sip of beer. "Him." A small, dark-skinned man hobbling on one wooden leg came, *tap, tap, tapping*, over to their table. "Who knows how Jim hears things? But he does."

The drunks parted for Beggar Jim as he made his way across the floor. He dropped into a chair across from Tucker and grabbed peanuts in a bowl on the table. "I heard you were out of prison."

"Do I know you?" Tucker asked.

Jim eyeballed him before scooping more peanuts. "Nope."

"Then how do you know I was in prison?"

"I keep an eye out," Jim said as he lifted the black patch over one eye and winked, his brown eye as sharp and clear as his other one. He pulled his patch down and leaned across the table. He tapped the table in front of Jack. "You *have* been beat."

"What do you know about that?" Jack asked.

Jim smiled. "These peanuts make my throat dry. I talk better with some liquid sloshing down there."

Jack called Monty's name and held up three fingers. Soon the bar dog brought three foam-filled mugs to their table. Beggar Jim inhaled the foam and took a short sip. He dabbed daintily at the corner of his mouth with a snotty bandana. "To answer your question, I hear all sorts of things. Like Jack's beating." He patted his shirt pocket, and Jack handed him his bible. Jim peeled off a paper and trickled tobacco into it before handing Jack his makin's back. "The McGintys don't want folks filing with the mining district. They'd do whatever it takes to prevent that." He tapped Jack's cheek, and Jack winced. "But they don't get their knuckles scarred nowadays. They're more likely to have folks do that for them."

"Then tell us who did it," Tucker said. "And we'll make sure they get beat much worse."

Jim lit his cigarette. It flared, and he managed to get two draws from the dried tobacco before sparks dropped onto his shirt front. "What do you see, Tucker Ashley, when you look around this here establishment?" he asked as he batted embers that had fallen on his tattered shirt.

"I see a saloon full of miners blowing off steam."

Beggar Jim chuckled. "What *I* see is only about one in ten of these fellers actually work a claim. Most came here too late to stake a claim, and they just hang around to make trouble. To see some action."

"That why you're here?" Tucker asked.

"I make my way wherever I am. I am too old to work *any* claim. Hell, you're an old man, too, compared to these kids. Most would as soon roll you and steal all your money when you're passed out than breathe. And most"—he winked at Jack—"would beat a man for the price of some beer as look at him."

"You saying the McGintys paid to have me beaten?"

"That's the rumor on the street."

"Who—"

Jim held up his hand. "Take your pick—any one of these young punks could have done the dirty deed."

A *whoop* went up from some drunks close to the staircase leading from the cribs upstairs. Jim looked starry eyed at the staircase. "Now that Helen is a vision," he said.

A woman—looking every bit the lady in her high-topped, pointed shoes and lacy skirt—seemed to glide down the stairs. Her auburn hair cascaded down the front of her low-cut dress, and rouge outlined her high cheeks. She looked even younger than Jack—though ladies in her profession were usually far older under the veil of heavy makeup.

Jack sucked in a breath. "Excuse me," he said and left the

table. Other men clustered around her, but Jack elbowed his way through them to stand at the bottom of the stairs when she reached bottom. He held out his hand, and she smiled before taking it.

Beggar Jim downed his beer and belched. "If you're his friend, you'll tell Jack to be careful with that upstairs girl he's sparkin'."

"A little itchy is she?"

Jim shook his head. "She's clean as a whistle. Madame keeps her girls that way. But another feller wants to put his brand on her."

"Who?"

"Him," Jim said and motioned to the door.

Trait McGinty—the top of his head barely visible over the taller miners in the saloon—shoved drunks out of the way to reach the bar. Drunks parted for him as he looked over the saloon. He finally spotted Helen and smiled at her. Until he saw Jack sidle up next to the bar girl and wrap his arm around her thin waist. Trait knocked one man down and tripped over another as he tromped his way to get to Helen.

Tucker stood abruptly, and his chair fell to the floor. "I better make sure Jack don't get beat again."

Tucker broke through the crowd just as Trait reached Jack, leaning on the bar, his head close to Helen's as they whispered and laughed between themselves. Trait spun him around and grabbed Jack by his shirtfront. Trait slapped him hard on the face, and Jack winced with pain, his lip starting to bleed anew. Trait had cocked his hand to hit Jack again when Tucker grabbed his hand. "Jack's been beat enough."

Trait shoved Tucker aside and grabbed Jack again, but Tucker threw Trait to the floor. He fell against two drunks, and the three rolled onto the peanut hulls littering the saloon.

Tucker eased Jack onto a chair and tilted his head up. "We'll get some of that salve Olaf uses—"

"Turn around, Ashley."

Tucker ignored Trait and took out his bandana. He handed it to Jack. "You okay?"

"I said turn around," Trait ordered. "I told you next time I saw you we'd find out just how fast you aren't any more."

Madame Marcie stepped between miners anticipating the entertainment. "This is enough. A fight now and then is just business. But drawing on an unarmed man is something else."

Trait reached for another drunk and snatched his pistol from his waistband. "There. Now you're armed," he said and tossed it to Tucker.

Tucker turned to Jack, keeping his eyes on Trait, standing with feet apart, hand close above his gun butt.

"Turn around!"

Tucker kept the miner's pistol away from his body where Trait could see it. "You shoot me in the back, and you'll hang."

"I'm giving you a fair chance," Trait said.

Tucker recalled the one time he'd seen Trait draw his weapon and knew he'd have no chance, even if he had his own Colt strapped on in the holster he had cut down. If he turned around now and faced Trait, Tucker knew he'd be a dead man. He glanced up at the corner of the saloon where Madame Marcie's guard sat with his shotgun pointed in Trait's direction. "See that man with the Greener?"

Trait looked up in the corner. "I got no truck with you," he called out to the guard.

"He'll cut you in two if you force this fight," Madame Marcie said.

Tucker used two fingers to lay the pistol on the floor before he turned and faced Trait. "Looks like I'm unarmed once again. If you shoot me now, that guard in the corner will cut you in two. Or you'll hang. Either way, you'll be just as dead as me."

Trait looked up at the guard, and Tucker saw his chance. He covered the seven or eight feet in one lunge and lashed out with a quick jab that landed on Trait's cheek. Trait's legs buckled, and Tucker hit him with a right cross that felled him.

Tucker bent over Trait and grabbed his pistol. He tossed it aside before he lifted Trait off the floor. Rage overtook Tucker's good sense, and he slapped Trait hard across the face. And backhanded him again, until Trait's eyes rolled back in his head. Blood dripped from Trait's nose, his eye closing from the bone-jarring slap that would stay with him for a lifetime. The kind that caused a man to want a rematch. The next time with guns. But Tucker didn't care—anger that had been percolating for the last two years came to the surface.

He had cocked his hand back to deal another blow when he felt cold steel jammed against his neck. Zell McGinty held his pistol tight against Tucker, and he let Trait go. Trait dropped onto his knees, and Tucker looked over his shoulder.

"You've made your point," Zell said. He worked his way around Tucker and bent to Trait. "You'll live," he said and faced Tucker. "You always slap smaller men around?" Zell holstered his gun. "Want to try me on for size?"

Though Zell had him by several inches and forty pounds, Tucker recognized in Zell the same flaw his son possessed—he was just a damned bully. "This is as good a place as any," Tucker said, and he felt anger overriding his common sense. He took off his coat and rolled his shirtsleeves up. "Stand back," he told the drunks in the saloon, and murmurs went around from men making bets on the victor. Tucker wasn't sure he could beat Zell, but that mattered little to him. He'd just stayed so angry since his arrest two years ago. And Zell offered a way for Tucker to take out his rage.

"You'd fight me?" Zell said. "When I got you on size?"

"You going to talk or fight?"

Zell studied Tucker for long moments, and there must have been something in Tucker's eyes that told Zell he faced a man who wouldn't stop until one or the other was beaten to death. He was used to bullying his way through men—Tucker was certain—and never expected Tucker to take him up on a fight.

Zell looked at the crowd. Money swapped between miners, talks among them favoring Tucker. The big man backed away, and he bent to Trait. "Another time," Zell said and hoisted his son to his feet "And soon. Right now, I need to get my son home."

Madame Marcie handed Zell Trait's gun, and he slipped it in his son's holster.

"The next time Trait sees you, you won't have that man with the shotgun watching your back." Zell wrapped his arm around Trait's waist and helped him out of the saloon. "I ain't done with you," Zell called over his shoulder as he left the Pretty Pony.

The drunks stood stunned, staring at the McGintys shuffling out of the saloon.

Madame Marcie laughed heartily and slapped Tucker on his back. "Drinks are on me," she announced, and drunks elbowed one another to be the first to the bar.

"Why the free drinks?" Jack managed to spit out.

"What for?" she said. "That was about the best—and cheapest—entertainment I could ever find here in Deadwood. And no one was killed."

"Yet," Tucker said.

CHAPTER 8

Beggar Jim poked his head inside the rooming house and shook Jack awake.

"What you doing?" Jack sat up and rubbed his eyes. "The sun's barely up."

"Wake up Tucker, too."

"I heard you," Tucker said. He rolled over and propped himself up on an elbow. He was used to men waking him for no apparent reason. "That wooden leg gave you away."

"I'll remember that," Jim said. "Now get up."

"For what?" Jack said, his lip thick and bruised.

"The best reason—money."

Tucker sat up and pulled his boots on. "We're listening."

"Ramona Hazelton," Beggar Jim said, smugly resting his hands on his meatless hips as if that were the only explanation needed.

Tucker looked at Jack. "This Ramona another old girlfriend of yours?"

"Hey," a grizzled old man sleeping next to Tucker said. "Do your talking outside." He covered his head with his blanket and rolled over.

Tucker helped Jack stand. Jack's balance still gave him fits, as he could see out of just one eye, the other being swollen shut.

Beggar Jim held the door, and they stepped outside. It was, indeed, early. No freight wagons fought to traverse the muddy street; no sounds of gaiety, or fights, erupted from the saloons.

It was—Tucker noted—quiet on the streets of Deadwood. Except for Jim and an occasional chamber pot being emptied from upstairs rooms. "Now who is this Ramona Hazelton?"

"I don't believe you never heard of her," Jim said. He snapped his fingers in front of Tucker's eyes. "Hazelton Oil Company?"

"Now I remember that name," Jack said, rolling a smoke and handing Tucker his makin's.

"Me too," Tucker said. Ramona Hazelton's late husband had got the oil bug when he lived in Pennsylvania. He was ridiculed when he said he thought oil could be found in Colorado and moved there. On a shoestring, he bought and begged drilling equipment and hit his first gusher in Canyon City. The Florence Oil Field would make him independently wealthy, with no care in this world. Until he wandered drunk on train tracks and was waffled by a freighter high balling through. And left his widow just as independently wealthy. "Now why would she be coming to Deadwood?"

"Think," Beggar Jim said, "where you've heard that name before."

"Can't recall—"

"Miller Hazelton should ring a bell, as Quasimodo once said. And he has nothing to do with oil."

"Of course," Jack said. "That dead soldier who had the claim next to mine before the Sioux killed him—Miller. His name *was* Hazelton."

"And his mother is here in Deadwood," Jim said.

"Why get excited about some woman coming here to bury her son?" Jack asked.

"She's not just some woman," Jim said. "She can buy and sell every miner in the gulch. And she'll be offering money for information on her son's death. Her coach is due here within the hour."

Tucker pulled his boots on, and the three men headed to

Lou's for a morning meal. He stopped before they entered. "What else you know about this Ramona?"

"You buying?" Jim asked.

Tucker nodded.

"Then let's talk," he said and brushed past Tucker on his way into the meal tent.

They finished eggs and left-over venison. Jim was regaling Tucker and Jack with his exploits during the war serving under General Johnson when a crowd outside grew loud. Tucker, Jack, and Jim stood and walked to the tent flap. Men milled about both sides of the street watching a black Concord stage pulled by six matched horses, white before the mud stained them dark. HAZELTON OIL COMPANY adorned the coach in muddy white letters, with the oiled curtains of the coach pulled down.

"Wonder if this Ramona Hazelton travels by herself," Jack said.

"Why?" Tucker elbowed him. "You going to sidle up next to her and see if she needs company? If you do, you'd better wait until your face heals. You weren't exactly pretty before you got beat up."

"Not hardly. The mother of a soldier would be too old for me. Too frumpy, too, if she has to ride cooped up in that coach."

The driver shared the seat with a man twice his size. His face had the haggard lines of one who had seen the elephant and was big enough to wrestle it to the ground. He held a double-barreled Greener across his lap with a Winchester propped up beside his leg. Two outriders followed, rifles resting across their saddles, their heads appearing to be on swivels, eying the crowd as they rode past. Tucker suspected more guards were positioned somewhere close by, to respond if need be. But the Deadwood drunks made no move to close on the stage and merely talked among themselves and pointed as the coach went by.

"Let's see where she's headed."

Tucker followed Beggar Jim, whose peg leg got stuck in the mud. Tucker and Jack jerked on it until it came free with a sucking sound. They watched the coach turn off Main Street onto a side street where the new Deadwood Dawn Hotel had recently been built. "Whowee!" Jack said as the coach stopped in front of the hotel. "What I wouldn't give to spend a night in that place. Even if it was with an old lady."

"Fat chance, unless I shoot a lot more deer than I have been."

"It's something to strive for," Jack said. "As soon's we make it big as ranchers."

When the coach stopped in front of the Dawn, the driver jumped down and opened the door. The shotgun guard stepped—he was so big he didn't have to jump to the ground—from the stage and cradled the shotgun in the crook of his arm as he watched the crowd that had followed. After a long moment, he nodded to the two outriders, and they disappeared somewhere across the street.

"Now we'll see what the old gal looks like," Jack said as the tall guard opened the coach door and took a white-gloved hand extended to him. A woman emerged wearing a long, black skirt, her features hidden by a black veil. Tall and lithe and straining her corset, she was no old lady, as Jack had assumed. She presented as stunning a figure of a woman as any who had found their way to Deadwood. She stepped onto the porch and turned to look over the crowd of two hundred miners waiting in the misty morning to hear what she had to say.

She pulled her veil back, revealing sharp, taut features, a certain hardness lining her face beneath her makeup. She wore her auburn hair in a coiffured bun, and a tendril of hair blew across her face. She tucked it behind her ear as the crowd hushed to hear her.

"Damn! That woman's a looker."

"Quiet," Tucker told Beggar Jim as Ramona Hazelton began to speak.

"I will get right to the point. My son, Miller Hazelton, was murdered two weeks ago, and I am here to bury him." She paused, gauging the effect of her words like a trained actress as she scanned the crowd. "But more than that, I am here to see his killer brought to justice. Brought to me." She nodded to the tall guard, and he motioned to the driver. He brought a strongbox from under the seat and opened it, handing Ramona a piece of paper. She held it high so everyone could see. "This is a draft drawn on the Bank of Denver for ten thousand dollars." She waited until the murmuring of the crowd died down. "And it belongs to the man who brings me the Indian who killed my son."

A miner stepped toward the porch for a closer look at the bank draft. The big guard shook his head, and the miner retreated.

"My son will be buried in two days, and for a week thereafter I will be staying at this hotel. You have until then to find the killer. After that week, I will rescind my offer and return to Denver." She handed the bank draft back to the tall guard, who put it back in the strongbox and followed Ramona into the hotel.

The crowd watched in stunned silence. When the offer sank in, they began talking among themselves before scattering in small groups toward the hills overlooking Deadwood. The hills where Indians had been spotted recently.

"Well, ain't you two going to look for that boy's killer?" Beggar Jim said.

"Let's walk," Tucker said, and they turned and headed back to the muddy street. "Did you not just see more'n a hundred fools go traipsing off to find that one Indian to kill? And how many more will join them when they wake up and hear of Mrs.

Hazelton's reward? Nothing good can come of this."

"But that is a powerful lot of money," Jim said.

"And how are they going to determine which Indian killed and scalped that soldier?" Tucker asked. "It's not like the Indian left a calling card."

"Tucker's right," Jack said, stopping long enough to roll a smoke. "Way I heard it, young Miller's body was found lying face down above Whitewood Creek with an arrow stuck in his back and his scalp sliced away. The only clue is that the arrow had the feathering of the Lakota."

"I wonder if that woman knows this could be a disaster," Tucker said, knocking gumbo off his boots. "Miners heading into the hills messing with the Sioux are most likely going to get their asses handed to them. Could be a real bloodbath for these fools."

"I see your point," Jim said. "But it's going to be a real disaster for me."

"How so?"

"With no one left in town," Jim said, "who am I going to beg off of?"

CHAPTER 9

Tucker threw an extra blanket on Soreback before setting the saddle and cinching it tight. Soreback nipped once at the saddle and went back to eying Tucker suspiciously. Tucker slipped the leather britching under the mule's tail to hold the saddle in place and grabbed the bridle hanging on a nail in the stall. Olaf had sold Tucker a spade bit and bridle one of his dead customers had left before he was shot in a saloon this last winter. Tucker coaxed the bit into the mule's mouth, talking softly. He grabbed Jack's rifle and took Daisy's reins.

"Take good care of her," Jack said as he patted his pony's back.

"If you do nothing else today," Tucker said, "make sure you find Perry Dowd."

"That's my goal," Jack said. "We *need* to get back to panning."

"And make it your goal not to get jumped and beaten again."

"I only need to have *that* happen once."

Tucker swung onto Daisy's back and held the mule's reins tight as he rode away from the livery. He still didn't know how much Soreback trusted him, but Tucker knew *he* didn't trust the mule yet. Certainly not enough to have ridden him when he went out hunting. Perhaps later, when they had been around one another, trust would develop. But Tucker was concerned enough about his self-preservation that he would take no chances with a critter that could kick him to death.

They walked past saloons, quiet now, empty now. On their way to the hills to the west of Deadwood, Tucker passed by miners working their claims, but not the usual hangers-around waiting for something—anything—to happen to bring excitement to their day. Tucker could only guess how many men had taken to the hills since Mrs. Hazelton's speech, looking for that one Sioux to kill and bring to her in order to collect the reward.

When they peaked out of the valley and were atop hills overlooking the town, Tucker stopped, listening. Somewhere in the forest men thrashed about, their voices faint but frantic, as if the specter of easy money had invaded their common sense. It would not surprise Tucker if half the men who tramped the hills were found with arrows sticking in them and their scalp locks adorning a Lakota's lodge. But Mrs. Hazelton had given them an incentive to find and kill an Indian—any Indian—and decency be damned. Tucker had no great love for the Indian—they had hunted him enough times—but he did respect them. And he knew when such decency and respect was overshadowed by revenge and greed.

By the time Tucker reached deep into the hills well away from the reward seekers, it was noon. The deer would be bedded down for at least several hours, and he hoped the hundreds of reward-thirsty fools tramping around the forest didn't scare the game away permanently.

"Ready for this little talk?" Tucker looked at Soreback, but the mule just eyed Tucker, the whites of his eyes as menacing as any bronc Tucker had ever thrown a loop over. The mule stood defiantly with his legs locked, challenging Tucker to try swinging himself into the saddle.

After tying Daisy to a birch tree, Tucker dismounted and led Soreback from the forest to a meadow, thick buffalo and grama grass providing *some* cushion for when the mule threw him.

"This is our come-to-Jesus moment," Tucker said and propped his rifle against a rock at the edge of the clearing.

He talked softly while he rolled a blanket up tight and lashed it to the cantle of the saddle. Tucker figured he'd need all the help he could get to stay on the mule's back once the big fella started bucking.

"Sorry to do this," Tucker said and slipped the end of his rope through the hondo and looped it around the mule's back leg. He ran the rope around the saddle horn, stopping when Soreback's leg was well off the ground, and tied it tight.

Tucker cheeked the mule, pulling the bridle hard, turning Soreback's head before Tucker swung into the saddle. The mule started crow-hopping—as best as he could on three legs— Tucker digging spurs into the flanks. Soreback brayed, screaming as if he were being tortured, jumping, trying to rid himself of the weight on his back. After twenty minutes, the mule stopped and hung its head, sucking in air, not looking at Tucker but at the lush grass just out of his reach.

Tucker stepped out of the saddle and ran his hand over Soreback's chest, but the mule paid him no attention. "Good," Tucker said. "Now let's see what you do in round two." He untied the rope and allowed the mule's foot to drop onto the ground before cheeking him one more time. "Here goes, big fella," he said and swung into the saddle.

The mule turned his head and merely looked at Tucker before dropping his head and beginning to munch on the lush grass. As if all he wished all along was to graze.

Which he did not.

The first great leap off all fours caught Tucker by surprise, and his legs flew too far forward on the mule's back. Daylight showed between saddle and rider, and he came back down hard against the horn. He nearly lost his balance before he double-gripped the reins. Soreback sunfished like he was a mean mustang and raked Tucker over the horn before Tucker could grab it and hold tight. With the next leap, Soreback switched ends, craning his massive head backwards, snapping jaws inches from Tucker's leg as the mule came back down hard and jarred Tucker's teeth.

The fight between mule and rider continued across the clearing, Soreback crow-hopping stiff legged, dipping to throw Tucker off, teeth snapping but never quite reaching Tucker's leg. And when Tucker thought his own teeth had been jarred loose, the mule stopped in the middle of the clearing, sides heaving, sweat lathering his flanks, his chest, and withers.

Tucker talked softly as he got out of the saddle. He stood on shaky legs while he took a parsnip out of his coat pocket and handed it to Soreback, expecting him to snap once again. But the mule took the tuber and munched calmly while he caught his wind, foamy sweat dappling his back.

After they had both caught their breath, Tucker talked to the mule quietly again as he stepped into the saddle. He held tight to the reins, keeping his feet deep in the stirrups, but Soreback remained calmly grazing on grama grass.

Cautiously, Tucker tapped Soreback's flank with a spur, and he started off at a slow walk, making a large circle around the clearing. When Tucker spurred him again, the mule started a fast trot, never breaking into a run, but not breaking into a rout either. After twenty minutes of riding, Tucker pulled up beside his rifle propped against the tree beside Daisy. He leaned down and patted the mule on the neck as he started grazing once again. "Hope we don't have to go through that every time."

Tucker was so fixated on the mule that the snap of twigs behind him startled him, and he lunged for the rifle. "I'll kill you where you sit," a voice behind him said. "Now step off that jughead and away from that Winchester."

Tucker did as he was told and got off Soreback. Zell McGinty sat atop his bay that seemed too small for him, rifle pointed at Tucker's chest. "Saw that little tussle you had with that mule. All you got for all that work was some pig-eared critter to take you places."

"He'll outlast that bay." Tucker's gaze darted around the clearing, trying to pick out some spot to dive when Zell started shooting. Not that Tucker would have any chance of walking away from this.

"It's too bad you won't get a chance to test your mule."

Tucker nodded to Zell's rifle. "You intend murdering me, here?"

Zell kept the muzzle pointed at Tucker as he slowly dismounted and walked closer to him. "You think I'm one of those savages who roam these hills, killing and scalping? A Sioux those dummies are hunting? Of course, I'm not going to kill you outright. But what I aim to do is . . ."

Zell thrust his rifle straight out, and the barrel caught Tucker on the temple. He fell out of the saddle into a piece of sage that dug into the side of his neck, vaguely aware as he struggled to stand that Zell had laid his rifle aside. "What I aim to do is teach you some manners. I didn't cotton to you beating up my boy in the Pony the other night."

Tucker got to his knees and stood on wobbly legs. His head felt as if Soreback had kicked him, and his vision was so blurry, he could barely make out Zell taking off his gun and Bowie and draping them over his saddle. Zell turned into Tucker, and he saw too late the big man's leg cock back, delivering a blow that landed in the pit of Tucker's stomach.

He rolled onto the ground. He spat grass out of his mouth and pushed himself away as Zell bent and hauled him erect by the lapels of his coat. He laughed and slapped Tucker across the face. "I'm a little bigger than my boy," he said and hit him full on the chin. Tucker's head snapped back, and he clenched his teeth against the next blow, fearing Zell would break his jaw. "I'm a bit heavier than you, but a few years older, so it ought to be an even match, don't 'cha think?" Zell asked and cocked his fist back.

"It might have been an even match," a voice said from the safety of the trees. "If you hadn't sucker-punched him with that rifle barrel. I've seen Tucker fight, and I'd put money on him. In a fair fight."

Zell looked toward the sound of the voice. "I don't know who the hell you are, but this ain't your fight, so you'd better clear out pronto."

"Drop the man."

Zell let go of Tucker and was diving for his gun hanging on his saddle when the man in the trees shot, kicking up ground an inch in front of Zell. "And you know me well enough when I say the next shot will drill a clean hole through your black heart." Simon Cady stepped from the trees holding a Rolling Block. The buffalo gun was tucked under one arm, as Simon fished in his pocket for another cartridge while he approached Zell.

"Trait will drill your ass," Zell said. "He's in the trees over yonder—"

Simon loaded the round and closed the breech block. "I don't think so, Zell. See, I would have stopped this beating you call a fair fight earlier, but I had to make sure that nasty little bastard you call a son wasn't anywhere near."

Tucker used his coat sleeve to rub blood from the blow to his head out of his eyes. He put his hands on his knees to stand as he watched Simon Cady calmly walk toward Zell. Though no taller than Zell, Simon appeared to tower over him. His wolf-skin jacket and cougar-hide cap sat at a rakish angle on his head, and his huge hands clutched his Remington rifle. A hundred years ago, folks would have called Simon Cady a mountain man. Now they just called him butcher and bounty hunter.

"Step away from those guns of your'n," Simon ordered.

Zell did as he was told. "Where did you come from?"

"Ohio," Simon said and smiled. "But I already told you that when we was at Sand Creek."

"I don't mean where you were born," Zell said. "I meant what the hell are you doing in Deadwood? Ain't no wanted men in these parts." He nodded to Tucker standing, swaying, after the beating. "Now you leave me and Tucker alone and mind your own business, and I'll forget this little misunderstanding."

"No misunderstanding to it." Simon took a step closer, and Zell backed away. "I hate to see a man suckered like you did him."

"What's Ashley to you—a pardner?"

"Not hardly," Simon said. "Any other time I couldn't care less if you beat him—or any peckerwood we find out here in Lakota land—to death. *If* the fight was fair. Let us just say I champion the little guy now and again." He chin-pointed to Tucker. "Besides, this is his lucky day." Simon stepped closer to Zell, who backed up and tripped over a log and went sprawling on the ground. "How about you?" Simon said as he pointed his rifle at Zell's head. "This your lucky day? This a day where you're just going to pick your ugly ass up and ride away from here with no fresh holes in you?"

Zell trembled. "I'm hoping it is."

"Good decision. You hop on that horse of your'n and light outta' here."

Zell stood and made his way to his horse as he kept his eyes on Simon.

"And Zell," Simon said. "Don't you dare touch those guns with bad intentions toward me, or I'll hunt you down and kill you slow." Simon cocked his Rolling Block. "Understood?"

Zell nodded and gathered his guns before riding out of the meadow.

Simon cocked an ear before walking to the trees. He returned leading his sorrel and slipped the rifle in the saddle scabbard. He took his water bladder off his saddle horn and helped Tucker sit on the ground. "That's a nasty bump he gave you with that rifle," Simon said as he soaked his bandana with water. "Here," he said.

Tucker took the bandana and pressed it gingerly against the side of his head. He winced but kept the wet cloth on his head. "Zell had one thing right—what *are* you doing here in Dead-wood?"

"Can't a man go where the wind blows him?"

"You're not just *any* man," Tucker said. "There has to be money here, or you wouldn't have come to the hills. And I doubt you came here to work a pan or sluice box."

Simon took a pull from the water bladder before capping it and draping it back over his saddle. He reached inside his coat and came away with a red-stone pipe and tobacco pouch adorned with Crow Indian beading, the bright blue and yellow glistening even in the fading light. "I am a bounty hunter," he said. "I make no apologies for that." He tamped his tobacco in the bowl with the stub of an antler. "And you are right—there is money to be made here for someone of my . . . vocation."

Tucker held the bandana to his head while he recalled the last time he saw Simon Cady. The bounty hunter had just killed an owlhoot wanted for stage robbery and murder in Montana, and Simon could have easily killed Tucker if he wished. But—like Simon told him then—there's no profit in killing a man without a price on his head. Simon had made the hair on Tucker's neck stand up back then with the easy way in which the man killed another without remorse, and that feeling hadn't gone away. Still, if Simon hadn't come along when he had, Zell might have killed him in this meadow with no one the wiser. "You're telling me you're after a wanted man hereabouts?"

"I am," Simon said, smoke rings drifting above his head. "A Lakota, if Ramona Hazelton's information is right."

"You're after an Indian who murdered her son?"

Simon nodded. His tobacco had gone out, and he relit it with a lucifer. "Ten thousand dollars is a powerful amount of money. In all the years I've hunted men, I've never saw a fugitive wanted for even close to that amount. But"—he pocketed the antler and held his hand over the bowl to keep it lit—"her offer is just a small amount with the money she has. Barely a week's oil royalties for her. I might even be able to shame her into a bonus. Once I catch the killer."

Tucker squeezed the bandana, the water feeling good trickling down his head and face. "Do you know how many men are out hunting that *one* Indian? Half the damned town—it's not even safe being in these hills with all those fools running around." He handed Simon his neckerchief. "I don't see how you're going to find one Indian. It would be difficult even if those drunken miners weren't tramping around, destroying any sign the killer might have left."

Simon smiled and tamped the burnt tobacco out on the heel of his moccasin. "I haven't hunted men this long not to have picked up some tricks. And if that Indian got away with killing and scalping a white man, I would wager he's got it in his blood—he'll do so again. That's when I look things over to see what sign he laid." He stabbed the air with his pipe. "But you stay away from that Zell McGinty. He'd as soon kill you as look at you."

Tucker held out his hand, and Simon helped him stand. His head still buzzed, but he was getting vision back to where he felt he'd survive. "It sounds like you two know one another."

"Unfortunately, we do. We both scouted down Colorado way

for the volunteers in '64.'"

"With Chivington?"

Simon looked away. "A dark spot on my honor."

It would have been a dark spot for Tucker, too, if he had scouted for Chivington. The colonel in Colorado's Volunteer Cavalry had taken it upon himself to attack Black Kettle's peaceful Northern Cheyenne and some Arapaho that had joined the chief. After massacring nearly a hundred and fifty Indians—mostly women and children—Chivington had paraded victorious back into Denver. "Word has it you were at the colonel's side when Black Kettle's village was attacked. Some mountain of a man—"

"Zell McGinty," Simon said. He looked down at his pipe, gathering his thoughts. "Sure, I scouted for Chivington—me and Zell and Jim Beckwourth, who was chief scout. Zell and me went out ahead of the rest of the volunteers. Colder'n hell that night when we spotted the Indian camp. The longer we watched, the more it became apparent there were just too many children and women to take the chance with an attack."

"But you *did* attack."

Simon nodded. "We returned to Colonel Chivington that morning and reported what we saw. I argued we ought to watch the camp, and when the warriors returned, then attack. After all, I figured they was the ones the colonel wanted anyways. Not the women folk and younguns." Simon spat, and his face became red as he recalled that morning. "But not Zell. He said we'd have the most impact by hitting the Indians where it would hurt the most—killing their families. When the volunteers attacked, Zell McGinty was right there alongside the good colonel."

"As were you?"

Simon kicked a rock with the toe of his boot. "I wanted no part of it. I didn't have a good word to say about *any* Indian, but I damn sure didn't want any part of killing their younguns. Their women. So I watched from the hillside, and it didn't take long to slaughter them." Simon put his pipe away and looked up at the sky as if gathering courage to relate the slaughter. "I rode down there afterward. Zell was kneeled over Black Kettle, unconscious, the man's white flag still flapping beside his lodge. Zell grinning up at me made my blood chilled, I'm here to tell you. He thoroughly enjoyed massacring those Indians." Simon leaned closer to Tucker. "And *that's* the kind of man who nearly killed you today. You watch your backside—he won't let this lay."

"You watch *your* backside."

Simon tilted his head back and laughed. "Hell, Zell thinks I am totally crazy. Unpredictable. He won't come after me unless he's sneaking up behind me."

Tucker walked around, feeling his balance return, the knot on his head throbbing in pain. "All I want to do is hunt deer now and again to keep me and Jack Worman's heads above water until he settles his mining dispute."

"So you're not up here with the rest of those fools looking for Indians?"

"Fools?" Tucker said, facing Simon. "A fool is a man thinking he can pick up sign of Ramona Hazelton's boy after hundreds of miners have already destroyed all traces of him."

Simon winked. "Don't count ol' Simon out just yet. After those miners fail to find that Indian and they adjourn to the saloon, I suspect there'll still be some sign left for me to decipher." He cocked his head and looked at Tucker's. "I think you'll live," he said and walked to his sorrel.

And when Simon Cady rode off, he did just what Tucker would have done—he rode off in a different direction than Zell.

CHAPTER 10

Tucker watched the spike elk from his vantage point behind ponderosa pine a hundred yards from the clearing. He had hobbled Daisy and Soreback another hundred yards downwind, unsure how the mule would react to another animal wandering in the forest. Not sure what the mule might do to spoil Tucker's shot. In time—Tucker knew—Soreback would get used to the sound of gunfire. Every mule he'd owned before Soreback would raise a ruckus the first few times when it heard shots. But every other one Tucker had ridden would eventually grow to where he could shoot off guns without exciting the mule.

The elk jerked his head erect, testing the wind. Had he heard Soreback's grunting or smelled Daisy, alien sounds and odors for the elk? After several moments, it returned to grazing on the tall buffalo grass that had benefited from the wet spring this year.

Tucker had waited for the better part of an hour, watching for doe followed the young buck. But none had come, and Tucker figured this fellow to be a bachelor driven out of another, stronger elk's herd. Unfortunate for him; fortunate for Tucker as he carefully cocked the hammer of the Winchester and let his breath out. The shot surprised Tucker as much as it surprised the elk, for Tucker never wanted to know when the shot would go down range. He never wanted to flinch with anticipation when the rifle discharged.

The elk humped up, and frothy blood dripped from his

mouth and nose from the lung shot. He staggered a few feet before dropping.

Tucker stayed still for several minutes, waiting for the critter to bleed out before he returned to Soreback. He took off the hobbles and led the mule to where the dead elk lay. The mule reared its head back, nostrils flaring at the odor of blood, and Tucker jerked down hard on the reins. "It's all right," he said as he stroked the mule's neck and handed him a parsnip. "That elk's going to be able to give you more oats tonight when we get you back to Olaf's stable. Get used to carting camp meat."

Tucker tied Soreback to an overhanging branch ten yards away and took out his Bowie, then returned to the elk to begin field dressing it. When he finished, he uncapped his canteen and ran water over his bloody hands, wiping them on his pants. "We'll get you used to gunfire," he told Soreback as he dug into his saddlebags and retrieved his Colt and holster. He buckled the belt around his hips and moved the pistol in and out of the holster. He had cut the side down with his Bowie, making it easier to grip the gun, and Olaf gave Tucker bear fat to smear inside the leather.

He dug into his saddlebags for a box of ammunition and bumped his face against the saddle. He winced and gently felt his cheek and head. The bump he'd received from Zell McGinty throbbed but was diminishing even now. Tucker was grateful Zell hadn't broken any ribs when he'd kicked Tucker. His lip was fat and swelling, but he had lost no teeth. He'd been beaten a lot worse in fights. But he also knew that if Simon Cady hadn't happened along, Zell would surely have killed him, like he'd killed defenseless Indians at Sand Creek.

But Tucker would still rather have run into Zell than Trait. Trait would love nothing better than to brag about killing Tucker Ashley in a fight. Now the little bastard would be even more determined to goad Tucker into a gunfight once his father told him about Tucker, and Simon saving his behind.

He walked to the edge of the clearing, grabbed five slender pine cones littering the forest floor, and set them on a rotted log. He walked ten paces away and turned, flexing his hand. It had started to stiffen, but he was grateful it hadn't been broken in the one-sided fight with Zell.

He slowly drew, cocked the empty Colt, and dropped the hammer once the sights were lined up on a cone. He holstered, repeating the drill, speed coming the more he dry fired. *Smooth is fast,* he told himself, and drew a last time before loading and holstering.

He breathed deeply and drew the Colt. The big .45 slug knocked a pine cone off the log, and Tucker holstered as he glanced at Soreback. The mule looked sideways at Tucker, the whites of his eyes still showing, but he made no fuss to get loose.

Tucker faced the cones again, breathing deeply, closing his eyes, imagining Trait McGinty the target, for surely Trait was the reason he was practicing. He drew and fired. Three times. And three cones flew into the air, shattered.

Fast.

Accurate.

Though neither as fast nor as accurate as he had once been. Certainly not fast enough to beat Trait McGinty, but fast enough to beat most men traipsing the hills looking for an Indian.

But then, he knew he would never be as fast as Trait.

All he had to do was avoid the killer.

CHAPTER 11

Tucker stripped the saddle off Soreback and turned him into the stall. The mule stood looking at one wall as if ignoring Tucker, but when he turned to leave, Soreback walked to the gate and hung his head over. Tucker had one snip of parsnip left, and he gave it to Soreback.

"A mule vill bide his time all his life," Olaf said as he walked out of his office rubbing sleepers out of his eyes, "yust to kill a man he hates."

Tucker ran his hand over Soreback's muzzle. "I'll remember that, even though I'm not sure I have much of a lifetime, the way things are going for me."

Olaf turned Tucker's face to the light. "I thought it looked like someone did a dance on your face."

"Zell McGinty."

"Ah," the fat man said knowingly. He grabbed a plug of tobacco and offered Tucker a chaw, but he waved it away. "Dat Zell McGinty is one nasty SOB, eh? He do not come around 'ere—boards his horse at Limey's Livery by da Badlands. Him and dat loud-mouthed whelp of his." Olaf motioned for Tucker to follow him into his small office in one corner of the barn. He pointed to a chair and poured Tucker a cup of coffee.

Tucker sat and stretched out the leg that had nearly been broken in a prison fight last year. "If I can stay away from both of them long enough to get that grievance hearing with Perry Dowd, I'll be happy."

"Good luck, with those two working for Perry."

Tucker sipped his coffee and set it on the floor while he started rolling a cigarette. "You sound like you have . . . intimate knowledge of the McGintys."

Olaf spat a string of tobacco toward a spittoon six feet away, but it fell a foot short and ran down the side of the barn. "Da McGintys used to board dere horses 'ere until Zell thought I was charging too much, and he vanted a discount. Free. When I told him he vas crazy, he got mad and t'reatened to beat me." Olaf laughed and jabbed his chest with his thumb. "With my size, do you think I worry about any man beating me, and I said yust dat to him. So ven he hit me, it vas little more than an annoyance."

Tucker lit his cigarette, careful not to get the flame close to any loose hay. "And he left you alone after that?"

Olaf smiled, recalling the fight. "No. He came at me. I knocked him down and tossed him into the side of the barn. Ven he staggered to stand, I vas ready to finish him when dat kid of his screwed his gun barrel into my ear. 'Count to ten, big man,' dat Trait said, 'and you'll be in hell.' He vould haf pulled the trigger, too, if three teamsters had not come into the barn vanting horses shoed. 'Another time, fat man,' Trait said and left. Every day I tank the Lord for teamsters." Olaf looked toward the wide doors of his livery as if expecting Trait to come in any moment.

Jack ran into the barn and spotted Tucker. He bent over to catch his breath. "I was worried about you," Jack said.

"Thanks," Tucker said, "but Zell just roughed me up a little—"

"I was talking about the shooting," Jack said and patted Tucker's pocket. He handed Jack his bible, and he began rolling a cigarette.

"What shooting?"

"A miner. Young guy. Was accidentally shot beating the hills hoping to cash in on Mrs. Hazelton's offer. Shot by another miner. Another feller was winged this morning. Damn fools are thicker than fleas on a coyote out in the hills. They was shot close to where you were hunting."

"I heard some shooting off to the south after I bagged an elk," Tucker said, "but never saw who was doing the shooting."

"You got an elk?" Jack said, glancing around the barn.

"Dropped it off at Lou's already," Tucker said and patted Jack on the back. "Relax—we'll eat good tonight."

Olaf motioned to the coffee pot, and Jack grabbed a cup hanging by a nail on the wall. "Dem fools are going to kill von 'nother, eh?" Olaf said. "Looking for dat Indian. How vill dey ever know vat Indian?"

"No way of knowing," Jack said. He finished rolling his smoke and handed Tucker his papers and tobacco pouch back. He tapped Tucker's cheek, and he winced. "Your face looks like mine now. What's the story with Zell?"

"He got the drop on me. Would have killed me, too, if Simon Cady hadn't stopped him."

"Simon Cady!" Olaf said. "Dat's all Deadwood needs is 'nother killer."

"What's he doing in the hills?" Jack asked.

"Looking for that killer of Miller Hazelton. Simon claims he'll be able to figure out which Indian did the deed, but I don't see how." Tucker brushed dirt and hay off the seat of his pants. "What did you find out about filing that grievance with the mining district?"

Jack snubbed his cigarette out under his boot. "Perry was in the office, all right, but he refused to open up and talk, no matter how hard I banged." Jack hit the side of the barn. "He *knew* I wanted to talk with him. I hung around most of the day, up until the commotion about the shot miners happened."

"Get up to Lou's Meal Tent and save us a spot. I got to visit someone for a minute."

"You got an upstairs girl you're visiting?"

Tucker shook his head. "Can't hardly afford a dance at a hurdy-gurdy house. How am I going to afford any alone time with a woman? No, I'm going up to that fancy hotel to talk with Ramona Hazelton. The longer her reward is out there, the more fools are going to get shot looking for her boy's killer."

Tucker walked the gauntlet of drunks staggering from one saloon to another, and past miners cursing themselves for losing their day's gold to some slick gambler. A man in a purple top hat sat on the walkway, miners clustered around, betting on where the pea was hidden under what nut shell. And never guessing right as they handed dust across to the guard towering over the con man.

Tucker stepped over a man passed out on the walkway and slipped. He caught himself, but not before one leg slid into the muck and mud up to his knee. He tugged on his leg. It finally came loose with a sucking noise, and he shook his leg to rid himself of the crap and goop before continuing on to Ramona's hotel.

By the time he arrived at the steps to the Deadwood Dawn, he was almost too exhausted to look up with awe at the new hotel. Tucker had walked past fancy hotels in St. Louis and Nashville after the war, and the Deadwood Dawn was as opulent looking as any of them, though on a smaller scale. He walked the eight steps to the porch running the length of the front of the hotel adorned with eight cannonades. He had started to walk inside, when the tall guard protecting Ramona Hazelton earlier emerged from inside. He turned up the collar of his raccoon overcoat that probably cost as much as Tucker made in a week panning gold with Jack. He stood in the doorway blocking

Tucker's way, the shotgun he displayed earlier looking small in the big man's arms. "Mrs. Hazelton doesn't want anyone in the hotel."

"Does she own it?"

"In a way," the man said. "She rented the whole hotel for as long as she is staying in Deadwood. And she doesn't want to be disturbed."

Tucker craned his neck up, looking into the man's gray eyes. Tucker estimated he was in his early fifties—an old man by Deadwood standards—but the lines on his face, the scars that dotted his neck and nose, told Tucker he had been around the horn. This was a man used to putting himself in the path of danger. Tucker did not desire to get beaten again, but he stepped closer to the guard. "I *need* to speak with Mrs. Hazelton."

"Shoo! She doesn't want to be disturbed."

"I thought she wanted information about her son's killer."

"What information?" the guard said. "You tell me, and I will pass it along."

"Not a chance," Tucker said, his gaze searching the buildings across the street. Somewhere on top of those buildings were marksmen in Mrs. Hazelton's employ, Tucker was certain. "That ten-thousand-dollar reward is something I keep close to my vest."

"Scat—"

"You want to tell your employer someone had information she wanted, and you put the run on him?"

The big man's face flushed, and he paused, mulling over what Tucker had said. He finally turned to the door and poked his head inside. He said something to another man in the hotel and returned to blocking the door. "Wait here."

"This must pay better than busting cows," Tucker said as he waited, making small talk.

"What makes you think I was ever a cowhand?"

93

Tucker got his makin's out and began rolling a smoke, all the while watching the guard. "You're missing your right thumb."

"So? Lot of men miss digits nowadays."

"You wear your pistol on your left side," Tucker continued as if not hearing him, "but you carry a shotgun. Like you never got the hang of drawing and cocking your pistol with your left thumb, 'cause you damn sure can't cock a hammer with a right hand with no thumb." Tucker struck a match on one of the colonnades and lit his cigarette. "I'd wager you missed a dally once when you roped a steer. Maybe a calf, and didn't get your thumb out of the way of the rope before the line went taut." Tucker snapped his fingers. "Take a man's thumb off just that quick." He grinned. "But I'm not telling you anything you don't already know."

"Is there a point to your rambling?"

Tucker drew in smoke and exhaled slowly. "Just that I observe things. All sorts of things. So here's a tip." Tucker pointed to the saloon across the street. "Tell your men on the roof to scoot back a bit. Their rifle barrels stick out like sore thumbs."

"There a reason you care?"

"Mrs. Hazelton's lost a son already. Not that it matters, but I'd hate to see her lose a guard because his men got sloppy."

Ramona Hazelton walked onto the porch. She had taken her hair down, its soft curls falling over her shoulders, her lithe movements catching Tucker off guard. When he'd first seen her getting off the coach, he had not thought of her as anything but a grieving mother. But here, with her dress casual, her manner more so, she seemed anything but an elderly mother looking for her son's killer. Tucker tried to guess her age but—like animal tracks one is not familiar with—it was difficult to know just how old she was.

"I heard what you told Chet, and do not worry about my guards—they are . . . gnarly is how I think you westerners put it." She looked Tucker up and down as if looking over a horse before buying it. "Chet tells me you have information about Miller's killer, Mister . . ."

"Tucker Ashley." He motioned to the far end of the porch. "If we can talk privately."

"It'll be all right," Mrs. Hazelton told Chet and followed Tucker. She sat in a wicker chair and motioned for Tucker to sit opposite her. "Now what information do you have for me?"

"Not so much information," Tucker said. "More like advice."

"Thank you, Mr. Ashley," Mrs. Hazelton said and stood to leave.

"Hear me out."

She paused.

"Are you aware one man's been killed and another wounded, stumbling around looking for your son's murderer."

"I have heard that, but it's none of my concern."

"Then you're aware more men may be hurt bumping into one another."

The woman shrugged. "All I want is for that Indian to stand tall in front of me so that I can look him in the eye before I see him drop from a scaffold. Unless his body is brought to me riddled with bullets already. Either way, my trip here won't be wasted."

"But there is no way to know which Indian killed your son. Even if he *was* killed by an Indian."

Mrs. Hazelton looked away. When she faced Tucker again, tears clouded her eyes. "Of course, Miller was killed by an Indian." She chin-pointed to Chet. "He said the Sioux often scalp a man while he is still alive." She ran a sleeve across her eyes. "Miller's twenty-first birthday would have been next month. The thought of a . . . child being scalped alive . . ."

"But how can you be certain the Indian these miners bring will be *the* Indian you want?"

95

"Mr. Ashley," Mrs. Hazelton said, "if these men bring me a hundred Indians, the killer is sure to be among them. Or two hundred. However many bodies they bring, the odds are good the one I want will be among them." She stood. "Now if you're done wasting my time—"

"One other thing," Tucker said. "Man down at the feed store said he's holding your son for his funeral."

Mrs. Hazelton nodded. "Mr. Grundy. His cellar, where he keeps . . . victims now and again, awaiting burial, is lined with ice. When I first heard Miller had been killed, he agreed to keep him—for a healthy sum, of course—until I could bury him proper."

She looked past Tucker, and he turned. Perry Dowd approached the walkway, his white suit pressed, his bowler hat perched atop his head at a fashionable angle. His full head of gray hair stuck from his hat and grew to meet his full, salt-and-pepper beard. He was little older than Tucker, but he looked much more so. He mounted the steps and walked past Chet to stop in front of Mrs. Hazelton. He ignored Tucker as he offered his arm. "Ready for dinner?"

The woman smiled and threaded her arm through his. Tucker laid a hand on Perry's shoulder. Perry looked at Tucker and tried shrugging off the hand, but Tucker clamped hard. Mrs. Hazelton waved Chet away as she looked with amusement at the two men.

"My partner, Jack Worman, has been camped out at the mining office to arrange a grievance hearing with you."

"What is this grievance hearing?" Mrs. Hazelton asked.

"Nothing for you to worry about," Perry said and tried shrugging Tucker's hand off again.

"The hearing," Tucker told the woman, "is when we miners have had our claims stolen and believe we have a right to have them returned."

Tucker dropped his hand, and Perry straightened his suit. "Miners have all sorts of cockamamie reasons for wanting a hearing before the district manager," Perry said.

"Jack Worman doesn't think it's a cockamamie reason," Tucker said to Mrs. Hazelton, "and I would wager—being a successful business woman—you wouldn't think proper business protocol is cockamamie either."

Mrs. Hazelton freed her arm and faced Perry. "Tell me you give these men proper service."

Perry's neck turned crimson, and his jaw clenched tight. "All right, then—ten o'clock tomorrow morning at the mining office."

"Thank you," Tucker said and turned to Mrs. Hazelton. "Last thing—is it all right if I pay respects to your son?"

"Even though you never knew him?" she asked.

"Let us say it is one former soldier honoring another."

"Very well, then," she answered. "See Mr. Grundy. He can show you where he is keeping Miller's body."

Tucker had turned to leave when Mrs. Hazelton called after him: "Is this something unique to Deadwood—paying respects to a total stranger?"

"Unique?"

"You're the second man who wanted to pay his respects," Mrs. Hazelton said. "The first was a bear of a man. Looked like pictures I've seen of mountain men."

"Mountain men?"

She nodded. "And he had the most beautiful, flowing white hair, kept so impeccably."

"He wanted to visit Miller, too?"

"He did."

"Simon Cady," Tucker said under his breath and started for the feed store.

CHAPTER 12

Tucker walked the three muddy blocks to the feed store, stepping over one drunk passed out across the walkway, running into another who had gotten the bum's rush from a saloon by the bouncer. Somewhere in back of Tucker two gunshots sounded, and he wondered if one or both men were dead as a result.

The lamp glowed from the feed and tack store, and Tucker was surprised the door was still unlocked tonight. A tiny bell tinkled as he walked into the store, and he looked around. No one attended the store filed with bridles and hackamores hanging on walls alongside a saddle propped atop a sawhorse with a price tag dangling off the pommel. Bags of chicken feed stood piled in front of a long counter. A bin of shovels and pickaxes stood awaiting anxious miners, fresh off the trail to buy them, even though there were no claims left. But no Mr. Grundy.

"Can I help you?" a deep voice called out from somewhere in back of the counter.

Tucker squatted in front of the long display case and looked through the glass at a pair of eyes staring back. "I need to talk with a Mister Grundy."

Tucker expected the man to stand and meet him around the counter. But he was already standing. A man twice Tucker's age but half his size wiped his hands on a feed-sack apron and walked the end of the counter. "You a buyer or a looker?" he asked, craning his neck up to see Tucker.

"Mr. Grundy?"

The man nodded. "Well?"

"I'm a looker. That's if you can tell me where I can pay my respects to Miller Hazelton."

"Damnit!" Grundy said and tossed his apron on the floor. He stomped it into the chaff littering the floor until he realized the spectacle he was creating. "Sorry." He straightened his bow tie and picked up his apron. He shook chaff and dust from it and put it back on. "It is just that . . . storing young Hazelton in my root cellar was a favor to the mourning mother—"

"One that has already proven quite lucrative, I would wager."

Grundy waved the air as if to dismiss it. "In any event, I wasn't supposed to have people parading through here while I'm working." He grabbed a lamp and turned to the back door. "But that's not your fault. Follow me."

Grundy stepped outside and walked twenty feet to one side of his store. He pulled a wide root-cellar door back and lit the lantern. "Here." He handed Tucker the lamp. Grundy grabbed a heavy coat hanging just inside the door and pulled it on. "Gets a mite chilly down here," he said and held the lamp in front of him while he picked his way carefully down the earthen steps.

"Mrs. Hazelton said the dearly departed had another visitor today."

Grundy stopped on the steps and half turned. "There was some big man." He shuddered, and Tucker didn't think it was from the ice-lined cellar. "That man gave me the willies."

"Did he threaten you?"

Frosty breath came from Grundy's mouth as he spoke. "He didn't have to—his look said it all. He wanted to be left alone with the body, and I didn't argue with him."

When they reached the bottom of the steps, Tucker thought the temperature had dropped forty degrees. He ran his hand over thick blocks of ice lining two walls.

"I get ice harvested from Whitewood Creek," Grundy said as if reading Tucker's thoughts. "Stays cold in here until mid-August."

Tucker broke off an ice chip and stuck it into his mouth.

"Duck your head," Grundy said as he led Tucker into a side room. "Something *I* don't have to do." He laughed.

The little man held the lamp in front of him as if to ward off spirits of the dead as he stopped at the threshold of the room. "Oh, young Hazelton," he called to the body underneath the horse blanket atop a table, "you have another visitor." Grundy handed Tucker the lamp. "Close the door and hang the lantern back when you're finished. I have work to do. Besides," he said, turning up his collar, "it's too damned cold down here."

Tucker waited until he heard Grundy close the cellar door after him before walking to the body. He peeled the blanket back and held the light to the victim. Miller Hazelton might have been twenty, but he looked even younger in death, with his wisp of blond mustache that had never grown full. A calico shirt clung to his dead torso, but he wore the woolen dungarees of a soldier. His lace-up boots told Tucker he had been infantry, used to walking long distances. The skin to one side of his face had been scuffed as if it had been dragged along the ground, and one arm had a deep laceration across it. Tucker turned the arm to the light: the wound had been made prior to Miller dying. A defensive wound? Both the man's face and arm had been thoroughly cleaned, part of Grundy's fee to the grieving mother, no doubt.

Tucker felt a cold draft and looked over his shoulder, but no one stood behind him. Like Grundy, Tucker started feeling a little morbid down here with the dead man as he rolled Miller onto his side. Tucker raised the shirt up, examining the spot where the arrow had been shot through a lung. Few men could have lived after such a terrible wound, yet Miller had lived long enough to fend off his attacker and receive a nasty cut to his arm. Tucker had been in Miller's boots more times than he wanted to remember, staring down the bow of a Lakota within arrow range, and knew the terror the young man had experienced before he died must have been maddening.

He gently rolled Miller onto his back once more and was pulling his shirt down over his bare torso when the head wound—the scalping of a man in his prime—caught Tucker's attention. He had seen dozens of men scalped in his time on the frontier, during his time scouting for the army, and times as a buffalo hunter. But he had never seen a man scalped so . . . cleanly.

He walked to the head of the table and turned the lamp up brighter. Miller's scalp had been lifted—cleanly. Like a surgeon would have done if given the duty. The victim's entire head showed where a sharp blade had been run under the scalp, slicing all the way around Miller's head until the whole scalp came off.

Neat. Almost surgical. And with that, Tucker left Miller to his icy tomb.

"What if Perry don't show?" Jack asked. He sat with his back against the mining district office. He wasn't going to get waylaid from behind again. "What will we do then?"

"Then I'll go visit Ramona Hazelton again," Tucker said, watching men stagger past, fighting off hangovers on their way to working their claims. "For no longer than she's been in town, it appears as if Perry's taken a liking to her."

"Haven't you?"

Tucker hadn't thought about Ramona Hazelton.

Since last night after visiting her, that is.

Sure, he'd thought about the lady, the strong businesswoman

who could put most men in their traces, coming to Deadwood with the sole purpose of burying her son and avenging his death. The woman—hard features made harder by the rough and tumble fights of business people—softened whenever she talked about her son. "I think Mrs. Hazelton will have enough influence on Perry. If she wants him here for our meeting, he'll be here."

"You two talking about me?" Perry said, walking up to them, his cane used for balance to keep him from falling off the wooden walkway. He opened the door to the mining district office and stepped inside. "Close the door," he said and hung his hat on a bentwood coat rack along one wall. He sat behind his tiny desk and motioned to two chairs.

Perry grabbed a file from a basket marked GRIEVANCES. He donned half glasses and wet a pencil stub with his tongue. "You want to file a grievance on your claim—"

"Our claim," Jack corrected.

Perry wrote "both claimants" across the form and jotted their names down. "I'm ready to hear your story," he said looking over his glasses.

"Ain't there like a jury or something?" Jack asked.

Perry shook his head. "Young Worman, there is no law here in Deadwood as we know it. We—Deadwood—isn't even legal to *be* here. Or didn't anyone tell you this part of Dakota Territory still belongs to the Indians?"

"Then where do we stand, Jack and me?"

"Stand, Mr. Ashley? Where we—or, I should say, you two—stand is this: I am the sole arbiter of mining disputes. Like it or not, that is a fact until such time as the Indians sell the government these Black Hills and we get an organized judicial system in place." Perry set his glasses on the desk. "So let us get on with this." He checked his Waltham and slipped it back into his vest pocket. "I have a lunch date." He ruffled through the papers and set one aside. "It says here in the Flynn brothers' application that you abandoned your claim next to theirs, and they filed on it."

"I didn't abandon it!"

Tucker laid his hand on Jack's arm. "What Jack is saying, is that he left the claim just long enough to pick me up in Custer City."

"Did you post on your claim when you intended returning?" Perry asked.

"Why the hell should I?" Jack blurted out. "It's my claim."

Perry put on his glasses and took out a small, green book from a drawer. He flipped pages, and finally turned it around so that Jack could read it. "Rule here"—Perry tapped the book—"says that if one leaves his claim for more than seventy-two hours without posting it, it shall be deemed abandoned and open for anyone else to file on. And that's just what the Flynns did."

"Let me see that." Tucker turned the book around and read the rule. "If I didn't know better, I'd say the ink dried on this cockamamie rule sometime yesterday."

Perry leaned back in his chair and smiled. "The rule book has been here in my office for all to see. And to follow these regulations."

Jack stood abruptly and leaned across the desk. His hand shot out, inches away from Perry's throat before Tucker hauled him back into his chair. "Since there are no laws here in Deadwood," Jack said, his hand resting on his gun butt, "there is nothing illegal in ventilating you right here in your own office."

"Nothing except him," Perry nodded to the door.

Zell McGinty filled the doorway of the mining office. He moved closer to Perry as he glared at Tucker. For a big man, Tucker thought, Zell moved awfully quiet. *I'll remember that.*

"These men are unhappy about our regulations," Perry said, "but they were just leaving."

Jack moved toward Zell, but Tucker shoved him toward the door. As Tucker passed Zell, the latter grabbed Tucker's arm. "My boy says he is looking forward to meeting you." Zell tapped Tucker's naked hip. "So you should start wearing that gun of yours."

Although it was mid-morning, the saloons along Deadwood's Main Street operated like it was midnight. Calliope music—erupting from one saloon, brash and echoing off the shanties and buildings thrown up in haste this last year—joined with a shrill voice coming from another saloon. Jack and Tucker bypassed them on their way to the Pretty Pony. At least there had only been four men killed in the Pony this year.

They started through the door, side-stepping a drunk being shown the door by Madame Marcie's bar dog. The drunk went sprawling in the mud. "And don't come in thinking you can cheat at stud again!" Madame Marcie called after him. She turned to Jack and Tucker as if seeing them for the first time. "Cheatin's reserved for the house." She slapped Jack on the back. "Come in and have a drink."

"We were doing just that."

"And can I interest you in a game of chance?"

Jack jerked his thumb at the drunk fighting to crawl out of the mud. "And wind up like that boob? Just beer, Madame."

"Monty," she called to the bar dog. "Two beers for these fellers."

Jack shoved two men out of the way, and another, who fell onto the faro table, as Jack stomped to a corner table. Tucker had seen Jack in this mood before. He knew his friend would love nothing more than to get into a knock-down fight just to get his anger off his chest. "Now what the hell we going to do?"

Jack slapped the table for effect.

"Drink up for now," Tucker said when Monty brought their beers, warm and three-quarters foam. "Then see if there are *any* claims the Flynns may have missed. Surely there are some not filed on—"

"I heard there are some claims way up Whitewood Creek, but they aren't producing enough color to buy a pouch of tobacco." Jack blew foam onto the floor. "The only ones working those claims are the heathens."

"If the Chinese are working the creek, color must not be too plentiful."

"My thought exactly." Jack leaned across the table. "We could go back to scouting for the army."

"Maybe you can," Tucker said, "but I sure as hell can't, or did you forget the army is the one that made me a convict? I'll have to keep hunting game for Lou until I find something else."

Jack downed his beer and held up his hand for another. "Just what am I gonna' do while you're off hunting? Don't take two of us to kill game."

Tucker waited until Monty had set two more beers on the table and was out of earshot before telling Jack, "You can start by nosing around. I want you to find out what Perry Dowd is really up to."

"He's the mining district rep."

"He's more than that if he has to hire the likes of Trait and Zell McGinty," Tucker said, sipping the foam slower this time, his split lip still tender. "Look—Perry denied that grievance a little too easily. Like he wanted the Flynns to keep the claim they stole. And believe me—those two idiots never had enough money to buy a shovel to work a claim, let alone afford the fee to file on one."

"You saying Perry is in cahoots with the Flynns?"

"I just don't know," Tucker said. "All I know is someone with money is buying up claims. And it sure isn't those two Irish bums."

Lowell Tornquist staggered into the Pony and made it to the bar before he fell against it. He looked around at the other drunks wasting their money at poker and the faro table and the roulette wheel. "Drinks for everyone!" he hollered.

The crowd elbowed each other in a rout to get to the bar and claim their free drinks.

Lowell dug into his pocket and handed Monty some coins before spotting Jack and Tucker sitting at the table. Lowell jostled his way through the crowd and plopped down across from Jack. He squinted through one eye swollen nearly shut. His nose had been broken, and bruises showed up black around Lowell's eyes, making him look like he was a raccoon.

"What happened to you?" Jack said and touched the young man's cheek. He drew back, and his hand gently caressed the side of his face. "And where did you get the money to buy a round for the house?"

"I s-s-s-sold my claim," Lowell said, stuttering in his Minnesota brogue like he always did. "A-a-and I figured I might as well spend it while it l-l-lasted."

Tucker motioned to the drunks drinking free on Lowell's money. "It won't last long at this rate. I thought you were like Jack—panning five dollars a day most days?"

"Was," Lowell answered, downing his beer. Foam ran down his dirty shirt front, but he paid it no mind as he held his mug high for another. "Until the Flynns bought me out."

"Lowell," Tucker said. "You didn't sell out to those peckerwoods? How much did they give you?"

"H-hundred dollars."

"Kid," Jack said. "Haven't you ever learnt figures? Many claims have brought fifteen hundred dollars. At five dollars a day, you'd have panned that hundred dollars in less than a month."

Lowell slammed his mug on the table. "I know how many days it would take to save up that amount." He pointed to his swollen and bruised face. "But just what the h-h-hell *could* I do? If I refused, the Flynns would beat m-me even worse."

"That's horse shit," Jack said. "I think I'm just going to stop and talk with that Perry Dowd. If his thugs were hired to enforce mining rules, they better damn well enforce this. It's nothing less than theft by the Flynns. What the hell do the McGintys get paid to do?"

"They were there," Lowell said. "Fact was, I went for my shotgun when that r-r-red-haired basted was kicking me, but Trait McGinty drew down on me like he was itching to kill somebody. I didn't want to be the somebody that gave him another scallop on that Colt of his."

"I told you they were dirty," Tucker said. "Maybe they're getting paid by both sides—the Flynns and whoever is feeding them money to buy claims."

"Or maybe the McGintys are the ones buying claims through the Flynns," Jack said.

"All's I know is, I *had* to sell." Lowell fished into his overalls and held a half eagle to the light. "And tomorrow, I'll have just enough money t-t-to get out of here. D-d-deadwood's beaten me to a draw."

CHAPTER 13

Soreback stopped and refused to go farther up the steep hillside dotted with ponderosa pine, birch, and juniper bushes. Mules were always smarter than horses, Tucker knew, and were smarter than some men he'd known, too. Beggar Jim had told Tucker just where Miller Hazelton had been found dead by a wolfer working the hills. Somehow, Tucker thought, the mule sensed a tragedy had occurred close by, and he slowed. As if by continuing up the hill, bad things would befall mule and rider.

Tucker found himself riding in this direction even though he hadn't seen any game trails in this part of the forest. "I need to hunt for meat," he confided in Soreback, "not traipse around looking for where young Hazelton was killed. Ain't none of my business what happened to him."

And it *wasn't* any of Tucker's business. But seeing the way in which Miller had been surgically scalped had piqued his curiosity. But he wished the mule could speak and talk him out of looking for the kill site. Perhaps Soreback refusing to continue up was his way of doing just that.

"That's a powerful climb up there if'n I was to make it afoot," he said soothingly, stroking the mule's neck and pointing up as if Soreback could understand. But the mule stood impassively, looking about, paying no mind to the man on his back. *At least he didn't try to buck me off today.*

Tucker reached into his coat pocket and grabbed a carrot. He held it in front of Soreback, and soon the bribe worked. He took the carrot and continued the climb. Tucker let the mule have his way, knowing he could figure better than Tucker the least difficult path to reach the top. And just what would he find if he located the spot Miller was killed? After two weeks, little sign would remain. If any. Unless some hapless Indian had left a note with his name on it.

When they reached the summit, Tucker reined the mule and looked down into the valley. The claims and the men working them were but large dots on Deadwood Gulch. Faint glimpses of town peeked through the trees, and the smoke of wet firewood could be seen between the pines. He strained to hear the men working, strained to pick out the saloon music. But he heard none of that. Except for the faint breeze rustling the pine needles, it was totally quiet. Yet he knew that at any moment the quiet could be shattered by passing Indians, and he could be fighting for his life. Like Miller Hazelton must have done.

He turned in his saddle and studied the hills. This was prime Lakota land. A half mile back, he had picked up tracks of unshod ponies working their way topside sometime this morning, if he aged them correctly. Yesterday when he was out scouting for deer, he had draped his bandana over Soreback's eyes to calm him when Tucker spied four Sioux warriors riding single file on a ridgeline seventy yards away. Tucker was sure they had spotted him when they stopped suddenly. But they hadn't, and they sat their ponies as they looked down on Deadwood and miners in the gulch. After tense moments, they rode on, as silent as if they had been gliding across soft, white powder that still dotted the hills.

Tucker stood in the stirrups and surveyed the area. It was as Beggar Jim had told him. Although the old man hadn't been out of Deadwood in over a year, he knew exactly where the wolfer had found Miller Hazelton's body. For someone who never went anywhere, Beggar Jim was surprisingly accurate in his description.

"Just how do you know where Miller was killed if you've never been there?" Tucker had asked him.

"Buy me a venison meal, and I'll explain it." Tucker bought Jim a steak and had to wait until the old man was near finished. "That wolfer told me when he brought the body in," Jim said as he speared a piece of venison with a fork missing two tines. Which was appropriate, as Jim had only two teeth left. "He said young Hazelton was right there beside a rock in front of a big lightning-burnt pine tree."

Tucker eased Soreback along the edge of a meadow swaying with grama grass and switch grass, buffalo berry bushes with their tiny fruit nearly ripe, feeling the cool, healing wind wash over his face when the spotted a pine tree—charred and lying across a boulder. He ought to be hunting for meat, he knew, for soon his money would run out.

He turned the mule away from the tree and paused. He checked the sun—there were still several hours left during which he could find a game trail, and he fought the urge to ride across the meadow to the kill site.

His urges lost. The memory of the young man's scalp still haunted Tucker, and he turned Soreback once again toward the tree. He had just enough time to feed his curiosity before the game was on the move once more.

When he neared the tree and the boulder beside it, Tucker dismounted. He took hobbles from his saddlebags and slipped them on Soreback's legs before looking at the sun. The meadow around the tree had been trampled down. Not gently, like deer or elk do for an afternoon nap, but violently, grass thrashed in every direction in an area nearly as big as a freight wagon.

Soreback jerked his head up and snorted. "I smell it, too," Tucker said.

Blood.

Putrid, fetid blood that had been rotting. But for how long?

Tucker squatted as he looked at the sun again. Blackened blood dotted the matted-down grass. More blood than there should have been here, if Miller alone had bled. A man's scalp bleeds profusely from a thousand tiny veins when he is scalped alive. But Miller could have only lasted moments with an arrow through his lungs. So why so much blood?

Tucker stood and stretched before walking in large circles around the kill site, always looking at the ground, studying the area, to figure out why so much blood . . .

A glint of something metal reflected the sunlight, and Tucker walked a dozen paces from the tree and bent to the object. A Green River knife lay partially buried under switch grass. Tucker grabbed it and held it to the light. There was nothing special about it: six-inch blade, leather-wrapped handle, dried blood crusted on the steel. Tucker brought it to his nose. The years in prison hadn't stunted Tucker's ability to age blood—this was more than a week old.

But this wasn't the knife that had scalped Miller Hazelton.

Tucker guessed Miller had owned the trade knife, probably picked it up in a sutler's store at some army fort before he deserted, its chipped blade hardly sharp enough to shave kindling.

Tucker stuck the knife in his waistband and had turned to the mule when the wind shifted, and the smell of rotting flesh drifted past his nose. He tilted his head up to catch the wind. He walked another dozen paces toward where the odor became stronger. Under a patch of cactus, hair fluttered. It was attached to a man's scalp that had been discarded. Tucker grabbed a branch and turned it over, spreading it out. Maggots had nearly consumed much of the flesh, but he could tell it was an entire scalp with blond hair fluttering. Tucker considered taking it back for burial with the body but dismissed the thought. Ramona Hazelton needn't see this. Seeing her dead son was enough.

Tucker returned to Soreback and took the hobbles off. "I've never heard of an Indian scalping a man and tossing the scalp aside." Soreback seemed to agree, as he jerked his head away from the bloody patch of hair and skin. "Any Indian would be proud to hang the scalp on his lodge pole." Tucker looked around and shuddered. "But which Indian?"

Chapter 14

Tucker bedded Soreback down for the night at Olaf's Livery and walked to the Deadwood Dawn. As he passed the saloon across the street, he glanced up. At first he saw nothing to indicate armed men were on the roof, until he spied the tip of a rifle muzzle and knew his approach had been covered every step.

He'd walked up the stairs when Chet emerged from inside, all three hundred pounds of him blocking entrance to the hotel. "Guess I didn't explain myself good enough last night," he said as he walked closer to Tucker. Before he had gone off to prison, he had been leery—even somewhat intimidated—by men Chet's size. But after two years of fighting men like Chet just for the right to continue breathing, Chet worried him little. "Mrs. Hazelton doesn't want to be disturbed."

"I have information about her son."

"Like the information last night? You wasted her time then, and I should have tossed you out that first time."

Tucker turned away from the hotel and started down the steps. "Suit yourself. But if the information I have is what she is looking for—"

"Stay right here," Chet said. "I'll get her."

Before Chet disappeared into the hotel, he glanced up at the roof across the street and nodded imperceptibly. Though the big man had gone inside, Tucker knew if he made a move to follow Chet, the outrider across the street would drill him with his

Winchester.

Ramona Hazelton followed Chet out of the hotel. She wore riding britches and a sheer, white top held tight by whale-bone buttons. Her auburn hair was pulled into a tight chignon, and—when she spotted Tucker—a smile crept across her face for the briefest moment. "Mr. Ashley—Chet tells me you insist on seeing me. Again."

Tucker motioned to the same wicker chairs at the far end of the porch they had sat in before. "May we?"

"I will be all right," she told Chet and brushed past Tucker towards the chairs. "And ask the staff to bring lemonade," she called to Chet.

She sat in a chair and motioned for Tucker to sit as well. "You had little information for me the first time we met. This better be good."

Tucker took off his hat and ran his hand around the brim, deciding what to say. There was just no easy way of telling the boy's mother. "Your boy was scalped—"

"Of course, he was scalped. I saw his body. And in return, men have delivered six Indian scalps to me, claiming to be from my son's killer."

"How do you know one of the scalped men killed Miller?"

Mrs. Hazelton met Tucker's gaze defiantly. "I don't."

"There is no way of knowing which Indian killed your son unless the whole Sioux nation is killed."

"Then so be it," the woman said and waited until the waiter had set the pitcher of lemonade and glasses on the table between the chairs. "It matters none to me." She sipped her lemonade. "I suspect that's the reason you came here again—to talk me out of offering my reward. I won't do it. The more Indians killed, the better the chance that one of them murdered Miller."

"I went to Grundy's cold cellar and looked at Miller's body. I don't think Indians killed him."

Mrs. Hazelton set her frosted glass down and wiped her moist fingers on her trousers. "Are you what they called an Indian lover, Mr. Ashley?"

"Indian lover?" Tucker shook his head. "Not hardly. I've fought Indians most my life, and near come to getting killed a few times. Scouted for the army against them. But"—he leaned forward—"I know when men are being falsely accused, and I don't like it. Even if it is Indians."

"Why do you think men other than those savages killed Miller?"

"Your son's scalp was . . . lifted neatly," Tucker said, choosing his words carefully. "With care and precision to make certain *all* his scalp was taken off."

"What has that got to do with your theory that Indians did not kill him?"

A gun shot from a saloon down the street echoed off the buildings, and Mrs. Hazelton jumped. "Have you ever seen a man scalped by Indians?" Tucker asked, not waiting for her response. "They often scalp in the heat of battle. Quick. Taking no time to be precise. They don't need an entire scalp to hang from their lodge. And they sure don't risk taking the time to scalp precisely."

The woman's eyes watered, and she turned away. Chet stepped toward them, but she waved him off. "Are you telling me this to make certain I remember the way in which my son was killed?"

Tucker stood and paced in front of the chairs. "Someone took the time to carefully cut Miller's *entire* scalp away, trying to make it look like Indians. But it was someone unfamiliar with Indian ways."

Mrs. Hazelton brought her glass slowly to her lips before putting it back down. "That is just nonsense. All he ever did was enlist in the army and desert. Why would anyone want to kill Miller?"

"Oldest reason in the world—money."

"He *had* no money!" the woman said. "When he enlisted in the army to spite me, I told him I would not give him a dime until he came back home. I wanted him to become involved in running the family business, but he insisted on going away anyway. Do you know what an army private makes, Mr. Ashley?"

"Sixteen dollars a month," Tucker said, "before deductions."

"Then why in the world would anyone kill Miller for sixteen lousy dollars?"

"For his claim on Deadwood Gulch."

Mrs. Hazelton dried her eyes with the sleeve of her blouse. "Perry says all a good miner makes is five dollars a day panning. If he's lucky. No man would kill another for five dollars."

"Prison is full of men who'd kill for less than that."

"That's right," Mrs. Hazelton said. "They say you were in prison these last few years. They also say you were a most dangerous man before . . ." She exaggerated a look at Tucker's shabby clothes.

Tucker flushed, ashamed at his torn and faded jeans with caked-on deer blood and mud; at his muslin shirt—the one the prison had issued him the day he got there—that had the pocket torn and should have been thrown away long ago. He had stuffed his boots with newspaper to shore up the holes, and his hat showed the bullet hole from a murderer he'd tracked in the Badlands a week before the army arrested him. "I think your son got his licks into his attacker before he died."

"How so?"

Tucker reached inside his vest and withdrew the knife he had found in the meadow at the kill site. Chet shouldered his shotgun, but Mrs. Hazelton mouthed "stay" when Tucker handed the knife to her. "My God, where did you get this?" she asked, her hand covering her mouth. "Miller's father gave this to him a week before the rig accident that crushed Thomas."

"I recovered that in the field where Miller was killed. There was a lot of blood on the grass—far more than could come just from your son. I think he sliced his attacker before he . . . died."

Mrs. Hazelton turned the knife over in her hand. "But there's no blood on the blade or the handle."

"I cleaned it. Didn't figure you needed to see it stained like it was."

"Thank you for that, Mr. Ashley, but my bounty still stands. Nothing you said proves Indians *didn't* kill Miller. Come back when you have something more substantial."

She had started for the entrance to the hotel when she stopped and turned back. She reached into the billowing pocket of her blouse and took out a bandana. She peeled it back to reveal an Indian's medicine bundle, cracked leather and shaped like a turtle. "Here," she said and handed Tucker the medicine bundle. "This might convince you an Indian killed my son."

Tucker balanced the bundle in his palm. The cracked leather was worn along the edges, and the thong a warrior would hang around his neck was brittle. It had broken at some point and been tied back together. "Where did you get this?"

"It was still clutched in Miller's hand when that wolfer brought his body in. Perhaps it might help to find that *one* Indian you say will be impossible to find."

Mrs. Hazelton walked toward the entrance and whispered something to Chet. And just before she disappeared into the hotel, she glanced back at Tucker. And smiled.

"What did you find out?" Tucker asked as he blew warm foam off his mug.

"Perry can't—or won't—let anyone see his books," Jack

answered. "But he did say someone he cannot reveal has been buying up mining claims all along Deadwood Gulch and Whitewood Creek. Some claims that have been abandoned."

"Or outright stolen. Like by those thieves, the Flynns," Tucker said.

"But, of course, Perry denied it was those fools."

"I'd wager he's right. Has to be someone with a whole lot of money," Tucker said.

"Like Perry," Jack said and lowered his voice. "Beggar Jim said Perry came to Deadwood right after the first gold strike with a couple of girls on his arm. Had no interest in breaking his back panning gold. But he was one of the few here who could tally books, and miners at the time voted him in as the mining district representative."

"That can't pay much."

"Especially since it's only part time. Seems like Perry comes to the district office only when there are ledgers to be filled out. Claims recorded or transferred. But those girls . . ." Jack smiled. "Those girls—they're running cribs out of the Miner's Paradise. Seems like Perry's got an arrangement with the owner—use his girls, and he gets a percentage."

Jack finished his beer and started to raise his arm for another when he put it back down. "Being out of work and broke like I am, I am at your mercy for another."

"I've got enough if you want another beer," Tucker said.

"I'm thinking about it," Jack said and nodded to a thirty-something miner downing shots of whisky faster than Tucker could count them. "Buckshot Blue there sold his claim yesterday for a song. Like Lowell, he was showing color every day he worked it. He didn't want to sell, and his face shows it."

Tucker squinted to peer through the smoke lingering just above the tables packed with drinkers and gamblers, until Buckshot Blue turned his head in Tucker's direction. Someone had danced on his face, making it look worse than Lowell's. Both eyes were swollen, and his jaw was disfigured, as if it had been broken. Sometime yesterday. "The Flynns made him an offer, but he put the run on them. When Buckshot went to the McGintys to report it, they just laughed at him. Told 'ol Buckshot they could do nothing. He blew his top and"—Jack nodded at Buckshot—"he made the mistake of throwing a punch at Zell."

"And I would bet Perry Dowd could do nothing, either?"

"Sure, Perry had some advice—don't attack his Protectionists, which is what Perry's calling his thugs. And Buckshot's been on the prod ever since."

As if to punctuate Jack's words, Buckshot shoved another drunk aside and elbowed up to the bar. The other man bulled up for a brief moment before walking away. "Buckshot's going to get his head split again if he doesn't cool off," Tucker said.

"Could be worse," Jack said, then added, "what the hell" and raised his hand for another mug of beer. "Buckshot's lucky he's not working his claim—another feller was shot when he was out looking for Mrs. Hazelton's Indian." Jack snickered. "Beggar Jim says the man was in the bushes doing his daily business when he was winged in the hind end."

Tucker waited until Monty had brought Jack another beer and left before telling him about his failed meeting with Ramona Hazelton. He explained that he'd found Miller's bloody knife in the grass close to his scalp, and how there was something odd about the arrow wound that supposedly killed him. "Too bad Grundy cleaned Miller up. We could have figured a lot by the blood seeping out of him. And I wish I could have gotten a look at that arrow, but she said the wolfer tossed it before bringing Miller into town. Something don't add up," he said.

"Damn straight it don't!" Jack said. "Indians don't waste

time to lift a man's hair like that. Rip and run, is what they do."

Buckshot started yelling and pointing to the door, shaking his fist like he was going into battle, and the drunks quieted. Trait McGinty elbowed his way through the crowd, limping like he'd gotten bucked off his roan gelding that was too skittish for him.

Trait stopped five paces in front of Buckshot and grinned at him. "I heard you were looking for me. Here I am."

"I want my claim back!"

"You already sold it to the Flynns," Trait said. "Duly noted at the mining office."

Buckshot pulled his tattered coat back to reveal a .36 Navy cap-and-ball pistol jammed down his trousers.

"This ain't going to end good," Tucker said. He shoved drunks aside, making his way to Buckshot just as he squared off to Trait. Tucker grabbed Buckshot by the arms and started dragging him away.

"What the hell you doin'?"

"You're drunk."

"Of course, I'm drunk," Buckshot said.

Tucker dragged Buckshot through the miners—who had parted to let the two men fight each other. They wanted the entertainment of a gun fight; they just didn't want to get drilled in the process. "You don't need this."

Buckshot jerked violently and nearly fell down. "Leave me the hell alone."

"That's right," Trait said. "Leave the fool alone." A piece of straw flicked from Trait's smiling lips. "This man wants a fight, unlike you." Trait raised his voice, ignoring Buckshot with his hand hovering above his gun butt. "Ashley here don't dare wear a gun—he knows he'll have to face me. The *great* Tucker Ashley—"

Buckshot yelled. He grabbed for his pistol and jerked on it. It hung up on his trousers, and Trait calmly drew his Colt. He waited until Buckshot freed his gun before Trait drilled him center chest, two shots sounding as one, and the miner was dead before he hit the floor.

Tucker knelt beside Buckshot, who had blood oozing from his chest, then he stood. "He was drunk," he said and stepped closer to Trait, still holding his smoking gun. He brought it up and pointed it at Tucker's head. "Anyone else want to lodge a complaint like Buckshot did?"

"I do." Madame Marcie stepped into the cleared circle in the center of the floor. She nodded to her guard sitting the chair high in one corner of the saloon. "You've killed enough for today. Next one gets ventilated is you."

Trait looked a long moment at the man with the double Greener pointed his direction before he backed away to the door. He holstered slowly and pointed a finger at Tucker. "Next time you be heeled, or I'll lend you one of mine. Either way, you and me gonna have a meeting."

CHAPTER 15

Tucker and Jack took a seat on the long plank at Lou's Meal Tent and set their plates of beans and venison beside their coffee cups. Jack was halfway through wolfing his food down when he stopped and stared at Tucker. "You tired of Lou's cooking all of a sudden?"

Tucker picked at his steak and dropped his fork on his plate. "Buckshot's been bothering me. Man did nothing except be angry at having his claim stolen."

"And thinking he could outdraw Trait McGinty." Jack held his plate to his mouth and shoveled the rest of his beans into the maw. "Buckshot wasn't smart enough to let it go. Don't you think I wanted to do just what he did?"

"You wouldn't have lasted any longer than him."

"Just my point," Jack said. "Buckshot knew he was taking his chances even coming to Deadwood in the first place. We all know the only law here is what we can enforce ourselves. One day there'll be order—if the Lakota don't wipe us all out first."

"Still sticks in my craw," Tucker said. "Like that son of a bitch Captain Roush in the bar in Cowtown—he needed to get taken down a peg. Or worse."

"And between him and that sergeant you fought, it earned you two years in prison."

Tucker pushed his plate away. "I'm not going to sit here and let the McGintys get away with murder. And that's just what it was—murder. That slob Buckshot wouldn't have had a chance even if his gun was already in his hand."

Jack stood and grabbed the coffee pot hanging on a tent pole. He refilled their cups and those of two miners across the plank from them before sitting back down. "This isn't our fight. Let's just light out of here. I hear tell there's silver showing color in Montana."

"Not our fight?" Tucker's voice rose, but none of the hungry miners paid him any mind. "Jack, he was like you—lost the claim he filed legally and"—he snapped his fingers—"lost it just that quick. It's an opportunity we won't see again, and I can't abide that."

Jack sopped the rest of his beans with a chunk of cornbread and washed the mess down with coffee. "Just *what* are you going to do about it?"

"I've been thinking about that—"

"Obviously."

"We know the Flynns have to be knee deep in stealing claims. With the blessing of Perry Dowd, it would appear."

Jack said, "Just means Perry is recording the claims when folks file. Don't make me feel better, but I'm not ready to point fingers at Perry. Don't mean it ain't legal."

"Legal," Tucker said. "What's legal here in Sioux country? I'll tell you—only the laws we make ourselves."

"I don't like that tone," Jack said.

"Then you're not going to like what I'm going to do in the morning."

Tucker gave Soreback a parsnip from Lou's tent, and the mule allowed him to slip the saddle on and run the crupper under his tail to keep the bit in place. Tucker had ridden enough mules to know that—on any given day—the critter could object to being ridden. And the results were usually not pretty, especially with a mule Soreback's size. For now, though, Soreback gave Tucker no grief as he swung into the saddle and rode out of Olaf's Livery.

When he got to the wide-open doors, he paused, searching the street. Olaf said Trait had visited him earlier this morning, wanting to know when Tucker usually rode out for his daily hunts. Olaf claimed dumb, and the hot headed McGinty promised he'd wait for Tucker. Somewhere.

Tucker's head was on a swivel, looking for Trait, as he rode slowly away from the town. Sounds filtered past him as he rode—of shovels and pickaxes hitting silt and rock in Deadwood Gulch mixed with an occasional holler as a miner found a speck of color in his pan or his sluice box. Tucker rode past men knee deep in creek water, bending over shovels, others washing the pan back and forth, others rocking the sluice box like they were rocking a cradle. The action halted only when a miner picked a fleck of gold dust out and put it into his poke. Just like he and Jack would be doing if Jack's claim hadn't been stolen. Though panning was back-breaking work, it was no different from breaking rocks in prison. At least he and Jack would have had enough money by winter time to buy a few cows and run them on open range to the east of the Black Hills.

Men in a hurry make mistakes, and Tucker walked Soreback slowly as he looked for Trait. He had strapped his gun on before leaving Olaf's. He might not have a chance against Trait, but he would be damned if he would allow the SOB to murder him without some fight if he came upon the killer.

As he rode along the bank, miners paid him no mind. He had ridden past a dozen claims and finally stopped thirty yards from the first claim marked with the Flynns' name. Neither Mick nor Red worked the long sluice box, but three other men Tucker had never seen before did. He eased the mule closer, and they finally looked up the bank. "You boys look like you're showing some color this morning," Tucker said.

The oldest of the trio—early twenties, perhaps—glanced up from the side of the wooden box as he agitated sediment one of the men in the creek fed to the box. "We're doin' all right. You got you a spot hereabouts?"

"Not me, brother. I'm not ambitious enough to do the work you're doing. Your claim?"

The youngest of the three laid his shovel aside and stepped from the bank to grab a canteen hanging off the sluice box. "Wish it were. It's the Flynn brothers'. They pay us three dollars a day, but we're bringing out twenty in flake. Found us a nugget as big as your little finger yesterday."

"By the by, where are the Flynns?"

The sluice box man jerked his thumb upstream. "They own the next eight claims. Ought to be up there working one of them."

The youngest capped the canteen. "Or telling others how to work them."

"Whoee!" Tucker said. "Eight. Heard some men couldn't even stake one nowadays. But thanks for the information."

He turned Soreback toward the upstream side, moving away from the bank so his approach wouldn't be seen. Now and again he stood in the stirrups until he'd gone past four more claims. Then he spotted Red, who stumbled, favoring one leg as he struggled to maintain his balance in the moving water. He worked the shovel, putting silt and sand into the sluice box, while another man beside Red worked a pickaxe. None of the miners was aware Tucker sat the mule thirty yards away, and Tucker was content to keep it that way.

He stood in the stirrups again, searching for Mick. He was nowhere near his brother, but that was all right, too. Tucker would talk with Mick alone, just like he would when he talked to Red when he got the chance.

Tucker's chance came an hour later. Red took hold of the

side of the sluice box to haul himself up the bank. He said something to the other two before he grabbed some loose paper and headed off into the woods twenty yards from the creek.

Tucker dismounted and tied the mule to a tree before following the path where Red had disappeared. The stench of Red's morning constitutional filtered up the pathway, and Tucker squatted beside a large birch, waiting. Within moments, Red appeared on the path. Tucker stood and blocked Red's way to the creek.

Red looked around, but none of the others had heard Tucker. "What do you want?"

"Just a friendly talk, you and me."

Red's glance darted around, as he looked for an escape route, but Tucker knew there was nowhere close where Tucker couldn't run Red to ground. Especially with Red's limp.

"Talk about what?"

Tucker stepped closer, and Red eyed a large birch branch lying beside the path. "Don't even think about it," Tucker said. "I just want to know about those claims you and your brother have been buying up. Last I knew, you peckerwoods hadn't a pot to pee in. Who's fronting you money?"

"It's our own," Red said. "We used money we made on our first claims—"

"Bull," Tucker said and stepped closer.

Red grabbed the branch. He swung it at Tucker's head, but his leg buckled, and he stumbled. Tucker walked up to Red and threw a right that landed flush on the side of his head. Red fell down.

Tucker bent to grab Red, but he kicked Tucker in the gut and swung the branch again.

It caught Tucker's knee, and he felt himself losing his balance. When Red rushed him, Tucker threw a right cross that connected with Red's nose. He staggered back, cartilage broken, nose flattened and gushing blood across his face. That's when Tucker kicked him in the belly.

Red staggered, blinking, fighting to focus on Tucker, who hit Red on the side of the neck, and he crumpled.

Out of the corner of his eye, Tucker saw the other two miners working with Red standing some feet away, watching the action.

Red looked past Tucker, and he slapped Red. "Those boys won't help you none." He hauled Red upright by the coat collar. "Now tell me who's been giving you money to buy those claims."

Red shook his head, and Tucker tapped his broken nose. Red howled in pain, and Tucker reared his hand back to hit him again. "I can't tell you," Red sputtered, blood flecking the front of Tucker's shirt. "I can't. I'll be killed if—"

Tucker backhanded Red, and he fell to the ground. Tucker squatted beside Red and grabbed his face, squeezing hard. "You won't last that long. There's no law here in the hills, is there? I have a notion to bury you right where you lie. Now tell me about Miller Hazelton's claim."

"We filed on it when he was found murdered."

"And Jack's claim? You've been forcing miners to sell to you two, or the poor slobs will be found beaten half to death or floating in the creek." Tucker cocked his hand.

Red curled up and covered his face with his hands.

Tucker wrapped his hand in Red's coat and drew him close. "Who has been funding you?"

"It was—"

"No one."

Tucker's blood chilled as he recognized that voice. He stood and faced Zell McGinty, who sat his horse on the bank above. He held his rifle pointed at Tucker. "Men come to Deadwood expecting to get rich, but few do so overnight." He got down from his horse, covering Tucker with the rifle. "And when they don't pan as much dust as they want, they sell their claims and move on. No one shoves them off their stakes." He motioned with his rifle. "Now back away from Red."

Tucker stepped back to where the other two miners stood wild eyed, watching the scene.

"Stand up," Zell said, and Red struggled to his feet. Zell brushed bloody dirt off Red's face and wiped it on the man's coat. "Go into town and get yourself something to eat and a long drink. *After* you've cleaned yourself up. When you come back, you'll feel like working your claims again."

Red snatched his hat from the ground and slapped dirt off it before walking toward town.

Zell watched him for a moment before turning back to Tucker. "You come here threatening miners again, and you'll have to answer to me."

"Red and Mick've taken over Jack's claim and damned near everyone else's—"

"Duly recorded by Perry. You might not make it back to town if you pull this again."

"That a threat?"

Zell leveled his rifle at Tucker and cocked the hammer.

"Even here in Deadwood, murder is murder," Tucker said, nodding to the other miners who had gathered to watch the scuffle. "You going to kill me outright and leave all these men to testify to what you done?"

Zell's muzzle drooped as he looked past Tucker to the men watching them.

"Of course, if you beat me in a fair fight, that wouldn't be murder." Tucker motioned to Zell's pistol. "You put that rifle down and face me square if you still want to press your point."

Zell shook his head. "Was a time when Tucker Ashley was the fastest man in the territory. But I hear a man gets almighty rusty in prison."

"Then you might have a chance if you face me."

Zell shook his head. "And spoil Trait's fun? No, I'll let him and you discuss the art of the quick draw whenever he catches up with you. But for now"—Zell's rifle came up again—"you leave, and let these men get back to their work."

Tucker untied the mule and kept Zell in his periphery while he crossed the creek on his way west to where he had spotted a small herd of deer yesterday. Only when he had reached the top of the hillside and was out of Zell McGinty's sight did he relax and rein in Soreback beside a stand of trees.

Tucker's legs shook as he stepped out of the saddle. He had enjoyed slapping the hell out of Red Flynn to the point where the thug would have told Tucker just what he wanted if Zell hadn't come around. But Red could be found most anytime, drinking himself into oblivion, usually in Nuthall and Mann's Saloon. Tucker usually didn't go into the Number 10, but he'd go in there tonight. Red had been frightened of Tucker a few moments ago. He'd be as frightened tonight after he got roostered up.

Tucker took a long pull of his water bladder and looped it back over the saddle horn before walking into a small clearing. He had just challenged a man to a fair fight, something he had not done in more than two years, and his legs shook as much from anticipation of a gun fight as from being scared. Being alive. As he unloaded his Colt and practiced his draw, he knew he *could have* beaten Zell. But Tucker also knew he could *not* have beaten Trait in such a fair fight, and he needed as much practice as he could get. That Trait would eventually trap him into a fight, Tucker had no doubt. And—this day—the outcome left no doubt either. But Tucker would work every day to increase his odds against Trait.

He spied pine cones hanging from a drooping bough, drew, and centered the sights on one. A satisfying *click,* a steady sight after the dry firing, and Tucker was confident his skills were returning. He holstered and snapped empty shots a dozen more times: smooth, quick. Satisfied, he loaded the Colt.

He placed a stone across his hand and held it at waist level. When he jerked his hand away, Tucker drew and fired, the pine cone disintegrating before the stone hit the ground. Smooth. Fast. Not like before he went to prison, but coming back to him.

He kept the pistol around his waist, getting used to the feel of having weight there again. He would need the gun to feel as natural as possible, with Trait gunning for him.

CHAPTER 16

Tucker rode the hills slowly, welcoming the faint breeze that had a cooling effect on his excitement of an hour ago. He hated to admit it, but he had enjoyed putting Red in his place, and he wondered how many miners Red had done the same thing to. He also wondered about how many men who'd supposedly abandoned their claims had been killed like young Miller. That Red knew things, Tucker was certain, but Zell had prevented the Irishman from telling him. Tucker doubted Red or Mick had killed Miller. They were about intimidation, about the joy it brought them when they could get a victim on the ground and put the boots to him until he was little more than a bloody mess able only to crawl away.

That left Zell and his evil son. Either would be good for Miller's murder, neither one having much use for anyone else's life, as Trait had demonstrated when he murdered Buckshot Blue in the Pretty Pony.

But then, Tucker could be misjudging the Flynns—they might have graduated to murder after these years of being mere strong-arm men.

A covey of partridge scattered from bushes fifty yards into the trees, and Tucker jumped. He slipped the rifle out of the scabbard and ran his hand over Soreback's muzzle, calming him before he dismounted. He hoped it was just deer that had scattered the birds, and not the Sioux he'd spotted in this part of the woods two days ago. Tucker had danced with death once today with Zell, who Tucker suspected would have killed him if the other miners had not been witness to the scene. Tucker had no desire to be that close to death again today.

"There are no Indians in those trees, if that's what you're riled up over."

Tucker spun around. Simon Cady put up his hands and laughed. "You're not going to shoot me with that rifle, now are you?"

"You scared me to death," Tucker said. "Probably scared the deer away, too."

"No deer there," Simon said. "Just birds taking flight." He whistled, and his sorrel walked from the tree line thirty yards away.

"You following me?"

Simon shrugged and took his pipe out of his pocket. "I could do worse. Seems like you have more luck finding out things than I do." He motioned to the direction of Deadwood Gulch with his pipe. "You were close to learning more about the miners getting killed until Zell stepped in."

"You saw that?"

Simon chuckled. "Hard not to, all the noise you made when you slapped hell out of that red-haired Irishman." He patted his pocket, and Tucker handed Simon a match.

"I thought you were hunting Miller Hazelton's killer?"

Simon lit the tobacco and cupped his hand over the bowl. "Haven't had any luck. So when I saw you riding out of town, I naturally figured you'd stir things up. Figured his killer would come wiggling from under a rock. What *have* you found out?"

"Maybe I'm after that reward, same's you."

Simon watched the smoke rings dissipate overhead. "You are not about money, Tucker Ashley. You have got some convoluted sense of justice that drives you. Some odd moral code."

"That you don't have."

Simon shrugged. "There is no profit in moral outrage." He tamped the smoldering tobacco with his piece of antler. "But if I find that boy's killer I wager I'll find out what is happening with these miners' deaths." Simon sat on a rock. "Tell me, what do you know?"

"We're not working together."

"Of course not." Simon waved the suggestion away. "That don't mean we can't . . . share information. Like I said, if you find out what's been happening to the miners, I'll probably find that boy's murderer."

"For one, Indians did not scalp Miller Hazelton," Tucker answered. "But you knew that after you looked at Miller slabbed out in Grundy's cold cellar."

"I knew that even before I talked with those Lakota yesterday—"

"You *talked* with Sioux around here?"

Simon waved the question away. "Not right here, but several miles to the south. Now, don't look at me like that—not every white man is in danger from the Sioux, especially if you've lived with one of the warriors I ran into. Besides"—he stroked his flowing white hair that ended just past his collar—"every brave hereabouts would like this hanging in front of their lodge. Let's say ol' Simon keeps a wary eye out whenever he's with his red brothers. Even *if* he knows them."

Tucker squatted beside Simon and took out his tobacco pouch and papers. "What did they tell you?"

"They still intend running the miners out of their sacred *He Sapa,* but they have made no overt move yet. At least not in force. They said they will when more Lakota converge on the hills. Cheyenne, too, if I believe their bravado." Simon knocked burnt tobacco off on the rock. "But they know about the deserter, the Miller boy, and how he died."

"Who do they say killed him?"

Simon shook his head. "You've been around Indians long enough, or have you forgotten their ways since you were in prison? They want nothing to do with white man's business, like that boy being killed. They will say nothing about it except they did not kill young Hazelton. And they did not kill any of the other miners working Deadwood Gulch. Yet."

"Believe them?"

"I do," Simon said. "If the Indians killed every man they get blamed for, there'd have to be a whole lot more Indians on the war path, that's for certain."

Tucker dug into his coat pocket and handed Simon the medicine bundle Mrs. Hazelton had given him. He explained it was clutched tightly in Miller's dead hands when the wolfer brought the boy in.

Simon turned it over in his hand. "Cheyenne." He handed it back.

"With a Lakota arrow stuck in Miller's back."

Simon shrugged. "The Lakota and Cheyenne are joined at the hip. Not unusual seeing them together in one war party." He stood and gathered the reins, stepping into the saddle. The horse seemed to groan and slump under his weight. "You keep stirring things up. You're bound to scare the killer out into the open, and when you do, I'll be there to collect Mrs. Hazelton's reward."

CHAPTER 17

Tucker unsaddled Soreback and rubbed him down with a clump of hay before turning him into the stall. He grabbed a pitchfork and gave the mule an extra ration before walking to Olaf's tiny office. He and Jack sat hunched over a small stove, jawing, when Tucker came in.

"Grab a cup," Olaf said, "and vill tell you about today."

Tucker plopped onto a sawed-off tree stump beside Olaf and sipped his coffee. "What about today?"

"Miners brought in another one of theirs," Jack said. "Another one with an arrow sticking out of his back. They didn't see the Sioux, but they gotta be close to town."

"I talked about the Indians with Simon Cady above the gulch today—"

"You are lucky to be on dis side of de grass," Olaf said.

Tucker smiled. "I'm safe. I don't have a price on my head, or I would be worried around Simon." Tucker took a prayer book from his coat pocket and began rolling a cigarette. "He talked with a Lakota hunting party he ran into yesterday. They didn't kill Miller, and they didn't kill any other miner."

Olaf refilled their cups and put the pot back on the potbellied stove. "You believe Indians?"

"Simon believes these Indians," Tucker said.

Jack scrunched his nose up at the burnt coffee and tossed the rest out onto the floor. "Lakota will fill you full of arrows and scalp you while you're still writhing on the ground. But if you're friendly with them—and respect their ways—they won't lie to you. Simon Cady lived with them long enough I believe him. Besides, there's something else."

Jack cut a corner off a plug of tobacco and stuffed it into his cheek. "I got a good look at the feller they brought in. Like most men hereabouts, he was barely dry behind the ears. Had an arrow stuck out of him, all right. But I suspect that ain't what killed him."

"Let's have it," Tucker said.

Jack lowered his voice as if there were people within ear shot. "There were ligature marks round the kid's neck, and not much blood."

"The kid was strangled, and the arrow stuck into him afterward," Tucker breathed. "You certain?"

"I got a good look at that feller they brought in. He was so damned young. A real shame—"

"Jack!"

"All right, I'm getting to it. There was a Lakota arrow sticking out of the kid's back, but not a lot of blood. Now I'm not the brightest feller, but even I could tell that the deep marks around the kid's neck indicated he was strangled."

"And the arrow stuck in afterward to make it look like Indians," Tucker said. "That's all this town needs—the Lakota are gathering to drive the miners out, and the miners think the Indians have already started." He stood and batted dirt off his shirt. "Let's stop at the rooming house. I need to grab a clean shirt before we eat."

"Do you have a clean shirt?" Jack asked.

"Cleaner than this one."

The sun had set—for all intents and purposes—behind the dark hills as they walked the gamut of drunks and panhandlers, men with no homes and even fewer morals, sizing up easy marks to roll or con out of their pokes. Jack and Tucker walked warily, watching the no-goods, as they headed to the rooming house, prepared to keep what little they had by whatever means necessary.

"Let's go the next block and talk to Beggar Jim," Tucker said and carefully kept to the wooden walkway as they crossed the street.

Jim sat with his back against a saloon front, his tin cup in front of him. When he saw Jack and Tucker, he stood and pulled the patch up over his eye. He stared at them for a moment with *both* good eyes before looking around and sitting back on the ground. "You boys not hitting the . . . drinking establishments?"

"Not a lot of money right now," Tucker said. "I never bagged any meat today."

"A shame," Beggar Jim said. "I was looking forward to a thick steak." He looked around once again at the men staggering by on their way to their favorite saloon. He rattled his cup and smiled. "At least I had a good day. You fellers need a meal?" He reached into his cup, but Tucker stopped him. "We can hold off for another couple days. But thanks. We will keep your offer in mind." A drunk walked by and dropped a half eagle into Jim's cup before stumbling past.

"Much obliged," Jim called after the miner and turned back to Tucker. "But you didn't hunt up ol' Jim to jaw about how broke you boys are."

"We need you to keep your ears open," Tucker said.

Jim laughed. "Don't I always?"

"This is serious. A miner was killed today—"

"Another Indian's doings, what I heard."

"We're not so sure," Tucker said. "We're thinking another miner jealous of the man's stake. Maybe someone connected with the Flynns or McGintys."

"Damned near everything nasty happens around here is connected to them. But I'll sharp up my hearing and see what I can find out."

They left Beggar Jim just as another drunk dropped money into his cup, and Jack held Tucker up. "Thought we were going to the rooming house?"

"We're making a detour."

"Where?"

"To visit a very cold witness," Tucker said and cut across the street.

When they arrived at Grundy's Feed Store, the lights were out, and Tucker walked around back of the store to the cold cellar. He threw the door back and grabbed the lantern.

"Feels mighty cold down there," Jack said.

"Thank God," Tucker said and picked his way down the steep steps. When they reached the floor, Tucker turned the wick up on the lantern as he ducked his head and walked into the side room where Miller Hazelton's body lay.

Jack turned the collar up on his coat. "I don't think I like this."

"Don't be a sissy. He's dead already. Not like he can hurt you. Hold the lantern."

Jack held the lantern while Tucker bent to the body. He pulled the blanket back and tugged on Miller's collar until it came away from his frozen neck. Tucker grabbed the lantern and shined it on the corpse.

"That's the same thing I saw on that feller they brought in today," Jack said.

Tucker traced a line around Miller's throat—a deep line his collar concealed—and cursed himself for not catching it before.

Miller had been strangled.

They walked into the rooming house where Mabel was waiting for them. She stopped them at the door and stood with her arms crossed. She glared at them with that stern look of hers. Or was it her pleasant look? They seemed the same to Tucker.

"You two owe me for a week's stay."

Jack hung his head and put on his best hound-dog look. Mabel had hung pictures along the wall of a son that had been killed at Spotsylvania in the war. A son who looked a lot like Jack. "We came onto a bit of hard times." He ran his hand across his eyes, looking away. Like a trained actor would to emphasize a point. Jack looked up at the old lady, and his mouth drooped. "We'll pay the first of the week. Promise."

Mabel wagged her finger at Jack. "You always do this 'poor me' stunt. But I warn you, Jack Worman, if you don't pay up by next week—"

"We'll pay—"

"You'll be out on your ears. The both of you."

"We will," Jack said, his voice breaking up. "And thank you, house mother."

Mabel's face changed to sadness, and she motioned down the hall to the large room they shared with six other men sprawled on the floor every night. "Some feller stopped by for Tucker this afternoon."

"What feller?"

"Big man," Mabel said. "Had to stoop to get through the doorway. That one what rode in with Ramona Hazelton."

"Chet," Tucker said. "What did he want?"

She shrugged. "Left a package for you."

"You ought to be ashamed of yourself, making that old woman sad like that," Tucker said when they were halfway down the hallway and out of Mabel's earshot.

"It bought us another week we don't have to sleep out in the rain."

They walked into their room. The other men who shared the floor were out working, and a paper-wrapped bundle lay beside the window. Tucker unwrapped it, and Jack whistled. "New set of duds," Jack said. He took a new muslin shirt and held it up to Tucker. "Who did you have to kill to get these?"

"Can't say." Tucker unfolded the note that had lain atop the shirt and trousers.

He handed the note to Jack, and he whistled again. "Ramona Hazelton requests your company for dinner tonight. You going?"

Tucker shook his head. "Even with new clothes I'm still a little . . . ripe." He sniffed the air. "And we don't have the dollar to spend at the bath house."

"I'll talk with Mabel," Jack said as he started out the door. "I am betting she can heat water for that tub of hers. But"—Jack faced him—"if Mrs. Hazelton serves any of those little tea biscuits you gotta' swipe me some. I just *love* 'em."

Tucker had started into the Deadwood Dawn when Chet stepped in front of him and blocked the door. "I see you made it."

"Did I have a choice?"

Chet grinned. "A man always has a choice."

Tucker started around Chet, but the big man remained in the doorway. "I have to pat you down first."

"I'm not carrying a gun."

"Then you're a damned fool in this town. I need to check you anyway. Can't be too careful with the owlhoots hanging around Deadwood thinking Mrs. Hazelton's carrying money all the time."

After Chet ran his rough hands over Tucker's belt line and under his armpits, he stepped aside and let Tucker enter the hotel. A mahogany reception desk waited straight ahead, the normal hotel clerk replaced with one of the outriders Tucker saw that first day Mrs. Hazelton entered Deadwood with fanfare. A Winchester stood propped by the desk, and the man eyed Tucker as he neared. "Down the hall," the man said. "Can't miss the wonderful odor coming from the kitchen."

Tucker walked down the wide hallway as he approached the smell of cooking, magnificent odors that smelled even better than Lou's Meal Tent. A waiter nodded to Tucker but said nothing, as if Tucker were the only customer that day besides Ramona Hazelton. Tucker walked past tables decorated with pearl-linen cloths with "DD" embroidered in pale blue on each corner. Wild prairie roses sat in water-filled vases on the center of each table, and high-hanging chandeliers lent a sophisticated atmosphere to the room. Like a few places Tucker had been to in St. Louis. Sophisticated.

Mrs. Hazelton sat in front of a bone china place setting. Light from the chandeliers reflected in the polished silverware. She was the dining room's sole occupant. She saw Tucker approach and stood. "You clean up pretty well. Please sit."

Tucker was looking about for a hat rack when the waiter took his Stetson. He held it away from him as he hung it on an antlered rack by the door. Mrs. Hazelton sat looking at Tucker, remarkably calm for a mother who had just lost her son.

"I'm sorry that you'll have to bury your boy," he said awkwardly.

"And you wonder why I'm inviting a man to dinner rather than grieving?"

"It crossed my mind."

She motioned to a chair across from her. "I began to grieve the loss of Miller the moment I got word he had been murdered. I got it out of my system long before I left Denver. Let us say I needed a distraction tonight."

"Hence the clothes?"

She nodded. "I thought we could visit. Perhaps we could strike a deal."

"What kind of deal?"

"After a good meal," she said. "I think clearer when I am not hungry."

Tucker order the steak—beef, not venison—he had eaten so much partridge and venison, he had forgotten what a juicy piece of beefsteak tasted like. As they ate, Mrs. Hazelton talked about her husband forming a drilling company and how he chased his dream across the country in failed attempts to find oil, leaving her and Miller to make what life they could. When her husband struck oil, and money started to flow as easily as the oil, she and her son still had to make their own way. "Thomas was a driven man. All he thought about was making money. Oh, he sent more than enough for us to live comfortably, but his love of black gold was paramount in Thomas's mind."

Tucker waited until the waiter brought custard dessert before asking Mrs. Hazelton, "Was Miller your only child?"

"I lost a girl in childbirth, but Miller was my only surviving son." She dabbed at the corners of her mouth with a linen napkin. "I fault myself for Miller's death."

"How so?"

"The Custer expedition," Mrs. Hazelton said, "ventured into these Black Hills two years ago. They claimed Custer went into the hills to scout for a place to build a fort, but we all know better."

"He and some archeologists with him thought there might be gold here."

She nodded. "Custer knew that if gold *was* found here, miners would flood the area and drive the Indians out. Do the army's job for them."

"Nothing angered them more than us *wasicu* invading their holy place."

Mrs. Hazelton waved the air. "It is too late now. Thomas

142

wanted Miller to join him in the drilling business after he graduated from boarding school. But Miller wanted nothing to do
with his father's business. I tried nearly everything to get him
interested. Thomas might not have been much of a father when
Miller was growing up, but he was sincere in wishing to make
up for it. When Miller was a year from graduation, Thomas was
killed in that rig accident. And Miller fought me every minute
since."

She lifted her hand, and the waiter hustled to their table. "We
will have coffee now, please."

"I hate to sound cynical," Tucker said, "but what has this all
got to do with Miller?"

"He ran away from the boarding school outside Philadelphia
and enlisted in the army. Falsified his age. And he did it because
I withheld money from his father's estate on the condition that
he join the family business. That's how he ended up in Custer's
expedition. And that's how he came to be here panning for
gold."

The waiter brought coffee and left with a slight bow. "Perhaps
he wanted to make it in the army—"

"He deserted, Mr. Ashley."

"Deserted for the lure of gold," Tucker answered. "Wouldn't
be the first man who did that."

Mrs. Hazelton sipped her coffee delicately, looking at the
ceiling as if gathering her thoughts. "I hired a man to keep an
eye on my son. When I heard he had deserted for the gold fields,
I quietly bought up a couple claims. I intended deeding them to
Miller." She looked away. "But, of course, he didn't live long
enough." She raised her voice, and the outrider Tucker saw at
the reception desk walked into the restaurant. But Mrs. Hazelton waved him away. "Which makes it all the more important
that I bring his killer to justice."

"Is that the deal you wished to discuss?"

"Listen, Mr. Ashley, I want to—no, I *need* to—have that murdering savage brought to me. If you can bring him in alive, so much the better. I just want to pull the trigger myself."

Tucker finished his coffee, eying the door, wanting to be anywhere but here discussing an impossible request. "We have been over this before. There is no way of knowing what Indian—*if* it was an Indian—killed Miller."

Mrs. Hazelton leaned forward and laid her hand on Tucker's. "I've had you checked into, Mr. Ashley. Apart from being a most capable man with a firearm—"

"Used to be," Tucker said. "Don't count me as proficient anymore."

"More important, though, is that you are the most proficient tracker in the territory. If anyone can find Miller's murderer, you can."

The waiter returned to the table and refilled their coffee cups. Tucker waited until he had left before explaining to Mrs. Hazelton, "I said before I believe Indians did not kill your son—"

"Chet tells me another miner was brought in dead yesterday with a Sioux arrow stuck in his back."

"Mrs. Hazelton—"

"Ramona."

Tucker nodded. "My friend, Jack, is also a capable man when it comes to reading sign. All sorts of sign. He saw the man the others brought in today—he was strangled. Same as Miller."

"I don't understand."

Tucker explained that he had returned to Grundy's cold room to look at Miller once again, and about the ligature marks around his neck, deep and crushing. "Indians do not strangle a man and shoot him in the back when he is dead. If a Lakota wants a man dead, he shoots him full of arrows, or knifes him to death in his sleep. What I am saying is that someone is killing miners and making it look like Indians did it."

Ramona stroked Tucker's hand. He resisted the urge to withdrew it. It had been two years since he'd felt the touch of a woman, even a manipulative one like Ramona, and he wanted to savor the feeling. "I do not think you are right. But whatever you do, find Miller's killer." She squeezed his hand. "No telling where our relationship would lead."

"You'd have a . . . relationship with an ex-felon?"

"Let us say you intrigue me, Mr. Ashley. And with my money, I worry not at all what people think."

Voices rose in an angry demand just outside the hotel, and Tucker jerked his hand away. He ran to the doorway and down the hall. "What's going on?" he asked the guard at the reception desk, but the man ignored him as he took up a position on one side of the door. "What's going on, Chet?"

"Mob wants in," the big man answered, his shotgun pointed at the crowd on the hotel porch and spilling onto the steps. "Now don't you wish you were armed?" he asked Tucker.

Mick Flynn and two dozen other miners advanced upon the hotel entrance. In the background shadows stood Zell McGinty urging the crowd on. Chet strode from the doorway and leveled his shotgun at Mick and two men beside them. "Mrs. Hazelton has this hotel rented," he said and cocked both hammers. "The *whole* hotel. And she doesn't want anyone else inside."

Zell shoved his way through the mob and up the steps. He stopped short of Chet and pulled his coat back, revealing two pistols slung low. "I say you're only one man."

Chet grinned. "Across the street on the roof of that saloon"—he waved, and two rifle barrels jutted out—"two sharpshooters are itching for target practice. And there are others—"

"What others?" Mick said and passed a whisky bottle to Zell. "I don't see them."

"That's the beauty of it," Chet said. "No one can spot them.

145

Now, what do you want in here for?"

"My brother was found on the bank of our claim," Mick said. "Beat to death. And his murderer is inside this hotel. We aim to have him at the end of a rope."

"What murderer?" Ramona had walked up silently in back of Tucker and brushed past him. She stood in the doorway beside Chet. "There's no murderer here. Only my staff."

"You got Tucker Ashley in there," Zell said. "I seen him go in."

"Mr. Ashley is my guest."

Zell took another step onto the porch, and Chet shouldered his shotgun. Zell put up his hands and stood back. "Even Perry Dowd put up a reward for Ashley."

"What's it to Perry if Ashley and the Flynns have disputes?" Ramona said.

"Because," Mick said, grabbing the bottle of whisky from Zell and taking a long pull, "Perry don't want to see miners murdered. The Indians he can't do a thing about. But when a white man kills—"

"He risks having the army sent into Deadwood. And we all know how that'd hurt business," Zell said.

"Since when was Perry Dowd elected sheriff?" Chet asked.

Zell turned to the crowd, urging them on. "Perry figures *somebody's* got to stand up for some order in town. Now, you giving up Ashley or not?"

Ramona backed into the hotel a few feet and whispered to Tucker, "You'd better slip out the back way. Chet can only hold this mob off for so long."

CHAPTER 18

The crowd yelling for Tucker could be heard fifty yards behind the hotel. Tucker paused to catch his breath as he crouched under a broken wagon down the street from the Delta Dawn. Chet stood beside two other guards in Ramona's employ holding the mob at bay. But for how long?

Tucker took a last look to make sure no one saw him before he left the safety of the wagon. He hugged shadows in the darkened alleyway until he arrived at the back of the rooming house. Lights shone through the dirty windows inside—miners sleeping, getting some rest until waking up with the chickens and going to their claims to work them another day. With hopes they wouldn't be the next one murdered.

He put his ear to the door and once again listened.

Silence.

He slowly opened the door, lifting on it to suppress the squeaky hinge, and duck-walked inside.

He shut the door, taking a moment to calm his heart, which threatened to burst from his chest. One day he hoped he would get the chance to repay Chet for holding the crowd back. Or at least thank the big man. Either option would require Tucker to stay alive to see Chet again.

Sweat rolled off his forehead and down his clean, new shirt. The lamp in the hallway was turned low, black smoke puffing every time Tucker got close to the fire. When he arrived at his room, he put an ear to the door. Jack snored as loudly as he always did, but there were no other sounds inside.

Tucker had cracked the door while he watched the hallway when he heard a *click* of a Colt's hammer cocking.

"You move, you die," Jack warned.

"It's me," Tucker whispered.

He entered the room and shut the door as Jack lit the lamp in one corner of the room. "Had to be sure it was you," Jack said. "Figured you'd come around when the coast was clear. One of the other roomers filled me in about Zell and Mick's mob, and I was just able to play possum when one of the mob poked his head inside to see if you fled here." He pulled his boots on. "Better fill me in."

Tucker explained about Ramona offering money and sweetness if Tucker found Miller's killer. "And if it wasn't for Chet holding those men back, I might have been taking a dirt nap right now."

"You say Perry put up a reward for you—how much?"

"You thinking on collecting?"

"It would be one way to make up for losing our claim—"

"You didn't lose it. It was stolen."

"Either way," Jack said. "I've had no luck getting it back with Perry. What do you plan to do?"

"One thing's for certain—I can't stay here. If it were me I'd post someone outside round the clock waiting for me. I need to get out of town fast. Can you saddle Soreback and bring him around back of the Pretty Pony? I'm wagering someone's watching Olaf's Livery, figuring I'll go for the mule."

Jack put on his hat and coat. "Twenty minutes, and he'll be saddled and waiting."

Tucker cracked the door an inch and looked out into the hallway. The lamp hanging halfway down the corridor flicked with the wind blowing through cracks in the rooming house. "I know the hills better than most of those peckerwoods looking for me. I'll hide out there and get word to you when it's safe."

"Just keep yourself on this side of the grass," Jack whispered after him.

Soreback's form was barely visible in the shadows in back of the saloon as Jack led him through the darkness. "Here," Jack said and handed Tucker a flour sack. "Lou sent along some sourdough biscuits and dried venison."

Tucker tied the sack around the saddle horn and dug out his revolver and belt. He cinched it tight, and Jack handed him his rifle.

"You best keep both guns handy. Wherever you're going, you'll most likely need them, wherever that is"

"The logical place would be where I've been hunting deer this last week."

"But that's where Zell and Mick'll figure you're running to."

"That's why I'll be heading toward Custer City. By the time anyone figures I went south, I'll have doubled back."

Jack slapped the side of the saloon. "Damn it, I should never have gotten you tied up with this mess."

Tucker laid his hand on Jack's shoulder. "It's nothing worse than what I went through the last couple years. But you be wary yourself. If Zell figures you helped me escape, he'll have his way with you. Now check and see if anyone's around."

Jack walked to the end of the alley and looked about before motioning to Tucker.

Tucker rode the mule onto the street, slow, like he was just another weary miner in from the gulch after a hard day panning.

He rode the dark alley. Soreback seemed to be looking a hundred yards up the side street at the Deadwood Dawn. The raucous crowd had no doubt raised his curiosity. Tucker turned towards the Badlands, with the nastiest cribs, the saloons hosting the most fights, the dead bodies that somehow seemed to rise from the saloon floors and walk into the street like modern-day Lazaruses, where they remained gathering maggots until some disgusted soul dragged the corpses out and hustled them to the cemetery.

Tucker noticed lights in the office of the mining district and reined the mule.

Between the mob forcing their way into the Deadwood Dawn and the fools still looking for Miller Hazelton's killer, the streets were unusually quiet tonight. Tucker stopped Soreback a half block down from the mining office and tied him to a rail in front of Mitchell's Mercantile. He calmly walked the half block, the few drunks still on the street paying him no mind.

At the mining office, he peeked in the window. Perry Dowd sat hunched over books, his half glasses perched on his nose, pencil in hand, making notes in his ledger.

Tucker ducked under the window and laid his hand on the door. When he burst into the room, Perry dropped his pencil, his eyes going wide when he saw Tucker still alive. He reached inside his open desk drawer, but Tucker's Colt was instantly in his hand, cocked and pointing at Perry's head. Smooth. Nearly as natural and quick as before he went to prison. "I'd take my hand out of that desk drawer were I you."

Perry slowly took his hand away and set his glasses on the desk. "Is there a reason for your visit at this time of night?"

Tucker pulled up a chair and sat backwards on it, his pistol in his hand dangling over the top of the chair. "A reason, like why am I still alive?"

"I don't understand—"

"Seems like we got us a little difference, you and me. About that reward you put on my head. Preferably dead, is what I'm hearing."

Perry leaned back in his chair while he kept his hands clasped atop his desk. "Not for killing you, Mr. Ashley. For apprehending you. For the murder of Red Flynn."

"How does Red's death concern you?"

Perry reached inside his vest pocket, and Tucker snapped his gun up. He came away with a cigar and held it up. "Mind?"

"Only if there's not another one in there."

Perry smiled and produced another cigar he handed to Tucker. Perry lit his cigar and waited until Tucker had bit the end off his before reaching across the desk and lighting it, too. "It concerns me," Perry said, blowing perfect smoke rings upward, "because miners getting killed by white men is something we can't abide." He waved the smoke away. "We can't do a thing about the Indians killing folks." He leaned closer. "You must know how it hurts the business around here when *white* men solve their differences with violence? Deadwood already scares off enough pilgrims. And we need fresh blood to make this community work."

"Still doesn't answer my question. Why you?"

"I am the closest thing to any law in the hills. Men voted me in because they trusted me." He leaned across the desk. "And you ought to trust me, too, and turn yourself in. Stand trial."

"You've already convicted me of murdering Red Flynn."

Perry shrugged. "Zell McGinty brought in four miners that witnessed you beating Red senseless."

"And Zell will tell you Red might have been bleeding, but he was very much alive when Zell stopped our fight."

"The other miners, they said you were mad. Killing mad, and you threatened to kill Red." He leaned closer again. "That's when you hunted him, stalked him like a cougar stalking a doe deer," Perry said. "Zell's words. Then you found Red drunk in back of the Gem and broke his neck."

Tucker took another draw of the cigar. Smooth. Sweet. Unlike cigars he occasionally smoked. "You ever meet Red Flynn?"

"No, but I've talked with his twin brother after they brought Red's body to Grundy's cellar."

"Then you know how powerfully built he was. It would be damned hard to break the neck of such a stout man."

"Not if you beat him near to death first." Perry rolled his chair back and propped his feet on the open desk drawer. Tucker reached over and snatched the small, silver pistol from Perry's desk drawer. "Take temptation away."

"You *don't* trust me?"

Tucker placed one hand on the desk top for Perry to see, then transferred his Colt to the other hand and showed that as well. "If I beat Red near to death like you say, don't you think my hands would be scarred? Cut up. Knuckles broken, even?"

Perry nodded and relit his cigar that had fizzled out. "I see your point. And it will make a good argument for you when we convene the miners' court. You turn yourself in, and I will see you get a chance to say what you just told me." He dropped his match in a spittoon beside his desk. "Trust me."

Tucker drew on his cigar and motioned with it. "Maybe there is something in me that resists someone who can afford fine cigars like this one. Someone who came to Deadwood to . . . exploit the miners—I'd wager—not help them."

Perry dropped his feet on the floor. "I'm no different than any other man here. I came to Deadwood to make money." He laughed. "Mine the miners, so to speak. Sure, I get a stipend for keeping the mining district books, and I . . . own a few ladies who make me some money, but that's the sum of it."

Tucker snubbed the cigar ashes on the corner of the desk and put the stub into his pocket. For later. He wanted nothing like smoke to cloud his assessment of Perry when he asked, "And you buy up mining claims that are abandoned? Or that miners are forced off or that become available when they are found dead?"

Perry looked into Tucker's eyes. A tiny tic caused one of his eyes to shiver. For the briefest moment. "I buy up claims for a group of investors—"

"What investors? Where are they?"

Perry pushed his ledger toward Tucker and grinned. "Look for yourself, but I can tell you their identities are not listed."

Shouts down the block got closer. Angry shouts. Drunken shouts. "I seen a feller ride a mule toward the mining office," someone yelled, and the sounds grew louder. Tucker cracked the door. Thirty men roamed the streets, lanterns illuminating their deadly faces as they staggered and stumbled toward the mining office.

"You can still turn yourself over to me. You don't have to go on the run. They'll find you."

"Those fools couldn't follow buffalo tracks in the snow. I'll take my chances."

He ran out the door and leapt atop Soreback as the crowd neared the office. One shouted. Another fired a gun that clipped the sign over the office. Soreback didn't run worth a tinker's dam, but tonight he must have sensed the urgency. He ran headlong away from the miners, who continued firing until mule and man disappeared into the night.

CHAPTER 19

Tucker rode clear of the hydraulic mining camp that had formed within the last month south of town along Deadwood Creek. He made no effort to hide his tracks in the soft ground until he passed Gayville, a few miles south. He went around the floundering mining camp and rode north for the next two hours until he entered that part of the hills littered with dead wood among the nearly impenetrable forest of pine and birch and aspen. Only then did he take pains to hide his back trail, careful to ride game trails rather than make his own prints trackers could find. And there were trackers among the men who followed him to collect Perry's reward. But none—he was certain—who could follow Tucker once he made efforts to hide his tracks.

Except Simon Cady.

As Tucker stripped the saddle off the mule and started rubbing him down with clumps of buffalo grass, he thought about Simon—in the business to hunt down wanted men and collect the reward. Would he come after Tucker? Of that, he had no doubt, if Simon knew there would be money at the end of the day.

Tucker made a cold camp, spreading his tarp and blanket on the ground between two huge pine trees that would provide excellent cover to return fire if somehow the miners found him.

He hobbled Soreback next to tall clumps of grama grass close to his bedroll. Mules, like horses, were better than any guard dog at alerting a man to danger. The mule would tell

Tucker if anyone approached. He would need Soreback's help. For Tucker was exhausted from riding the hills these last few hours. He knew that, once he shut his eyes, even imminent danger would be hard pressed to break through the fog of sleep.

He grabbed the corn dodgers and dried venison Lou had sent along and wrapped himself in his blanket as he thought about what Perry had told him. Red was hurting when Zell broke up the fight with Tucker yesterday, but he stumbled off toward the saloons under his own power. And even if Tucker *had* beaten Red senseless, the man was still so powerfully built, Tucker could not have broken his neck if he'd wanted to. If Tucker hadn't gotten in the first blow, stunning Red, keeping out of reach of his powerful hands, the outcome might have been different.

Tucker contemplated the men he had met in the hills who might be capable of killing Red. Zell was certainly strong enough, and rumors of him taking on two men at the same time in a fight and prevailing were the stuff of legends. But it made no sense for Zell to kill one of the men who was helping him— Tucker was certain—take over the mining claims along Deadwood Gulch.

Tucker's list narrowed to include Simon Cady, perhaps the strongest man Tucker had ever met. But why would Simon kill Red? The man had no price on his head. If Simon thought Red knew something about whoever had attacked and killed Miller Hazelton—under the guise of an Indian—Simon might have questioned him. In his own special way. But Tucker was sure Simon didn't think Red was Miller's killer, or else the body of the Irishman would have been dropped at Ramona's feet. A ten-thousand-dollar reward can make a man do evil things.

The last man Tucker believed to be powerful enough to kill Red worked for a millionaire businesswoman. Chet was definitely strong enough to snap Red's neck, but his having done so made no more sense that the others. Chet was devoted to keeping Ramona safe. He wouldn't get sidetracked by local toughs. Unless Ramona and the Flynns had some history together. She had admitted buying claims in the early days, presumably to deed to Miller. Was there a connection between her and the Flynns that Red tried to exploit? Was that what he was about to tell Tucker before Zell shut him up? If he had, it would have been only a matter of time before Chet caught wind of it. And protected his employer.

With no more answers than he'd had when he entered Perry Dowd's office, Tucker folded his bedroll over and lay inside. He momentarily forgot the chill of the Black Hills, lulled by the warmth of the blanket, a light breeze whispering through the pines, and the knowledge that the mule was standing guard close by.

Tucker fought the urge to open his eyes immediately when Soreback snorted. He felt under his bedroll for his Colt while he lay immobile, listening to the morning sounds. But he heard nothing and opened his eyes. The mule stared intently down the hill in the direction they had ridden last night. Tucker eased from his blanket and low crawled toward the edge of the tree partially concealing him. Two hundred yards down, five Lakota sat their ponies, while a sixth squatted on the ground beside his horse, running his hand over the earth. He said something to the others, and they looked in Tucker's direction before they mounted and started up the hill.

Tucker talked soothingly to the mule, calming words that held little conviction. If the Lakota caught him—here, alone in their sacred Black Hills—he'd be the next one brought into town shot full of arrows.

He crouched behind the tree and shook dust off the saddle blanket before slipping it on Soreback. Within minutes, Tucker had the mule saddled and had swung onto his back. Through the trees he saw flashes of white and brown, ponies little more than twelve or thirteen hands high, but ponies that would ride a thoroughbred into the ground. Tucker knew he could never outrun the Indians, but he could out climb them on the mule.

He looked about, spotting a steep, granite peak two thousand yards higher than his camping spot, and he spurred Soreback toward that summit. If he could get a moment's head start—enough that arrows wouldn't find him—he would have a chance. For his mule would ride their ponies into the ground in that rugged country.

Tucker let Soreback pick his own way up the hill until he heard shouts below. Four Sioux dug their heels into their ponies' flanks when they spotted him, while the last two peeled off and started working their way around Tucker's flank.

Soreback, for his part, plodded steadily upward, not excited, not worrying about those who would do Tucker harm. Within minutes, the Indian ponies below had faltered among the sharp rocks and slowed. One Indian raised his rifle and hollered in Lakota before the four dismounted to attend to their ponies' bloody hooves.

Tucker had ridden halfway up the mountain. The Lakota remained below, where they had broken off the attack. Tucker breathed relief.

Until the first shot clipped his hat.

The two Indians who had flanked him had gotten ahead of him—probably using a game trail known only to them and the deer—and now rode hard for him, their voices trilling the eerie sound many men had last heard before arrows ended their life. One warrior shot arrows over his pony's back, arrows that veered wildly, while the one armed with a rifle shot under his horse as he clung to its mane. Three more quick shots nearly hit Tucker, and he snatched Jack's Winchester before diving for the ground.

157

The shots had come rapidly. Winchester? Spencer, perhaps? Few Indians possessed guns in these parts of the country, yet in most circumstances Indians were far more proficient with their bows than they ever were with guns. They rode toward him, trilling, snapping shots. A bullet kicked off a piece of boulder next to him; an arrow stuck into the tree next to where he crouched.

Tucker darted from behind the tree and snapped a shot that clipped the single feather sticking out of the bowman's hair. He shot again, hitting the horse. Indian and horse went down in a tangle. The warrior rolled with the horse. He gathered his legs under him as the other Lakota rode past him, his hand trailing toward the ground, snatching the downed man and swinging him onto the horse behind him in a smooth, practiced motion. *No wonder the army has such a damned hard time taming these people,* Tucker thought.

The two riders had disappeared through the trees when Tucker heard the four other Lakota down the mountain. They hollered at Tucker as they picked their way on foot up the hill among the rocks.

He caught sight of the eagle feather he had clipped earlier for the briefest moment as the Indian maneuvered his way to one side of Tucker, but he did not see the other Lakota. Glancing down the rugged hillside, he realized the four warriors would get to Tucker's position in ten minutes. Perhaps less. He cursed himself. The two flankers hadn't planned on killing him—they'd attacked to slow him, distract him, while the other four made it up to Tucker.

He took out his Colt and laid it on the ground in front of him along with the last three cartridges for the rifle. When his Winchester ran dry, he would shoot the pistol. And when that ran dry . . .

He laid Perry Dowd's little pocket gun on the ground in

front of him. It packed little punch, but it was enough to penetrate a man's brain at point-blank range. In case the Indians overran his position. He would *not* have his scalp lifted while still alive.

Tucker waited, and the waiting was worse than the fighting. It always had been. Whether waiting for the order to charge the Confederate line at Gettysburg or waiting until cutthroat thieves sprang to rob him in Nashville, waiting was the hardest part.

Two rifle rounds echoed off the granite hills, the four shots that followed even louder. Coming quicker. Tucker scooted farther behind the tree, but no bullets impacted it. More shots followed, shots that were not aimed at him. Shots that came from the warriors down the mountain.

Screams joined the cacophony of chaos happening on the hillside, and he chanced a peek around the tree. Down the hill, a battle had erupted, and Tucker crawled to where he could look from behind a cactus. Two men lay scalped beside a small clearing, their bloody faces contorted in pain, one squirming as a man does prior to death.

Three Indians crouched behind a huge boulder snapping arrows toward white men they'd caught out in the open, while other Sioux, armed with rifles, flanked the survivors. *Survivors for now,* Tucker thought as he recognized one man who had stood beside Zell McGinty as he shouted for Tucker to surrender outside the Deadwood Dawn. Fools. The miners had smelled easy reward money. They had followed Tucker, hoping to catch and string him up in order to earn Perry's bounty. Instead, they found this band of passing Lakota out scalp hunting for *wasicu.*

For the briefest moment, guilt crossed Tucker's mind for not rushing to the rescue of the miners. For the *very briefest* time. He holstered his Colt and slipped the Winchester into the saddle scabbard before he swung onto Soreback. He looked downhill a final time. One more miner lay dead as the others, caught in the open, frantically levered rounds into their rifles. Their fates were sealed.

"Keep 'em busy for me, boys," Tucker said under his breath. And he spurred the mule up the mountain before the Indians turned their attention back to him.

CHAPTER 20

Soreback snorted, and Tucker opened his eyes as he felt for the Colt under his bedroll, straining to hear what had alerted the mule. More Lakota? A twig snapped. Black birds took flight with shrill protest.

Tucker slid from under his blanket. He moved behind a boulder, keeping low to the ground. He was clutching the rifle when a flash of white and brown passed through the thick forest of trees like a painted ghost searching for him. *An Indian pony.*

He shouldered the rifle and eased the hammer back, while the pony made its way higher among the granite boulders and thick pine. When the head of the horse broke free of the foliage, Tucker's finger took up slack on the trigger just as Jack ducked under a low-hanging pine bough.

Tucker stood and set the rifle against the tree as he approached Jack. "Thought I'd never find you," Jack said as he dismounted. He tied the horse beside Soreback, who promptly kicked Jack's pony in the flank. The paint hunched up, blood coming from a superficial wound, and Jack led his horse away from the mule. "Kind of contentious, ain't he?"

"Kind of an a-hole at times is what I figure. Kinda like some men."

Jack gathered branches and laid them on the faint embers inside Tucker's fire ring. Within moments, the campfire blazed, and he grabbed a cup out of his saddlebags. "Saw eight miners back down the mountain. All scalped, and not an Indian among 'em. I was worried one of those bodies was you."

"Would have been if those miners hadn't come along. Lakota musta figured they'd rather kill eight white men than one straggler."

"Then I come onto a cold camp this morning down at the base of Gay's Peak," Jack said. "Had the mule's tracks pasted all over the ground."

"Been moving campsites every couple hours," Tucker said, pouring Jack and himself a cup of coffee and setting the pot back over the fire. "I was afraid Simon Cady would smell the reward money."

Jack chuckled. "Probably not, since Perry only offered a hundred dollars for your hide."

"Hundred dollars!" Tucker said. "That's almost an insult."

"But it explains why Simon isn't here looking for you—not enough money in it for him. But enough for out-of-work miners to beat the woods looking for you. Beggar Jim talked with a couple who make a business of robbing drunks. They figure they'll never collect on Ramona Hazelton's reward but figured they could hunt you up for whisky money." Jack motioned around Tucker's camp with his coffee cup. "But finding you is harder than they know."

"I've had a chance to think these last few days," Tucker said, scrunching up his nose at his own burnt coffee, "about Ramona's reward. I don't think she ever figured on having to pay out."

"I don't follow you."

"She has to know there is no way anyone could identify the Lakota who murdered her son," Tucker said. "She could have offered the reward without coming to Deadwood. She could have remained in Denver, safe and secure, without facing the dangers of this place."

"Then why the pomp and circumstance of making such a

show of it? Why even come here, if you're right?"

Tucker tossed the rest of the coffee grounds in the grass and stood. "Perry said someone has been buying mining claims on behalf of the Flynns." Tucker grinned. "Make that one Flynn now, with Red dead. Someone with money. Who else in Deadwood has enough funds to keep buying up claims? I think Ramona came here—to bury her son, yes—but also to oversee the claims she was snapping up."

"If you're right," Jack said, "*she* has to be the one paying the McGintys for strong-arming the miners into selling. But here's a problem with your theory—Beggar Jim heard Ramona's been outbidding Perry's anonymous buyer. So there have to be more folks involved. Like that group of investors Perry claimed is fronting the money."

"Think Jim got it right?"

"Wondered that myself," Jack said. He sat on a rock and cut off a piece of plug tobacco, stuffing it in his cheek. "So I nosed around the saloons. I ran into four men who sold their claims to Ramona. *After* Perry made them an offer. That kind of piqued my curiosity, so I . . . broke into the mining district office. Perry Dowd keeps his books in remarkably good order."

Tucker stowed the coffee pot and cup in his saddlebags. Soreback took no notice but returned to eying Jack's paint like he wanted a rematch. "You gonna' tell me what the book showed, or do I have to guess the rest of the day?"

"All right," Jack said as he spat a string of juice. "I'm getting to it." He stood and paced in front of the fire. "Beggar Jim was right. Ramona has bought out six more claims since she arrived in Deadwood. She now owns a fourth of the gulch, if Perry's records are right."

"She told me she'd only bought two claims, which she intended deeding to her son."

"Well, she lied," Jack said. "After I talked with those fellers, it got to working on me, so I hunted up the other two miners who had sold their claims to Ramona. They wouldn't say how much she paid—part of the deal was to keep their mouths shut. But they weren't angry at selling, like Buckshot Blue was, so her offer must have been fair."

"I still can't figure out why she has such an interest in Deadwood when she has made a fortune in black gold."

"Oldest reason in the world," Jack said. "Greed."

Tucker cinched the crupper under Soreback's tail. He'd be riding down the steep mountain, and the last thing he wanted was the saddle to ride forward. "How close are the miners to catching me?"

Jack laughed. "Not very."

"Well, those eight fools the Sioux killed down the mountain got close."

"They had some boob who tracked for the army at one time with them. He might have been a tracker, but he wasn't much of an Indian fighter. But most miners trying to corral you are young kids who have no idea how to cut sign. They'll probably end up like those fools down the mountain. Now, Zell McGinty's different."

"You don't have to tell me. If Simon scouted with Chivington, he must be good. The colonel only recruited the best trackers."

Jack nodded and spat another string of tobacco juice. "He's done enough scouting for the army that he damned well can read a track. And he bought a four-year-old Morgan yesterday. Musta cost him a bundle, by the looks of that horse. He's been bragging in the Miners Paradise that it'll run your mule into the ground. Best be wary of Zell. And of Trait."

"Where'd he buy a Morgan?"

"Had it delivered from an Indian breeder outside Ft. Robinson yesterday." Jack wiped his mouth with the back of his hand.

"That's another thing I saw when I looked at Perry's books—Zell and Trait are paid eighty dollars a month. Sure not enough to afford a fancy critter like that. Beggar Jim hasn't heard of any stage being held up lately, so they must be making money on the side—Perry or Ramona?"

"Zell must be getting a cut of the claims that are . . . abandoned or sold from one of them."

Jack eyed Soreback suspiciously as he untied his pony. "I'd better be getting back to town and see if there's *something* I can do to raise money. Mabel says this is the last day to pay rent, or she's giving me the bum's rush."

"You mean giving *us* the bum's rush?" Tucker said.

Jack shook his head. "Miners are taking bets on whether or not you'll live out the week. Mabel's a born gambler—she figures Zell and Trait will find and kill you before you get a chance to lay your head in her rooming house again."

"What a sweetheart that Mabel is," Tucker said.

He waited until Jack had left for town before kicking out his campfire and leaving the safety of the trees. He rode Soreback down the mountain, the mule plodding along, never faltering. Zell's Morgan would play hell keeping up with the mule in the mountains. Flats were a different story, for Soreback was like any other mule Tucker had ridden—he wasn't too champion in the running department. Then again, there weren't many flats to run here in the Black Hills.

But more telling for Tucker was that Zell had wanted to capture Tucker so badly, he had shelled out big money for a fancy horse. How much, he didn't know, but surely more than the paltry hundred dollars Perry was offering. Tucker's escape must have worked on Zell enough he wanted to catch and kill Tucker that badly.

He had started down a steep game trail—all but hidden in the thick forest that at times prevented a man from seeing deer ten yards away—when the mule balked. He stopped, his ears twitching, looking toward a thick stand of trees twenty yards from the game trail.

Tucker slipped the rifle out of the scabbard as he continued watching the trees. After a few moments, Soreback dropped his gaze and started munching on grama grass. If Lakota were in the trees, they had gone without spotting Tucker. He breathed deeply and let the mule graze for long moments before coaxing him down the trail.

When he had gone another five hundred feet, the game trail skirted a flat meadow a hundred yards across. He pulled up Soreback short of the clearing as he watched his back trail. No one followed. No one hunted him. Yet he *felt* he was being hunted, the hairs on his arms standing at attention as they often did when Tucker got that feeling of dread.

When he turned back, Simon Cady sat his sorrel twenty yards away in the clearing. Tucker drew his Colt and aimed it at Simon's chest.

Simon held up his hands and chuckled. "If I wanted to kill you, I could have when you were watching those trees so intently."

"Come on down here so's I can see you better."

Simon walked his horse toward Tucker and stopped a few feet away.

"So now you're here to cash in on Perry's reward for me?" Tucker asked.

Simon slowly pulled his pipe from his coat pocket and began filling it. "If I wanted to collect on Perry's measly reward, I'd have done it before now. Wouldn't even pay for me to come after you for a hundred dollars."

"But while you're here, you thought you might cash in on it?"

"The thought did cross my mind." Simon motioned with is

pipe to Tucker's Colt. "Until a moment ago. You *are* getting better." He lit his pipe. "But if you point that hogleg somewhere else, we might talk civil like."

Tucker holstered the pistol but kept the hammer loop off. "Talk."

Simon stepped down from his horse and dropped the reins. The gelding meandered to tall grass and began grazing. Simon put his hands at the small of his back and arched, stretching. "I'm not as young as I once was. Was a time I could follow a bad man all the way across the territory, turn the body infor the bounty, and be on the trail after another the next morning. Not anymore."

"I don't figure you tracked me down because you wanted to rehash your glory days."

"Who's to say I didn't just happen on you and that jughead you're riding?"

Tucker stroked Soreback's muzzle. "Simon Cady doesn't *happen* on to anyone."

Simon squatted on the ground and rubbed a knee. "You stir things up."

"Still doesn't tell me why you're here."

"Sure it does," Simon answered. "I figured if I followed you, you'll lead me to Miller's killer. Or he'll come after you. At which time I'll shoot him and drape him over my saddle."

Simon lit his pipe, and his mouth turned down in sadness. "Ashley, I need that one big payday. Catching that one *hombre* that will let me . . . retire. Do you know that a man can live for pennies a day along the beach in Mexico? With *senoritas* waiting on him hand and foot?"

"Unless the *rurales* find and kill you."

Simon waved the suggestion away. "Ramona Hazelton's reward will put me on that beach, and I'll pay off the *rurales*." Simon shrugged. "If I follow you, the murderer of her son can't be far behind."

Tucker dismounted and tied Soreback to a large rock. "I thought we figured it wasn't an Indian who killed Miller."

Simon nodded. "That's what we figured, all right."

"Then just how can I help find his murderer? I don't know who the hell he is."

"Sure you do," Simon said. "And if I stay close to you, you'll lead me right to him."

"You're not making any sense," Tucker said. "What does make sense is, I want you nowhere near me. I find you on my back trail, and there's likely to be one less bounty hunter in these Black Hills."

"Or one less ex-con with a price on his head," Simon said. And winked.

CHAPTER 21

All the way into Deadwood, Tucker kept checking his back trail. If Simon was following him, he was concealing himself mighty well. But then, a man who has been hunting other men successfully for forty years could be almighty cagey.

Tucker entered the Badlands of Deadwood long after the sun set. He'd planned to board Soreback at Olaf's, but thought better of it. Zell might have the livery watched, expecting Tucker to return. Besides—depending on how this played out tonight—he might need the mule in a hurry.

Ramona held the key to all the intrigue, Tucker had concluded on the way into town. She had bought up far more claims than anyone else, stiffing Perry's anonymous buyers, paying more than the claims were worth. Tucker recalled what Jack said, suspecting Ramona had come to Deadwood when she did for reasons besides burying her son.

Tucker rode the muddy streets slowly, past drunks who paid him no mind and con men too busy fleecing others in their games on the walkway. He rode, passed by others too busy with their own vices to notice him, and he stopped in the shadows of the alley in back of the Salty Dog. He let his eyes adjust to the darkness as he peered from the corner of the saloon at the Deadwood Dawn a block away. He scanned the rooftops surrounding the hotel. A rifle barrel—more difficult to spot than the last time—poked out from the edge of the roof—but still remained visible. Tucker imagined the bored shooter, sleepy and lying behind his rifle for hours at a time, watching the front of the hotel.

Tucker couldn't spot Chet, and he dearly wanted to spot Chet. The man was an ominous presence, one Tucker wanted to avoid at all costs. But Chet had to sleep sometime, and one of the outriders peeked from inside the front of the hotel where Chet usually stood guard.

Tucker walked hunched over as he made his way toward the back of the hotel. Tall grass waved in the light breeze, casting eerie shadows along the rear porch, any one of which might be a man in the pitch blackness. But Tucker saw none, and he stepped from the safety of the shadows. Then he paused. There *had* to be a guard watching the back somewhere. Chet didn't strike Tucker as one to leave anything to chance; surely he'd have stationed a guard at the back door as well as the front.

A faint clicking sound, of metal to metal, reached him then, and he cocked an ear. Ten yards from the back door of the hotel, among a pile of broken chairs and a busted table top, a man sat immobile on a broken bar stool. The clicking sound came again, and Tucker finally identified it—the metal sling swivel on the man's shotgun he held across his lap. It slapped the barrels of the gun every time the wind picked up. The guard's head did the pecking-bird polka, his head dropping onto his chest every now and again, as he fought to remain awake.

Tucker took off his boots and worked in a lazy arc around the man's backside, avoiding dead branches piled beside a rusted-out Franklin stove. He tested every step he took, careful not to step heavily, careful not to put his weight down when . . .

The man's head snapped up, and he looked around the night.

Tucker froze.

Startled, the man strained to see in the darkness.

Tucker squatted slowly, avoiding the man's gaze. *The eyes*

170

draw the eyes, he told himself. *Don't look right at the man; look at him in your peripheral vision.* After long moments, the man—satisfied no one was there—sat back in his chair and rested the shotgun across his legs once more.

Tucker eased the Bowie knife from the sheath and took hold of the long, wide blade as he stepped toward the man. Another step, testing the ground. Another step . . .

. . . a twig snapped under Tucker's foot.

The guard sprang up. The stool crashed against the stove. Tucker rushed the last few feet. Swung the heavy knife handle at the man's head. It caught him on the temple, and he crumpled to the ground.

Tucker squatted beside the unconscious guard and looked about, waiting. When no one emerged from the hotel to check on the sound, Tucker untied the man's bandana and cinched it tightly around his mouth. He dragged the guard behind the pile of rubbish and took the sling off the shotgun, using it to hog tie the guard's legs and arms.

Satisfied the man would be busy for some time, even if he regained his wits, Tucker walked to his boots and slipped them on. He waited in the darkness for long moments, expecting somebody to come outside to check on the guard, but no one did. He crept inside the hotel's back door. Unlike the dingy rooming house he and Jack slept in, the Deadwood Dawn had lamps illuminating the spacious hallway every ten feet, light flickering off paisley-papered walls. Tucker's boots fell on cushioned carpeting.

He kept glancing down the hall where the reception desk stood just off the hallway as he looked at the doors of the rooms. Each had the name of a past president engraved on a mahogany placard above the door, each looking identical to the one on the next room.

Except the Lincoln room.

A painting of Honest Abe above a door in the middle of the hallway looked down at a silver tray on the floor. A white linen napkin covered what the room's occupant had left of supper before sliding the tray into the hallway.

Tucker eyed both ends of the hall as he inched along the wall, careful not to brush against the side, careful not to telegraph a sound as he stopped to one side of the door. He put his ear to the wall, straining to hear. He heard no movement inside, and he laid his hand on the door knob. It turned, and Tucker cracked the door while he peered inside.

Ramona Hazelton lay sleeping, the faint light from a tiny table lamp illuminating her face. One hand lay over her head, the other under her pillow. Tucker eased the door shut and . . .

"You want to die tonight?"

Tucker slowly turned to the sound of the voice. Ramona held a derringer aimed at Tucker's chest as she threw the covers aside. Tucker averted his eyes as she slipped on her dressing gown and turned up the lamp. "If you wanted romance, you didn't have to sneak in here. But I suspect you didn't come for a late-night visit with romance in mind."

"I hear that you have been buying up a lot of the miners' claims."

"And you couldn't come around at a decent hour to ask me about that?"

Tucker rubbed his collar. "And get my neck stretched? I'm not exactly popular in Deadwood. Now, about those claims—"

"Is it a crime to invest? Because that's just what those claims represent: an investment."

"It is a crime if you intimidate—threaten—men to sell."

Ramona laughed. "Threaten them with what, this?" She tapped the gun.

"Not you, but someone like your man Chet. He could intimidate anyone into selling."

"How's about we call Chet in here and ask him? Besides being angry at being woken up, he'd be doubly mad when he learned you sneaked in here. After waylaying the guard outside. Am I right?"

Tucker nodded. "Had to be done. He'll be all right once the swelling on his head subsides."

She motioned for Tucker to sit in a chair. "Chet won't take kindly to you hurting one of his men. He might just get angry enough to kill you with nothing more than his hands."

Tucker looked down at his holster. "He wouldn't get a foot in the door before I drilled him."

"You forget I have this gun aimed at you? I won't have Chet killed by you or anyone else if I can help it."

Tucker slowly reached inside his coat pocket and withdrew his prayer book. He began trickling tobacco onto the paper. "You ever kill a man?"

"No," she answered. "But I would have no qualms about killing the man who beat that miner, Red Flynn, to death."

"You really believe I did what Zell McGinty accused me of?"

"Perry thinks you did. Even offered his own money in a reward."

Tucker laughed. "A hundred dollars is all."

Ramona agreed. "I suppose if he *really* thought you killed Red, he'd put up more money."

"Good. Then lay that gun aside and we can talk."

Ramona lowered the derringer but kept it beside her on the bed. "Okay, talk. And this better be better than what I've heard so far—sneaking into a lady's room—or I yell for Chet."

"All right," Tucker said. "Here's the problem—you lied when you said you only bought a *couple* of claims. You bought a lot more than you told me."

"I figured it was none of your business how many claims I bought up. What's your point?"

"Miners have been dying—"

"Not my doing—"

"And being made to look as if Indians killed them."

"Mr. Ashley, you have told me this more than once."

Tucker was looking around for something to snub his cigarette out in when Ramona dragged a spittoon from behind a nightstand. "You have enough money. You don't need to buy up claims. See, it struck me as odd that you bought them since you *came* here. You could have done that from the safety of your Denver home."

"I told you the truth before—I bought two claims to give to my son. But he died before he could enjoy them. And when I came here to bury him, I had every intention of paying money for the Indian who killed him. But you've convinced me it might not have been Indians."

"Then why not cancel the reward?"

"The reward still stands. Whoever brings in Miller's murderer can collect it."

"That doesn't explain all the other claims you've bought since you came here."

Ramona took Tucker's tobacco pouch and papers and expertly rolled a smoke. "Perry told me it would be dangerous for me to buy up claims. He said his group of anonymous buyers would be killing mad." She blew smoke towards the open window.

"But you bought them up anyway?"

"Perry is rather . . . over dramatic. I believe he tried talking me out of buying claims because the fewer claims he buys for his clients, the less he makes."

"This buyer appears to have some powerful allies here in Deadwood, given the number of miners who have been killed or run off their claims. What if this anonymous group comes after you?"

"That's just what I'm counting on. When he does I—not Chet—will put a big hole in him."

Tucker mulled that over, considering Ramona's logic. Buying up claims to force Perry's buyer to eliminate the competition—Ramona—might force her son's killer out in the open. Or this latest tale of hers might be just another lie.

"Look," Tucker said, "all I want to do is get Jack's claim back so he and I can work it before the big mining companies come in and push us little guys out."

"You should think bigger than that three-hundred-foot claim."

"Think bigger how?"

Ramona stood from the bed and walked to the chair. She laid her hand on Tucker's and squeezed gently. "You *have* been in prison too long. What I'm thinking about is that this"—she waved her hand around the room—"gets boring without someone to share it with. A man."

"You have Chet."

Ramona laughed. "Chet is like a . . . loyal dog. One that stays loyal as long as he is paid well. But you're different. You can give up on that little claim and come to . . . work for me."

Tucker had thought of being with Ramona these last couple days. Even without her vast wealth, she would have been a catch for any man, let alone an out of work ex-con. Even after being awakened in the middle of the night, she was lovely with her tousled hair and face devoid of makeup. But right now, he needed to be rid of the thought of her offer that had just fogged his common sense. Right now, he needed time and space to process her words. And her claims.

"Any other time your offer would be tempting. But right now, I have men who want to hunt me down and kill me." Tucker stood from the chair, but Ramona made no overtures with her tiny gun. He cracked the door an inch and looked out into the hallway. "But—for the record—I'd love nothing better than to remain here with you until the wee hours of the morning."

"I understand," Ramona said as she stroked Tucker's cheek. "You know I will have to sound the alarm that you were in my room. Especially if you hurt the guard out back."

"He'll be all right when that knot on his head goes down."

Ramona laid her derringer on the nightstand and stood on her tiptoes. She took Tucker's face in her hands and kissed him lightly, then kissed him deeply. "Come back to me," she said as he opened the door and looked down the hallway. "You have five minutes before I start hollering. And, Mr. Ashley, think my offer over."

"It's all I have been thinking about for the last few minutes," he said and walked into the hallway and the dark night.

CHAPTER 22

Tucker stepped into the empty hallway and paused. Hearing nothing from the guard at the reception desk, he made his way out the back door. He waited in the darkness, his eyes slowly adjusting to the night. He strained to see the guard he had trussed up.

But didn't. The man should have been lying on the ground beside the pile of rubbish.

But he wasn't.

And that worried Tucker.

He looked around the back of the hotel but saw no one. Heard no one. He had no time to wonder where the guard was—whether he had freed himself or had thrashed about and rolled down the hill away from the rubbish pile. Tucker had only five minutes to get as far away from the Deadwood Dawn as he could before Ramona sounded the alarm. Five short minutes before Chet and his men started looking for him.

He jumped down from the porch and ran around the side of the hotel. He started down the alley to where he had tied Soreback, only a few minutes away.

Just a few minutes when . . .

. . . the cocking hammer was loud in the still night air, and he turned toward the sound. Zell McGinty pointed his revolver at Tucker's head as he strode from the corner of the saloon and out of the shadows. He motioned to the mule. "You're easy enough to find—only one hereabouts who rides a mulie rather than hitches him to a wagon. Damn fool."

"And you got careless with that guard out back," Mick Flynn said. He came out of the shadows on Tucker's backside and hit him with the butt of his rifle. Tucker's knees buckled, and he fought to remain on his feet as flashes of light illuminated the night in front of his eyes.

Zell snatched Tucker's Colt from the holster and stuffed it in his own waistband. "When we heard that feller yelling in back of the hotel, we figured it had to be your doing."

"Where's the guard now?"

Mick smiled. "Let us say you'll get blamed for his death along with Red's."

Zell chin pointed to the hotel. "Let's get moving before that big bastard of Ramona Hazelton's finds his man with his throat slit and comes after Tucker."

Mick shoved Tucker north toward the Badlands. He stumbled, catching his footing in the dark. He tripped over a man lying dead in the alley and went sprawling.

Tucker gathered his legs under him, gauging the distance to Mick. He could reach the Irishman in time to knock him on his keester, but not in time to disarm Zell before he parted Tucker's hairline with his Colt.

"Get to your feet!" Mick hoisted Tucker erect and kicked him in the behind, herding him along the alley. A half block over— from the direction of the row of saloons and hurdy-gurdy houses and cheap cribs where women made little money unless they rolled their johns—a calliope joined the sounds of a woman's voice. Men hollered and laughed, and a cry of pain followed a gunshot, the sounds of chaos growing louder the deeper into the badlands—the seedier side of Deadwood—they walked. As if *all* of Deadwood wasn't seedy.

Zell swung open the wide door to Limey's Livery, and Mick shoved Tucker hard. He fell to the floor, and Mick kicked him in the gut. Tucker took the blow deep in his belly and held his gut when Mick stood him up. "Get him into the tack room," Zell said.

Mick pushed Tucker into a small side room. Saddles sat on boards along one wall, with bridles and hackamores and tapideros on another wall. Zell held his gun on Tucker and took the piggin' string from his belt. He handed it to Mick, who tied Tucker's hands. Mick grabbed a rope dangling from a saddle in the corner and tied Tucker's feet tight before looping it through the rawhide around Tucker's wrists and securing it to a ring in the wall.

When Mick was finished, Zell started to the door, then stopped and turned back. "You coming?"

"In a bit," Mick said while he lit a lantern hanging on one wall. "Me and Ashley have some things to discuss."

Zell grinned. "Understood. Just make sure there's enough left to try him at the miners' court in the morning. I'm going to hunt up Perry and collect that hundred dollars."

"You go out that door and leave me with this crazy bastard, and I'll kill you," Tucker yelled after Zell.

"I don't believe you're in any position to kill anyone," Zell said. "Besides"—he turned and slapped Tucker across the face— "you'll hang in the morning. For killing Red and murdering that guard out back of the Deadwood Dawn."

"I'll kill you!" Tucker yelled at Zell as he shut the tack room door.

Mick put on thick gloves and took his jacket off. "It's a real shame you'll hang tomorrow. That means I only have one night with you."

"I didn't kill Red—"

Mick hit Tucker in the belly, and when the air rushed out of him, hit him on the chin. Tucker's head snapped back and bounced off the wall. Mick squeezed Tucker's cheeks hard and cocked his fist. "You didn't kill Red, you say?"

"I didn't. But if I had got the chance, I damn sure would have."

Mick bellowed like an old bull and hit Tucker flush on the jaw. His head hit the wall again, and he felt himself losing consciousness, but Mick's blow to his cheek snapped Tucker awake. "All doomed men claim they're innocent right before the noose is pulled tight."

"Look at my hands, you idiot. See scars? If I'd beaten him as badly as folks say he was, don't you think my hands would be cut all to hell?"

"No," Mick said. He took off his gloves and showed Tucker his hands. "Mine aren't cut either after our little visit tonight. Don't prove anything."

"Then look at me," Tucker said. "Do you think I could have broken Red's neck, as powerful as he was?"

Mick spit in Tucker's face. "Tomorrow you'll hang, and I'll be there to cheer it on. And if you figure your friend Jack Worman's gonna help you, he's trussed up in Limey's office. Aim to keep him that way until he can witness the hanging in the morning."

Mick had started out the door when Tucker called after him. "Trait's not going to like this. He set his sights on a fair fight between him and me—"

"Trait's away on his own job that Zell gave him. He'll just have to get mad that he missed your final words."

Mick doused the lantern and slammed the door, plunging the room into darkness. Tucker saw flashes of light across his eyes as he recovered from his head hitting the wall. A knot was forming on his head where Mick had hit him with his gun butt, and he ran his tongue over swollen and bleeding lips. But his injuries were minor compared to the thought of swinging by a piece of stout hemp in the morning.

Tucker tried working the rawhide strap loose, but Mick had done a good job of securing his hands to the ring attached to the wall. The more Tucker struggled to free his hands, the tighter his legs cinched up, attached to the rope. He strained one last time, feeling the joints in his shoulders pull tight, and he backed off.

And sometime after that immense struggle, sleep overcame him, his head dropped onto his chest, and he fell into a fitful sleep.

CHAPTER 23

Footsteps approaching just outside the tack room woke Tucker. He shook his head to clear it, dizziness still lingering. He didn't know how long he'd dozed, but he knew another visit with Mick might do him in. For a moment he forgot how securely the Irishman had trussed him up, and he struggled for a bit before giving up.

The footsteps stopped outside the room, as if Mick was gathering his strength to beat Tucker again. The door opened, and someone filled the opening, blocking out light from a lantern glowing somewhere in the barn. "You come to finish the job, Mick?"

"Don't ever call me Mick," Simon Cady said. "And keep your damn voice down."

"What the hell—"

Simon clamped his hand over Tucker's mouth and leaned close. "I said hush," Simon whispered. "You want that damned crowd out there to hear you? They're already getting roostered-up enough, thinking you might not have lasted until daybreak before they strung you up." Simon took his knife from his belt sheath and sliced the rope, then the rawhide securing Tucker's wrists. Tucker slumped, and Simon caught him. "Work some circulation back into your legs and arms. You're going to need 'em if you're to survive this night."

"You're taking some chance coming in here and cutting me loose."

Simon sheathed his skinning knife. "Not really. Besides, I enjoyed it. I laid Limey out cold—that old bastard musta looked the other way while that ape of Zell's worked you over."

Tucker turned up the lantern. "Where's Zell now?"

"Beggar Jim said he took off long before I got to town. But Mick and the others are getting knee-walking drunk, bragging what a lovely thing it'll be to see you swing."

Tucker rubbed his wrists and followed Simon from the tack room. Then he stopped Simon. "Why are you helping me?"

"It's not 'cause I like you so much," Simon said. "It's a purely selfish reason—you'll lead me to Miller Hazelton's killer. *If* you are free."

"I don't know who the hell his killer is."

"You will."

"Where do they have Jack tied up?"

"Limey's office," Simon said. "They didn't beat him like they did you. Slapped him around some, but he'll survive. But if you're going to get the hell out of here, you'd best cut him loose and get as far away from Deadwood as you can."

Tucker started to go around Simon, but Simon stopped him. "You'd better hurry. They tied your mule in back of the saloon and plan to butcher him for the celebration after the necktie party."

Tucker ran to the far end of the livery barn and paused outside Limey's office. He chanced a look inside and saw Limey, still unconscious where Simon had left him. Jack looked up, and Tucker pressed his finger to his lips as he looked about for a knife to cut Jack's ropes.

"How the hell'd you get free?"

"Simon Cady." Tucker motioned over his shoulder, but Simon was gone, as if he'd never been there. "In the drawer." Jack nodded to Limey's desk. "Our guns and knives are in there."

The second desk drawer Tucker opened held his gun and

Bowie knife. He sliced Jack's ropes before he strapped his belt and holster on.

"Better hurry," Jack said, rubbing his wrists and rifling in the drawer for his own gun. "I heard Zell and Mick talking. They're headed into the hills to meet up with Trait."

"Why?"

"Can't say for sure, but it sounded like Zell was meeting with a couple fellers, and Mick would be meeting up with Trait. And it sounded like they intended meeting up with their claim buyer tonight."

"Someone besides Ramona?" Tucker told Jack what Ramona said about buying up claims, hoping the killer would decide to put her out of business. Then she'd have her son's murderer.

Jack strapped his gun and knife on and took his coat off the nail in the wall. "Brave lady. She must want to catch her son's murderer awfully bad."

"If she's telling me the truth," Tucker said.

Tucker tied Limey up before they left. Last thing they needed was for that fool to sound the alarm before Tucker and Jack had a chance to escape.

They opened the wide barn door a foot. Drunks whooped in revelry inside the saloons along the Badlands, anticipating a quick hanging and a celebration afterward. Tucker and Jack walked the alley to the opposite side of the street. They found Soreback tied behind the Salty Dog, the saddle still on him. It was the only time the mule seemed to appreciate Tucker. He nickered as Tucker approached.

"Ever eat mule?" Jack asked.

"Shush," Tucker said. "Don't want to spook Soreback."

"Well, have you?" Jack pressed.

"Burro once," Tucker said and checked the cinches and the crupper. "Soreback would never forgive me."

Tucker led the mule along the alley and made it to Olaf's

Livery. The big man met them at the door and ushered them inside. "Vat haf you boys got into?" Olaf said. He told them Simon Cady had woken him an hour ago and nearly given him a heart attack. "I thought I was a goner, but I am not wanted." Simon had asked if Olaf had seen Tucker, and Olaf had told Simon to talk with Beggar Jim. "Don't be mad, but I yust thought Simon could help you better."

"Just don't tell anyone we were here getting Jack's pony."

Olaf nodded.

"Where is Beggar Jim?"

"Sleeping in back of the Pretty Pony. But be careful," Olaf said. "That mob is about to erupt. Once they see you are not in Limey's, they vill tear the town apart."

"Get your pony saddled," Tucker told Jack. "I'll be back soon's I hunt up Beggar Jim."

Tucker found Jim sleeping under a horse blanket in back of the Pretty Pony.

"Thought you'd have your neck stretched by now."

"You, too?" Tucker said. "Have you heard where Zell rode off to?"

Jim uncorked a bottle of foul-smelling spirits and took a long pull. "Overheard him talking with that ape, Mick Flynn. Zell said he was going out to visit the Courys."

The Courys—two men claiming to be brothers, but as different physically as night and day—were suspected to be wanted men in Montana, where a string of stage robberies was attributed to them. They had drifted to Deadwood, where they staked their claim upstream from Jack's. They had refused to sell to the Flynns.

"I suspect Zell is going to do more than just a friendly visit. When'd he leave?"

"An hour ago. He told Mick Flynn that, if he wasn't back in town in another hour, to go find Trait and join him."

"Where is Trait?"

"What am I, a soothsayer?" Jim said. "I can only hear so much. All's I know is he rode off alone."

"Thanks," Tucker said and handed Jim his last quarter eagle.

"Keep it," Jim said. "There's no telling where all this is going to lead. You might need it more'n me."

Tucker kept to the alley, stopping in the darkest shadows now and again to check if anyone followed, or if any of the sloppy drunks staggering past recognized him. But by the sounds of the laughter and fights and the occasional gunshot, most of the rowdies were still inside the saloons getting roostered up enough to enjoy the necktie party starring Tucker Ashley—a party Tucker would have to skip.

He crouched across from Olaf's Livery. Soreback stood tied where Tucker had left him. But something was wrong— something he couldn't identify right off. His instincts had often saved his skin, and right now those instincts told him he'd best wait and watch.

Another gunshot from the Salty Dog, followed by a dozen more, interrupted the stillness of this part of Deadwood. Yet Tucker saw nothing out of order outside Olaf's barn, the mob still working up courage to hang Tucker. He stared into a pile of hay bales stacked high in one corner of the livery. A freight wagon loaded with cut lumber waiting for Olaf to fix a broken wheel was parked beside the bales.

After Tucker saw no movement in the alley, he was sprinting across the street, passing the bales of hay when . . .

. . . strong hands, powerful hands, grabbed him by the throat, lifting him off the ground. His legs flailed the air as his attacker slammed him against the side of the livery.

"Not just yet." Spittle flew from Chet's mouth, inches from Tucker's. "I want you to know I'm killing you for murdering

Rance in back of the hotel. He was a good man."

Tucker tried speaking, but Chet's hand encircled his neck. He loosened pressure for the briefest moment. "Zell McGinty and Mick Flynn killed your guard—"

"Bullshit. There are witnesses in the saloon—"

A loud *thump,* and soft *grunt* from the big man, and Chet looked behind him. Jack had cocked his Colt again, holding it by the barrel for another blow to Chet's head, when Chet dropped Tucker and turned to Jack. He grabbed Jack by the shirtfront and flung him against the side of the livery. Jack slid down the side of the barn, and Tucker stumbled toward the wagon. He grabbed a four-inch-square piece of rough lumber and staggered toward Chet. When he bent over to grab Jack again, Tucker cocked the board over his shoulder and swung with all his weight. The blow landed on the side of Chet's head, and the huge man crumpled to the ground. He groaned once before going limp.

Tucker picked Jack up and leaned him against the barn. "You hurt?" He breathed, catching his breath, his voice raw.

Jack rubbed the back of his head. "Just where I landed against the barn." He squinted and touched Tucker's throat. "But looks like you got the worst of it."

Tucker agreed. His throat had been on the verge of collapsing when Chet let up for that one brief moment, but it would be days until the hoarseness left him. "Hope you didn't damage your Colt when you hit him."

"My gun!" Jack said. "You worry about my gun?"

"Friends, I can get." Tucker forced a grin. "Good Colts are harder to come by."

Tucker filled Jack in about Beggar Jim hearing Zell brag he was going to visit the Courys. "Anyone else, and I'd say they'll have their hands full with those two. But Zell . . . I suspect he's caught more than a few men unawares in his lifetime. We better get after him before that little visit takes place. Don't need any other miners turning up dead."

Before they went after Zell, Tucker motioned for Olaf, as he stuck his big head out the barn door. Tucker said, "Take his feet." Together, Tucker and Olaf managed to carry Chet inside the livery. "His head is split from that board," Tucker said. "Maybe you can do what you can to fix him up, even though you usually work on horses."

Olaf looked down at Chet. "I do not recall the last time I doctored a horse that big."

They crossed the gulch, riding slowly past tents dotting the bank, filled with weary miners waiting for the sun to rise so they could resume working their claims. The water in the creek was icy cold despite it being mid-summer, and Tucker drew the collar of his coat tighter around his neck. When they had gone a quarter mile, Tucker dismounted and handed Jack the reins. He walked along the creek and looked into the moonlight. "Horses crossed the creek here within the last couple hours."

Jack followed Tucker at a distance and kept an eye on the trees. He had walked another twenty yards when he spotted hoofprints disrupting the sediment in the creek, and he crouched, studying them. The tracks went up the steep hill toward where Tucker had seen a Lakota hunting party last week. And where the Courys' camp was.

They mounted and rode the last hundred yards until they came to a coulee next to where the Courys had pitched their tent a few yards from their claim. Tucker waited to approach the tent, holding back, watching within shouting distance.

Jack dismounted and squatted beside Tucker. "Scared to death, is what they are," Jack had said to Tucker that first day in Deadwood Gulch. Jack repeated it tonight. "We go busting in there, we're likely to get our butts shot off. They don't cotton to anyone coming around their place. What do you think?"

"I just don't know," Tucker said. "Back at the creek I picked up sign of two riders crossing sometime in the night. Hard to age them, but one set rode straight for the Courys'." Tucker squatted and ran his hand over the hoof tracks.

"The stride of this one," Jack said, circling a hoofprint with a twig, "is longer than the other. That new Morgan of Zell's, more than likely."

Tucker took his reins and mounted the mule. "That was my thought, but I needed you to confirm it. If I'm looking at these tracks right, Mick followed Zell on that rangy mustang of his."

"And Mick's no more than half an hour ahead."

"But that Morgan rode towards the Courys' tent." Tucker studied the terrain. "We'll approach from the west. Only place with decent cover, if those hot heads decide to wing rounds our way."

Jack mounted, and the two men rode the coulee past where the tent was pitched, past where a thick stand of birch petered out and allowed them to ride up out of the ravine undetected.

At the trees, Tucker took a deep, calming breath. "Now's as good a time as any," he said. "Get ready to hit the ground if they hear us approaching."

They rode at a slow walk, Tucker prepared to kick himself out of the saddle. The Courys were dangerous men, if he could read dangerous men. Being in prison the last few years had made Tucker an authority on bad people, and he had no desire to shoot it out with these two. But—by the tracks—Zell on his new horse might have ridden past here, and the Courys might know where he'd gone.

When they arrived within yards of the tent, Soreback snorted, his legs locked, and he refused to go farther. The wall tent showed no light from inside, no movement from the Courys. Yet the mule had told Tucker something was not right.

Tucker dismounted and tied Soreback to a pine. He drew his Colt. He motioned to Jack to circle to one side of the tent while Tucker approached front-on, wary of what lay in ambush. Even before Tucker reached the tent, the reason Soreback had locked up reached Tucker—the odor of fresh blood.

Tucker dropped to the ground and crawled to the tent. He pulled the flap back and peeked quickly into the tent before holstering. He stood hunched over and entered the tent for a closer look. He spotted a lantern hanging by a tent post and lit it.

"Doubt they'll hurt us any," Jack said as he poked his head inside the tent flap.

Two men lay dead inside the tent, one face down, the other looking up at the tent center, his eyes open in that stare reserved for the dead. Arrows stuck out of both Courys.

And neither one of them died from arrow wounds.

Tucker bent to the bodies and played the light over the corpses. "Look here."

Jack squatted beside the two men, left where they had been killed. Except for blood dripping from their scalped heads, there was little blood. And there should have been more blood if they had been shot with arrows while they still lived. They should have bled out where they lay.

Tucker ran his hand over the fletching of an arrow that jutted from one Coury's back into his lungs. The other Coury had an arrow in his chest over his heart.

Jack turned one man over. "Look at these marks." He pointed to deep marks around the man's neck. "He was strangled like Miller Hazelton."

"And the other one had his neck broken," Tucker said, cocking his head, looking at the odd way in which the man's head was turned nearly backwards on his shoulders.

Tucker stood and started walking large circles around the

bodies, studying the area. Mick's mustang had ridden up to the bodies sometime after the men had been killed. Boot prints—half again as long and wide as Mick's—had made deep sign in the soft earth. "Mick didn't kill the Courys—Zell did," Tucker said. "Mick come on to them afterward. They'll probably pick up the bodies on the way back to town and bring them into Deadwood to prove Indians are still hereabouts, killing miners."

"At least we now *know* who's been killing these miners," Jack said. "Just like we suspected. And Mick will file on the Courys' claim, if I believe Perry's ledger. Mick probably filed before the Courys were even murdered."

Tucker left the tent, grateful for the fresh air. As many times as he had seen dead men, the odor of their corpses never left his nose. He walked a large circle around the tent and spotted where Mick's mustang had peeled off and gone in a different direction from Zell. "I think we should stick with Mick," Tucker said. "If he's supposed to meet up with Trait, we might get the drop on them and finally get to the bottom of the murders."

The Black Hills at night can be especially treacherous, the thick forest seeming to block the very moonlight from fighting its way through the trees, making cutting track difficult. Tucker and Jack did more crawling on hands and knees and walking than they did riding, looking for the next broken twig, the next hoof-print, as Mick's horse stepped over a fallen log or around a boulder. So the flicker of a campfire—no matter how far away—shines as brightly as a blood moon.

Tucker stood in the stirrups and eyed the campfire no more than a hundred yards away. "Jack," he whispered and pointed to the light.

Even in the darkness his smile was evident. " 'Bout time. How you want to play this?"

"Best go on foot," Tucker whispered, but Jack had already

tied Daisy to a tree.

Tucker tied Soreback to a tree away from Jack's pony, and they made their way toward the campfire. They took time to avoid dead, loud branches, ducking under overhanging boughs. Two figures, illuminated by the fire, were now visible twenty yards through the trees.

Tucker motioned to Jack, who bent over as they approached within earshot. Mick Flynn and Trait McGinty squatted around the fire as they talked over coffee. "I need you to go back into town," Trait said. "Tell the buyer the last two holdouts have been taken care of."

"I saw the Courys in that tent of theirs." Mick chuckled. "Bet those boys aren't so damn tough now. If they had only sold out to us—"

"If they had sold out, we'd be a hundred dollars poorer," Trait said. "Better this way, don't 'cha think?" Trait tossed coffee into the fire and stood. "Best get into town and tell the buyer the last of the holdouts have been dealt with."

"Where'll you be?"

"Meeting up with my pa, then into town in time for the hanging. Almost tempted to spring Ashley just so I can have him in front of me."

Mick stowed his cup in his saddlebags and untied his mustang. "See ya in town for the festivities."

Tucker motioned for Jack to back away. "Follow Mick," he whispered. "See who the buyer is who's bankrolling this venture of theirs."

"What're you gonna do?"

Tucker nodded to Trait stuffing a coffee pot into his bags. "If I follow him, he'll lead me to Zell."

"And take them on by your lonesome? That's not very smart."

"It is if I get the drop on them first." Tucker patted Jack on the back. "The fool will never know I'm riding his back trail."

Jack waited until Mick had disappeared through the trees before following him, leaving Tucker watching Trait. He rolled a smoke and leaned against his horse until the cigarette was down to a stub, then tossed it aside.

Tucker returned to the mule and untied him, talking soothingly. Tucker sat Soreback, watching Trait through the trees until he mounted his own horse and walked slowly through the forest. And toward Zell.

CHAPTER 24

Following Trait was easy. The man made no attempt to hide his trail; nothing in his riding indicated he even suspected he was being followed. *He still thinks I'm trussed up in Limey's barn,* Tucker thought. And Tucker would be the only one Trait would worry about following him.

Trait threaded his horse through thick forest, riding bent over in the saddle as he rode under overhanging pine boughs, oblivious to Tucker fifty yards behind him.

When Trait rode another half mile, he pulled up short and looked warily around, his form barely visible in the moonlight. Tucker stroked Soreback's muzzle while he talked softly, and the mule made no sounds. After several moments, Trait dismounted and tied his horse to a boulder before kicking loose, dry pine needles into a pile in a clearing. He walked around the trees, picking up small branches to lay over the needles. A lucifer flared, illuminating Trait's face for a moment before he dropped the match onto the kindling. The fire blazed high and hot when Trait laid larger pieces of wood across it.

The mule suddenly snorted, his muscles twitching. Tucker bent over and whispered, "No need to get riled. You've smelled a campfire before."

"I'll give an amen to that."

Tucker drew his gun as he turned in the saddle. But a gun cocking gave him pause.

"If you think you can turn and fire that Colt before this

194

buffalo gun cuts you in two, feel free."

Tucker dropped his pistol back in the holster and turned to the sound of Zell's laughter. "I was worried Trait would lose you in the dark, so I told Mick to tell my boy to make sure he'd leave an easy trail."

"Now you're going to kill me like you did the Courys back there a mile or so?"

"Not if you tell me what I want to know," Zell said. He eased his Morgan closer to Tucker, grabbed Tucker's pistol from the holster, and stuck it in his waistband. "Might as well go into camp and say howdy to your old friend." He motioned to Trait. "On foot."

Tucker dismounted and let the reins drop. With Zell a step behind him on his horse, Tucker broke through the trees and stood at the edge of the campfire. "Thought you'd never bring him in," Trait said. He walked up to Tucker and exaggerated a look up and down. "You started packing a gun, I see." He took the Colt from Zell and hefted it. He brought the hammer back and aimed it at Tucker's head, closing one eye as he took aim.

"Not just yet," Zell said, stopping him. "He ain't told us what we want to know."

Trait carefully lowered the hammer and hefted the pistol again. "I wouldn't think of killing Ashley outright," Trait said. "Not without a fair fight." He hefted the Colt once again. "I see you've done some filing on this piece. Sweet. Too bad the last time you'll hold it again is when you face me."

A commotion behind Tucker caused him to turn. Mick shoved Jack ahead of him and kicked him when he broke through the clearing. Jack went sprawling and landed at the edge of the campfire. "Sorry, Tuck. Mick was waiting for me."

"Then we've both been snookered tonight," Tucker said. Zell had gotten the upper hand at every turn, all because Tucker had become complacent, thinking he could outwit a man who had spent his entire life surviving in the woods by being cautious. Zell hadn't become sloppy in his old age like Tucker figured.

"I don't know how you two got loose from Limey's," Zell said, "but I don't care right now. All I want to know is who you told about us—"

"Murdering the miners?" Jack said, and Zell kicked him in the side. He rolled over the fire, his coat flicking embers, and he batted them out.

"I'll deal with you soon's me and Ashley here have our little visit," Zell told Jack.

Zell grabbed Tucker by the coat front and lifted him off the ground. He shook him and slapped Tucker hard across the face. "I want to know who you told!" Zell dropped Tucker, who fell to the ground next to Jack. Tucker had no illusions about their fate—Zell and Trait would kill them here, now, in the Black Hills. Unless Tucker could convince Zell that he had told others his suspicions about the McGintys and the Flynns. If Tucker failed, he and Jack would never leave this campfire alive.

"We have told . . . the authorities how you murdered those men these last few weeks—"

Zell squatted beside Tucker and took his cheeks in his hand. He shook his head while he squeezed Tucker hard enough for his eyes to water. "Those idiots working the creek had no idea what they had—pan a few ounces of dust from the gulch, get drunk and gamble it on the tables, or blow it on ten minutes with some upstairs girl. Then back the next morning, panning with the damnedest hangover they ever had. And then do it all over again that night."

"And by buying out the small guys," Trait said, "one person will control all the gold that comes out of Deadwood Gulch. One person will own enough claims to set up a viable commercial operation that will bring in more gold than a hundred of those fools do every day."

"That's enough," Zell said. "You don't have to tell them everything." He stood and lifted Tucker up again. Zell pulled Tucker close enough that he smelled the whisky on the killer's breath. "You two have been nosing around town and have found out just a little more than I'd like. Now you say you told the authorities—who are these *authorities* you claim to have talked to?"

"I'll tell you what," Tucker said, looking around for something—anything—he could use for a weapon. If he could distract Zell, Trait, and Mick long enough for Jack to escape . . . "You tell me who the major investor is who keeps buying up all the claims, and I'll tell you just who I told about your murders."

"*We* don't even know who the buyer is," Mick said, "though we wouldn't tell you anyways."

Zell backhanded Mick, and he backed up, tripping over Jack, who lay beside the campfire. Mick fell on his back and scrambled to stand. "I said shut the hell up!" Zell yelled.

"Ain't that just something," Tucker said. "I'd wager you boobs have been murdering miners and haven't got paid anything yet. Promised a cut of the gold, maybe? You fellers *are* stupid."

"Perry Dowd pays us," Trait said and backed away from Zell. "Hell, Pa, it's not like these two are going to walk away from here. Might as well tell them just to make them feel like the fools they are."

"So Perry is your investor," Tucker said. "Where does he get his money? Far as I know, he just runs a few girls in the Miner's Paradise. Surely not enough to buy up half the gulch."

"Perry pays for getting the claims registered, is all," Zell said, "on behalf of a group of investors he won't tell even *us* about." He stepped closer to Tucker and drew his gun. "Now, who did you tell?"

Tucker remained silent.

"Nothing to say?" Zell cocked the gun and pointed it at

Tucker's head. As long as Zell thought Tucker and Jack had told someone . . .

"Not today."

"No?" Zell said and motioned to Mick. "Stand Jack up and prop him against that there pine tree."

Mick hoisted Jack erect and leaned him against a pine tree.

"Now step away," Zell ordered. "I wouldn't want blood to splatter all over you." He aimed the pistol at Jack's head and sighted down the barrel.

"Wait!" Tucker said. "We sent a wire to the U.S. marshal in Yankton—"

"Wrong answer," Zell said. "I have a . . . contact at the telegraph office. You two didn't send *any* wire."

"All right. All right," Tucker blurted out. "We *didn't* tell anyone. Now let Jack go."

"Just what I thought," Zell said and cocked the hammer, his Colt inches away from Jack's head. "Say goodbye to your friend . . ."

. . . a shot—loud, coming from a buffalo gun—erupted from the trees. The bullet entered Zell's chest from the side, blowing heart and veins and blood from his other side, and he dropped dead on the ground.

Mick clawed for his gun as Trait drew his and crouched, looking in the direction the shot came from. Tucker spotted Zell's pistol lying ten yards from him. He'd started inching toward it when another shot from the tree line kicked up dirt between Trait and Mick's feet. "Next one is in your head," a voice hollered. "Want to gamble which one of you will die first? Now drop those guns."

"I'd do as Simon says," Tucker said. As soon as Mick and Trait dropped their guns, Tucker bent and picked up Zell's pistol.

"Step back," Simon Cady ordered as he emerged from the

stand of birch and aspen. He stuffed a fresh cartridge into his Rolling Block as he approached the campfire. "You, too, moron," he said to Mick.

Mick and Trait stepped away from the campfire while Tucker held his gun on them. Tucker grabbed his own Colt out of Trait's waistband and holstered it.

"Better see to your friend," Simon said.

Tucker bent to Jack, draped an arm around his shoulders, and helped him stand.

"Careful," Jack said. "I think Zell broke some ribs."

"You can go and boo-hoo over your old man," Simon told Trait, " 'cause in a minute me and his body will be going *adios.*"

Tucker carefully eased Jack onto a fallen log and turned to Simon, keeping Mick and Trait in his peripheral. "You've been following me."

"I have," Simon said. He took his pipe from his coat pocket and began filling it with tobacco. He looked around Tucker and motioned with his rifle. "You two fools sit on the ground beside what's left of Zell."

Tucker's hand shook as he rolled his own cigarette. "I don't understand . . . why kill Zell."

"Not 'thanks, ol' Simon, for saving our bacons'?" Simon smiled.

"Thanks for saving our butts," Tucker said. "But why Zell now? It's not like you really care about what happens to Jack or me. There's no profit in it. Ain't that what you always say?"

Tears streamed down Trait's face as he glared up at Simon. "I'll kill you."

Simon grinned and kicked Zell's body. "But not today, sonny." He turned to Tucker. "I had to get Zell away from town. He's got too many cronies who'd step in and spoil the fun if I tried taking him in Deadwood. Besides"—he blew smoke rings upward into the trees—"I work better out here anyways. Never did cotton to towns. Besides, there is a *lot* of profit in killing Zell." Simon cupped his hand over his smoldering bowl of tobacco.

"What profit?"

"Ramona Hazelton's reward for her son's killer. Hand me that medicine bundle she gave you."

Mick scooted back from Zell's corpse when Tucker turned his Colt on him. "Another foot, and you'll join your brother." Mick sat still, and Tucker fished in his coat pocket. He handed Simon the medicine bundle Miller had clutched in his hand the day the wolfer brought his body in.

Simon tossed it into the air and caught it. "This medicine bundle belonged to Black Kettle—"

"I'll kill you—"

Simon lashed out with his foot and caught Trait in the belly. Trait rolled away and lay clutching his stomach.

"Have some manners. I'm talking to Ashley." He turned back to Tucker. "Like I was saying, this was Chief Black Kettle's medicine bundle."

"Black Kettle who was attacked at Sand Creek?"

"The same. This piece of crap"—Simon kicked the body again—"stole Black Kettle's bundle from the unconscious chief that day. Zell slipped it around his neck. He's worn it ever since."

Simon's tobacco went out, and he relit it. "Damned moisture," he said and drew in smoke. "Zell McGinty was proud that he led Chivington in that dawn massacre of those Cheyenne and Arapaho. Proud they never had a chance against those Colorado Volunteers. He would wave this bundle around like some badge of honor. The last I saw it many years ago, it was dangling from Zell's neck."

"When I showed you the medicine bundle—"

"When you showed it to me, I *knew* who Miller Hazelton's

killer was. I just needed to get to Zell somewhere unaware."

"And you used me and Jack for bait?"

Simon shrugged. "I knew Zell would be hunting you, all the snooping you two have been doing around Deadwood. Just a matter of time before he caught you."

"Why not just kill the man outright? Not like he was making himself scarce around town."

"Like I said, he's got too many friends in town. Besides, Zell was a lot like me—spent his entire life watching his back trail with caution. I knew I'd have to bide my time to get to him."

"Miller Hazelton must have snatched the bundle from Zell's neck the night Zell attacked him."

Simon nodded and walked to Trait. He scooted away from Simon. "Not that it matters none now, but who came onto your old man the night he killed Miller?"

"Screw you—"

Simon stepped on Trait's leg, and he howled in pain. "Who?"

Trait grimaced as he rubbed his leg. "Who says anyone did?"

"Only reason Zell wouldn't have reclaimed Black Kettle's bundle is if he were interrupted. Now you want to dangle a broken ankle around town—"

Trait looked up at Simon, wild eyed. "I wasn't even there."

"Of course, you were," Simon said. "You scalped young Miller to make it look like Indians."

"Bull—"

"Now, sonny . . ." Simon stepped on Trait's leg again. Tucker feared his screams would alert every Lakota within miles.

"Your old man knew enough about Indians to know they never take the time to scalp a man surgically. They rip and run. But you didn't know that, now did you, because you'd never been around men after they'd been scalped like Zell had? You took your time and lifted the whole scalp, thinking that's the way Indians work."

Trait remained quiet.

Simon dropped his rifle butt on Trait's leg, and he screamed in pain.

"All right. Pa thought Miller was dead when he strangled him. But the kid came to life when I went to scalp him. He lashed out with a knife. Cut me on the leg. That's when Pa got mad and finished the job."

"And stuck a Sioux arrow into him?" Tucker said.

Trait rubbed his leg. "Pa went out every night until he finally found two Sioux alone. He killed them and stole their arrows, so we could . . . use them later."

Tucker cursed himself under his breath. He had noticed how Trait limped. And how—with time—the limp had become less pronounced. Tucker should have figured it out, remembering how much blood was at the scene where Miller was killed. And it wasn't blood from his scalp or the arrow Zell had stuck in the body afterward.

"Did somebody find you two," Simon asked, " 'cause Zell wouldn't leave the bundle?"

Trait nodded. "Indians came along about the time we finished the deserter off. Four in a war party. We hightailed it out of there before they spotted us, and Pa was almighty angry that he lost that medicine bundle. We rode back the next morning to get it off that deserter, but the wolfer had already brought the body into town."

Simon tamped burnt tobacco out on the heel of his moccasin. "Now the conundrum—that's one of those ten-cent words I learned as a youngster—is how do I prove all this? I need proof for Ramona Hazelton to pay up. I could take Trait into town, but I suspect he would recant all he's said, and I'd be out my reward money."

"You got that right, old man."

"See?" Simon said and threw up his hands. "Now all I got is

this fool to tell folks just what Trait here just said." Simon stepped closer to Mick, but he scooted back. "About Miller Hazelton and the other miners."

"Mick won't say a thing," Trait said and glared at Mick. "Right?"

Mick looked up at Simon. "I *can't* say anything." He pointed to Trait. "He'll kill me."

Simon lifted Mick off the ground with one strong paw and shook him. "Ol' Simon here's done being nice to you boys. Here's the deal: you come into town with me and spill your guts, and I won't kill you."

"But Trait—"

"Trait will kill you quick." Simon dropped Mick into the campfire, and he rolled off, batting embers from his shirt and trousers. Simon drew his Bowie, the fire flickering reflections in the sharp blade. "I'll kill you slow. Believe me, when I say *slow*, I mean *Kiowa slow*. I learned interesting things from them. No one tortures a man and draws it out like the Kiowa. Now what do you say: come into town and worry that Trait here might find you one day, or have pieces of your flesh flicked off an inch at a time?"

"And what happens if I tell the truth?" Mick said. "All's me and Red did was file the claims when they came available. I didn't kill anyone. Just . . . knew about Trait and the old man knocking off miners. The miners' court will convict me same as if I did the deed."

"I'll wire the U.S. marshal in Yankton to come and take you to trial. Best I can do."

Mick shook his head. "I don't know—"

"Would it help if I told you Zell murdered your brother?" Tucker said.

"How's that?"

"I looked at Red when he was on ice at Grundy's cellar.

Strangled." He squatted beside Trait. "His neck had been broken by a powerful man. Red was fixin' to tell me about your operation that day I beat him up by the claim. Only your old man conveniently came along and prevented him from spilling his guts. Your father *had* to kill him before I could find him and squeeze the information out of him."

"Tell him he's full of shit," Mick said, but Trait looked away.

Mick's jaw tightened, and he spat at Trait. "You . . . I'll tell the truth all right," he told Tucker.

Trait lunged at Mick. "You son of a—"

Simon kicked Trait, and he rolled away from Mick, holding his stomach. "Keep away from my star witness."

Tucker motioned to Trait, who was holding his side. "What should we do with him? Can't hardly kill him outright, and he's too dangerous to allow to live."

"Get his boots," Simon said at last.

"What?"

"His boots," Simon repeated. "Take off his boots."

Tucker squatted at Trait's feet and grabbed a leg. "You kick me, and you *will* have a broken leg to worry about." Tucker took off Trait's boots and stepped back.

"Now stick them in his saddlebags," Simon said.

"He'll just put them back on."

"Not if his horse isn't here."

Trait stood and limped toward Tucker. "You are *not* taking my horse."

"Your turn." Simon winked, and Tucker threw a roundhouse right that connected flush on Trait's face. Blood spurted from his broken nose, and he slumped to one knee.

"Best stop that bleeding," Simon said. He hoisted Zell's body over his Morgan and lashed him to the saddle. "Some Indians I've known can smell blood."

Trait looked about the clearing. "What Indians?"

Simon waved his hand to the trees encircling the clearing. "Indians you're bound to run into wandering around these hills."

"You setting me afoot?" Trait asked.

"Boy's not as stupid as I thought," Simon said to Tucker. "I *am* setting you afoot. It's only three miles to Deadwood, but it will seem longer without your boots or your horse. Be my suggestion, you best travel these hills cautiously. 'Cause if you run into a Lakota war party, a little feller like you won't stand a chance. Especially since you're unarmed now."

"That's murder!" Trait shouted.

Simon stepped closer to Trait and jabbed a finger in his chest. "No. Murder is what you and your piece of crap old man intended doing to Tucker and Jack. And what you been doing to miners hereabouts. At least you'll have *some* chance of survival. More than you gave those poor bastards."

"When I get to Deadwood—"

"By the time you get to Deadwood," Tucker said, "word will have gone out that you and your old man're the ones been murdering miners. You'll be lucky to stay one step ahead of a noose. But come on into Deadwood if you still want to."

"What chance do I have, unarmed? Walking with no shoes and Indians close by?"

Tucker smiled. "Very little, I'd wager."

CHAPTER 25

Tucker marveled at the way Madame Marcie kept the crowd of angry miners subdued as they listened to Mick Flynn tell about how the McGintys had killed the miners, leaving their claims open to file on. As Mick told of the scheme to bilk gold miners out of their claims—those the McGintys didn't murder—the men in the saloon became more vocal, and still Madame Marcie held them back. But when Mick came to the part where all the murders, all the strong-arming of the miners to abandon their claims, were solely done to allow a big conglomerate to waltz into Deadwood Gulch and set up a large, commercial operation, the crowd closed in on Mick.

"I didn't lay a hand on those fine men," Mick said from the safety of Madame Marcie's back. "It was all the McGintys. All me and Red done was front for them. We didn't know it was all for some big investor."

"Let's string him up," a drunk hollered and brushed past Madame Marcie. Her guard, sitting his chair in the corner above the crowd, touched off one barrel of his shotgun and pointed it at the rowdies.

"Say the word," he said to Madame Marcie as he waved the double shotgun at the mob of drunks.

"Yeah," Monty said. The bar dog stood in back of the bar holding a Henry repeater at the crowd. "Say the word, boss."

"Boys. Boys," Madame Marcie said. "Let us have some civility. Let Mick say his piece. Then, if you want to string him up afterwards, the drinks are on the house."

"Where's your partner?" one drunk shouted. "Seems like he ought to be here with you telling us his story."

"He is still wandering somewhere in the hills," Mick said, and when the crowd hushed, he continued. "Trait McGinty is without shoes and without a gun. And him and his old man murdered my brother, same as he murdered many of your friends."

Tucker admired Mick. In another time, Mick might have been an itinerant preacher, going from town to town, stepping onto a soapbox whenever he drew a crowd, hat on the ground to collect coins from those hearing him preach. But right now, Mick had turned the mob's attention from him to the real murderer—Trait. "He can't be far away, boys!"

A dozen men downed their beers and shots of whisky and rushed out the door. They would start hunting for Trait. As soon as they were sober enough to sit a horse.

"That was pretty slick," Jack said. He stood hunched over, the wrappings Olaf had encircled Jack with were tight, restrictive. Like a horse with broken ribs Olaf had worked on last year. "Mick might just live long enough to see trial in Yankton."

"Think again," Tucker said. He nodded to four men who had stood up from a corner table. One man drifted close to Madame Marcie's guard, while another worked his way around to within grabbing range of her bardog. One of the remaining men began fashioning a noose as he walked, hidden by his partner walking close beside him as they picked their way through the crowd. "If those guys get the drop on the guard Mick can pretty much kiss this world goodbye." Tucker finished his beer and motioned for the door. "This is something we don't want any part of."

"I thought you told Mick you'd see he got to trial in Yankton?"

Tucker shook his head. "I told Mick I'd *wire* the U.S. marshal to come pick him up. Which I did. I never said anything about protecting the fool," he said as he started out of the Pretty Pony. "I'd like to say I feel sorry for Mick. But I don't. Shame, too, him opening up about Trait and Zell like he did."

On the way into Deadwood, Mick became more agitated about Zell and Trait killing Red. He told them it was Zell who had killed the guard Tucker had trussed up that night in back of the Deadwood Dawn. "Twisted his head like a twig," Mick said.

Mick explained that Zell had put the sneak on the Courys.

Tucker said, "Zell had to be careful with those two, Mick told me. He made it into their tent without being seen and snapped the first Coury's neck before the other woke up. When he did, Zell slipped that piece of leather around his throat and strangled him."

"At least we know how Zell took out those two bad asses," Jack said.

They walked outside and away from the Pretty Pony, listening to the boisterous mob getting more worked up by the minute. "Did you find out where Perry went to?" Tucker asked.

"I hung out at the mining office half the morning, but he never showed," Jack said. "No one's seen him since we brought Mick in. He probably lit out, now that Mick's spilling his guts."

"We—or anyone else—can't prove anything against Perry. Apparently, he just accepted money and paid it out when the investors bought a claim. Too bad Mick didn't know who Perry's investors were."

They crossed the street, deserted today. Many of the usual hanger-around bums were off the street and in the saloons, drinking free beer and anticipating Mick's probable hanging. "If Perry is being paid by a group of investors, he'll hang around town, I'm certain," Tucker said. "You stake out the mining office in case he comes back."

"Where are you headed while I watch for Perry?"

"To pay Ramona Hazelton a visit," Tucker answered.

Jack nudged Tucker. "You fixin' to take Ramona up on her offer to go back to Denver with her?"

"No," Tucker answered. "Though it is still a tempting offer."

"Good, because I'm still putting my money—what little I have left—on Ramona as the investor working with Perry."

"I'll soon know," Tucker said and headed down the back street toward the Deadwood Dawn.

The din of the crowd grew fainter as Tucker neared the hotel. As usual, a rifleman lay on the roof across the street, and a hulking form was visible just inside the entrance to the Deadwood Dawn. Tucker stepped onto the porch, and Chet emerged from inside. A wide muslin bandage circled his big head, and he glared at Tucker.

"By now you ought to know it wasn't me who killed your guard out back," Tucker said.

"Don't matter," Chet said. "What matters is you split my head open."

"I had to do something, or you'd have killed me."

"I'll kill you anyway," Chet said, his finger inching toward the side hammers of the shotgun cradled under one arm.

"You think you can bring that scattergun to bear before I can draw and kill you?"

Chet forced a chuckle a moment before he brought the muzzle of the shotgun up. But he was too slow. Tucker had drawn and cocked his pistol before Chet leveled the gun. "Wave your man off on the roof or you won't see your next birthday."

Chet paused, seeming to mull over Tucker's words. "If you tell me what the hell you want here."

"I need to speak to Ramona."

Chet lowered his shotgun and waved to the rifle on the roof.

Tucker slowly holstered his Colt.

"Mrs. Hazelton is busy packing."

209

"Tell her I am here. She'll talk to me."

Tucker leaned against a colonnade supporting the porch and rolled a cigarette. He was nearly finished with his smoke when Ramona came outside onto the porch, following by Chet a half step behind her. She wore tan riding britches and a white top. Her hair was formed into a bun, and her lace-up boots were spit-shined. Chet loomed over her until she motioned to him that she would be all right.

She led Tucker to the chairs at the far end of the porch and sat. "You have reconsidered my offer then?" She smiled.

Tucker shook his head. "I cannot. As enticing as the idea is." He leaned forward. "Ramona." He laid his hand on her hand and squeezed lightly. "I have been out of prison less than a month. I am not ready to commit to *any* woman right now. Let alone one as intriguing as you."

"That *is* a polite way to brush a woman off."

Tucker smiled. "Can I take a rain check on the relationship thing?"

"Do I have a choice?" Ramona stood and paced in front of the chairs. "If you did not come to accept my offer, why did you come see me?"

"I heard you are leaving Deadwood."

"No reason to stay now," she said and patted Tucker's pocket. He rolled her a smoke and handed it to her while she looked over her shoulder. "While you were avoiding men up in the hills, I buried Miller," she said. "Chet doesn't approve of my smoking." She waved the air when she exhaled. "And that big man came by to claim his reward."

"Simon Cady."

Ramona nodded and kept her back to Chet. "Mr. Cady explained about the medicine bundle Miller had clutched in his hand the morning the wolf hunter brought him into town. And about that associate of Mr. McGinty—Mick Flynn—admitting down at the saloon what happened to the miners. Including my Miller."

"Took you by surprise, I would wager."

"What did?"

"Anyone actually finding Miller's murderer." Tucker stood and met her eyes. "You never actually intended paying out that reward, now did you?"

Ramona looked away.

"You knew that if you made the reward for an Indian, there was no way to prove which one."

Ramona nodded. "Mr. Cady did surprise me. Even when you argued it was no Indian who killed Miller, I never thought for a moment anyone would actually catch who did it."

"You just wanted to inflict maximum damage on the Indians, even when you *knew* no Indian killed your son."

"Stirring things up here was the only way I would ever know who killed Miller. But you make me sound like such an awful person."

Tucker shook his head. "No, just someone used to . . . manipulating others."

Ramona shrugged. "Call it the business woman in me. I am used to getting things done my way." She laid her hand on Tucker's arm. "One last plea—I still need someone strong to be close to me. To help me so that I don't make such poor decisions in the future."

"Like buying up all those claims in Deadwood Gulch."

Ramona snubbed her cigarette out and tossed the butt over the railing. "I had to buy up as many claims as I could to force Perry Dowd's hand."

"I don't understand."

"Perry was buying up miners' claims for pennies—those were the ones who weren't murdered—with the claims filed upon by the Flynns."

"I know all about the group of investors from Chicago Perry said was buying up claims for—"

"There is no group of investors," Ramona said. "He was in business strictly for himself. Don't you understand?"

"I'm beginning to," Tucker said and sat back in the chair. "Perry was the one buying up all the stakes along the Gulch. For *himself.*"

Ramona smiled. "Now you're getting it. He even made the idiot McGintys think he was buying claims on behalf of a third party. Remember that investigator I said I hired to keep track of Miller? He posed as a miner and worked a claim for a few weeks. He found out Perry's upstairs girls were making more than enough money for him to buy up mining claims. But when it got a little too expensive even for him, it was cheaper to pay the McGintys to murder the miners and have the Flynns file on the deceased miners' claims."

"There never was a big conglomerate waiting to mine the entire gulch?"

"Not right now, but there's talk of a big company coming into Deadwood." She looked over her shoulder. Chet stood rubbing the side of his head. "Chet said you had nothing to do with Rance's death the other night."

"Did you ever think I did?"

Ramona shook her head. "Not for a minute." She reached inside her blouse and Tucker looked away. "Here." She handed Tucker a slip of paper.

He unfolded it. "What's this?"

"What's it look like?"

Tucker read the deed to one-hundred-sixty acres of homestead land Ramona had bought from a rancher south of Custer City. "There will be a fine bull and eight bred heifers waiting for you and Jack on that land."

"I still don't understand."

Ramona looked away for a moment. When she turned back, tears filled her eyes. "I would not have seen my son's killer brought to justice if it hadn't been for you and Jack—"

"But it was Simon Cady who figured it out."

"With your help, he explained."

Tucker handed the paperwork back to Ramona, but she refused to take it. "Isn't that what you and your friend always wanted—your own spread to start a cattle ranch?"

"We talked about it," Tucker said. "But it was always just talk. I can't—"

Ramona pushed the paper back at Tucker. "Let us say I am being selfish. I believe that one day you *will* decide you want to be with me. This way"—she snapped the paper with her fingers—"I know just where to find you when I make my next attempt at your heart."

Tucker thanked Ramona and slipped the paper into his coat. "And you bought up all those claims to force Perry's hand?"

"My investigator suspected Perry had no anonymous group of investors he was fronting for. And when my man was found murdered shortly after he reported this to me, I *knew* Perry was involved. I just had to force his hand.

"There is a new mining district representative starting today. I have instructed him to divest my claims—sell them back to miners at a fair price. It's not going to be long before the gulch is taken over by big mining companies. But for now, I think I like the romantic idea of men panning for gold in that creek. Except for Miller's claim. I'm holding onto that one for sentimental reasons."

Ramona turned and started for the hotel entrance. Tucker called after her, "Did you say there is a new mining rep?"

"As of this morning."

"Then Perry did flee the hills?"

Ramona faced Tucker. "No. I heard Perry Dowd is resting in

213

Grundy's cellar. Seems someone practically turned his head around backwards."

"Perry dead? Where did you hear that?"

Ramona nodded to Chet. "He heard about it when he went into the saloon for a drink."

"I thought you said Chet was a teetotaler?"

"Did I?" Ramona said, and a wry smile crossed her face before she disappeared into the hotel.

"Why didn't you tell me there was a new mining representative?" Jack asked as they crossed the street to Grundy's feed store.

"Just heard about it my ownself a few minutes ago."

"Well, he is one grouchy bastard," Jack said. "But at least he gave me my claim deed back." Jack stopped Tucker. "But now that I've got it back, I don't think I want another damned thing to do with Deadwood Gulch."

"Good, 'cause I'll need help with *our* cows." Tucker handed Jack the deed to the quarter section south of Custer City where a bull and heifers waited for them.

Jack read the letter, turned it over, and reread it. He slapped Tucker hard enough on the arm that it hurt. "This is ours! Just what we wanted all the time."

"And the way land is traded and swapped and sold, I'm guessing we'll be able to pick up another quarter or two down the road."

"For now, this is a start." Jack threw the deed in the air, but Tucker caught it before it hit the muddy street. "Let's go to Grundy's before Perry is carted up the hill."

They found the little man behind the counter standing on a stool and looking at them when they entered the feed store. "It's you." Grundy hung his head. "I am betting you boys don't want any chicken feed."

"I wouldn't want to bet against you," Tucker said. "We'd like to look at Perry Dowd."

"Seems you like to look at a lot of dead folks," Grundy said, drying his hands on his dirty apron. "You have a fascination with dead bodies or something?"

"I have a fascination with my own survival," Tucker said. "Can we look?"

Grundy waved to the back door. "You know where it is. And say a kind word to Perry for me."

"By the way," Tucker said, "how did Perry come to be in your root cellar? My guess is he didn't walk here of his own accord."

"You *do* have a grasp on the obvious," Grundy said. He stepped off his stool and came around the counter, looking up at them. He snapped open a peanut shell and dropped it on the floor with the thousands of other hulls. "His body was laid across my doorstep this morning. Had a note with instruction for burial and five double eagles in his pocket."

Tucker led Jack out back and toward the cold cellar.

"You can rest assured that is about four times what Grundy will be spending to bury that man," Jack said when they were out of Grundy's earshot. "Might be the first time someone actually *made* money off Perry."

Jack bent to the cellar door, but his breathing came hard, and Tucker opened the door. "Do that one more time, and Olaf will have to wrap you back up again."

"Let's just get this over with. You know this place makes me queasy."

"Well, it's not my favorite spot to spend a morning either, despite what Grundy claims."

Tucker snatched the lantern off the wall just inside the cellar door and lit it before descending the steps into the cold. He held the light high and walked to the back room where a blanket covered a corpse. Tucker laid the blanket aside and looked down at Perry Dowd resting on a wooden table. His suit remained impeccably cleaned and starched, the tag from the Chinese laundry on Main Street sticking out of an inside pocket. Perry looked like he was ready for a fashion parade. Except for his neck.

Tucker pulled Perry's collar away. Deep finger marks encircled his neck, nearly breaking the skin, and his head lay at an odd angle, broken. Jack whistled. "Took some powerful feller to do that. Only one I can think of around here who could do that is Simon Cady, what with Zell being dead and all."

Tucker rubbed his neck where Chet had almost strangled him a couple nights ago. "Either way, it's justice." Tucker pulled Perry's collar down. "He knew just what Zell and Trait were doing with the miners. I suspect he just chose not to ask questions."

Jack shuddered. "Let's get out of this place. I hear Lou's had a whole cow delivered for butchering."

Tucker was picking up the lantern when something light-colored caught his eyes, and he bent to the table where Perry lay. A piece of muslin cloth—crumpled up as if it had gotten caught on something—had fallen from Perry.

Cloth looking a lot like the cloth circling Chet's injured head.

CHAPTER 26

Jack and Tucker had hauled the last of the logs in from Custer. Tomorrow—they agreed—they would start building their house. Tucker sat Soreback and stood in the stirrups, looking about. "Something's been troubling you," Jack said. "Is it me?"

Tucker forced a laugh and tried to sound optimistic. "Not hardly." He looked carefully around their small ranch. "It's just that I'm not used to being tied down to one spot like we are here."

"You having second thoughts about this little venture?"

Tucker had been having second thoughts since the moment Ramona had handed him the deed. He *was* beholden to her, even if she wouldn't have agreed. She had given Jack and Tucker their dream—handed it right to them in the form of the deed to their own ranch, albeit a small one. Would she ever come and claim the land? Tucker doubted it, telling himself that she'd bought the land and cattle for them for the precise reason she'd told him—in case she wanted to come visit and try to convince Tucker to join her. Again.

No. What had Tucker on edge these past months since they moved here was Trait. Tucker had put out feelers, trying to find out what had happened to him, trying to find out if Trait had been killed by Indians or by miners out for revenge, but he'd heard nothing. The thought that Trait might be in the trees somewhere looking, waiting for the right time to jump Tucker unawares, had given him nightmares. He had even started wearing his Colt when doing ranch chores.

"You going to be all right?" Jack asked.

Tucker smiled. "If I don't have to eat any more of your cooking, I will."

"You want to cook then?"

Tucker nodded. "I think I will do just that."

While Jack unsaddled his pony and double-checked the rope corral they had hastily erected, Tucker rode into the thick forest, watching the ground, as much to pick up game trails as for hoofprints.

A twig snapped behind him, and he threw himself to the ground, rolling, coming up with his pistol in his hand. A startled doe looked at Tucker for a brief moment before bounding off into the forest.

Tucker sat on the ground and holstered, holding his head in his hands. He had gone over that night they had left Trait afoot and unarmed. And every time he did, he thought how he wished he had fought a duel with Trait then and there. Now, all he did most hours of the day was keep looking over his shoulder. That no one had heard anything of Trait McGinty after that night helped none. "Trait's revenge," Tucker said aloud and startled himself.

He stood and walked to Soreback. The mule merely looked at Tucker as if he were crazy and returned to grazing on buffalo grass. "Lot of help you've been," Tucker said and mounted the mule.

Later, after he had bagged a dry doe for supper, he thought how Trait's presence was still with him, taunting him, as surely as if Trait were here in front of him. *Damn him*, he thought, *a dead man's not going to get under my skin any longer.* Because Tucker was certain Indians had found Trait wandering in the forest. Tucker had a life to live that didn't include thoughts of Trait McGinty.

He field-dressed the deer and rode back to camp. As Tucker broke from the tree line, he saw Jack talking with someone hunched over a fire beside their tent. Someone vaguely familiar, but Tucker could not tell who at this distance.

He made a wide circle coming into camp, the Winchester resting across the saddle, his hammer loop off his Colt. When he got closer, the man stood and smiled at him. Simon Cady tipped his hat and bowed. "Least I can do is show respect to you ranchers."

Tucker dismounted and turned Soreback out into the rope corral. "Thought you were going to retire down on some Mexican beach."

Simon grabbed his pipe and tobacco pouch from inside his coat. "I plan to as soon as I find one more man."

"What man?" Tucker asked.

"Cheyenne to Deadwood stage has been robbed three times," Simon said. "By some young feller folks on the stages say is meaner than anyone else in the territory."

"Figured you were done chasing bounties."

"I was," Simon said. "Until I heard about this one. He's especially brutal to stage passengers after he stops them. Killed one guard, wounded another. He pistol whipped a man at every robbery, laughing all the time. There's only a five-hundred-dollar reward so far, but I'd find this one for nothing. Even if it goes against my principles." Simon topped off his coffee cup. "I'd like you to come along."

"I don't hunt other men for money."

"Then hunt this one because he's terrorizing folks along the stage route. Think about it while I help Jack build a fire."

As Tucker butchered the doe, he thought about Simon's offer. The man worked alone, yet he had offered Tucker a chance to join him. But Tucker had no intention of riding with Simon Cady.

Tucker sliced off steaks and handed them to Jack to cook once more, figuring the odds were that eventually Jack would cook a decent meal. Tucker was wrong, and Jack burned the venison. But Simon didn't complain about Jack's deer steak. Nor about the wild onions mixed with a parsnip he had dug up at the base of a birch, or bread cooked on a stick over the fire.

Before they turned in for the night, Tucker stood looking at the trees, imagining that any dark shadow might be a man. Might be Trait.

Jack patted his stomach and walked up on Tucker. "Pretty good meal wasn't it?"

"You certainly outdid yourself this time," Tucker answered, his gaze returning to the trees.

Simon lit his pipe and joined them. "You looking for your nemesis? That's another dime word I learnt in school. He *could* be out there behind any one of those trees."

"Who?"

"Trait, of course," Simon answered.

"Not hardly," Tucker said. "Even men like us would have had a hard time eluding Indians *and* miners set on vengeance for their brothers. No, Trait is fermenting the soil somewhere in the hills, and I'll not waste one more minute thinking of him."

"You'll *always* think of him," Simon said. "Same as me—I got that *one* man I expect will catch me sleeping one day. That *one* man from my past."

"What man?"

"Let us call him my Trait McGinty." He glanced at Jack. "If you got meal clean-up duty, me and Tucker's going to take a little walk. To settle our stomachs."

Simon and Tucker walked the meadow, Tucker always looking, always searching, all the while Simon told him about that stage robber who needed to be captured. Or killed.

"How long will you be gone?" Jack asked, eyeing a slab of bacon as if deciding whether to eat his own cooking or not.

Tucker hefted the saddle and blanket and walked to Soreback, who was grazing inside the corral. "When I talked with Simon last night after supper, he said he'd heard the man he's hunting has been hanging around Hat Creek Station where no one knows him."

"How will you know him then?"

"Simon knows," Tucker said.

"I still don't understand it," Jack said, slicing off a piece of bacon and wrapping it around a stick as he bent to the fire. "Why does Simon want help now? He never worked with anyone before."

Tucker shrugged and cinched the crupper under Soreback's tail.

Jack looked over his shoulder at Simon putting the saddle on his own horse. "I don't like it."

"You just don't like Simon."

Jack lowered his voice. "I don't trust Simon. You sure you don't have a bounty out on you somewhere? 'Cause he's taking an almighty interest in you."

Tucker patted Jack on the shoulder. "I'm not wanted that I know, so relax. I'll be back here soon's we find this stage robber. I figure if me and Simon split the bounty money, we'll be able to buy up some more cows. Maybe a mower if'n we can find one used. You going to be okay until I get back?"

"As long as you tell me you're *coming* back."

Tucker stopped and thought of that. Nothing in life—he knew—was guaranteed. "Look, if I'm not back, this place is yours. You know what?"

"I don't want to work it if you're not here with me."

Tucker smiled and led Soreback out of the corral. "Then I'd better make sure I'm coming back."

Tucker and Simon made camp that night twenty miles south of Custer City, Jack's words returning to Tucker many times throughout the night. Simon *never* worked with anyone when he was man hunting, yet he had filled Tucker in about the robberies, emphasizing he just might need help this time. Tucker was praying help was all Simon wanted him along for, and he vowed he'd not let his guard down around Simon.

They reached the ridgeline above Hat Creek Station and looked down. A major stage stop since the Cheyenne to Black Hills route was opened, the stop boasted a brewery and post office, bakery and butcher shop. An operator maintained a telegraph office, and the station was secure against Indian attacks, with its underground tunnel leading to Sage Creek for water in case of siege.

"There's a small saloon of sorts attached to the brewery." Simon pointed to a low-roofed building across from the livery. "I received word that our man drinks himself silly there most days and crawls out from under his rock at night to attack the stage."

"How will I know him?"

"Cocky young bastard, I'm told," Simon answered. "But I'm going down to scout things over. You stay here."

Tucker stepped off Soreback. He led him to a large clump of grama grass and hobbled his front legs. He watched Simon disappear into a deep coulee to skirt the stage station and approach it from the far side of the blacksmith shop. Tucker grabbed his canteen and sat under the shade of a maple tree, the leaves turning various colors. Soon, Tucker and Jack would be battling winter, getting feed to their cows, fending off wolves and the wandering bear after an easy meal of heifer. But that was all right by Tucker—he had fended off bad *men* for enough years; he welcomed fighting the elements.

He thought back to what Simon had said of the man they hunted, wondering what kind of man pistol whips an unarmed man. Tucker thought of a few people he'd known in life cruel enough to do that, and his thoughts turned back to Zell. Zell and his crazy whelp had been responsible for twenty murders in and around Deadwood Gulch. Perhaps more, if one tallied up the men who had disappeared and never been heard from again. If Perry Dowd had been successful in driving out most of the miners from the Gulch, Zell and Trait would have had a major role in doing more harm. The thought of those killers being in any position of authority made Tucker shudder.

But more than anyone else, Simon Cady had prevented Dowd's scheme from working. Sure, he was after the reward money from Ramona Hazelton, but more than that, he genuinely hated Zell McGinty and what he had done at Sand Creek. Simon said the massacre had haunted him at the time. And for many years since.

A brief flash of white hair through the trees on the far side of the stage station was the only sight of Simon Tucker caught as he waited for Simon to return. While he sat wondering what kind of man they hunted, Tucker took his Colt from the holster that he had smeared bear fat inside before he left. He cocked the hammer and blew dust from the action, from the trigger before loading a round into that last chamber that he normally kept empty under the hammer.

And even though Tucker knew Simon would ride in any moment, he still jumped when his bay broke through the trees. "He's there." Simon stepped from the saddle. "Been nursing a beer for the last two hours, so he's not as drunk as the station master figured he would be."

"What's your plan?"

Simon filled his pipe with tobacco and sat on a rock. "I've told the station master to quietly get as many people away from that saloon as he can without tipping off our man. The only other man inside that makeshift saloon is the bar dog. Believe it or not, I'd rather not ventilate some innocent bystander." He stood and grabbed the reins trailing on the ground where his horse grazed. "I'll ride around the station and approach from the back door."

"You want me to take the front door, where it's going to be more dangerous?"

Simon threw up his hands. "Sorry for me being old and helpless—"

"Helpless, my butt," Tucker said. "What *are* you going to be doing while I'm walking into a bad situation?"

"I'll come in the back door. Give me a few minutes to ride around back, then come in the front. With any luck, our man will be concentrating on you and not the back, and I can cold-cock him without firing a shot."

"That'd be a first for you," Tucker said, but Simon had already mounted his bay and started toward the back of the station.

Tucker waited for what he figured was fifteen minutes, giving Simon a chance to approach the saloon from the rear.

Tucker took the hobbles off Soreback and rode down the hill to the stage stop.

He had been through here once, when people wandered the grounds, going from one shop to another, station hostlers playing horseshoes in the middle of the yard, others taking a *siesta* in the late afternoon. But no one walked the grounds today. No one was foolish enough to be anywhere near the saloon with a shooting match about to happen.

Tucker stopped the mule at the blacksmith shop down from

the brewery with its tiny saloon and tied him to a rail. He took the hammer lock off and slid his Colt in and out of the holster, the bear fat making it glide easily. He walked the last few yards to the saloon and peeked through the open door. A man stood behind the bar, towel draped over his shaking shoulders. He stared wild-eyed at his lone customer leaning over the plank bar.

Tucker took deep, calming breaths as he stepped inside. As he looked around the small room, he realized there *was* no back door for Simon to sneak in.

Tucker was on his own.

"Don't know who the hell you are, mister," the man at the bar called over his shoulder, his voice familiar, "but I don't cotton to folks sneaking up on my backside."

"Simon Cady said you'd be here."

The man stiffened and stood slowly.

The bartender stooped low and duck-walked past Tucker and out the door.

The man set his drink on the bar and turned around, his long hair flowing past the collar of his duster. Trait McGinty eyed him for a moment before a wide smile crossed his face. "I asked all over about you," Trait said, moving away from the bar. "No one knew if you lit out of the country or not. I looked all over hell for you, but here you are. You're like an early Christmas present for me."

"Folks say you're a wanted stage robber."

Trait laughed and spread his feet wide. He pulled back his duster, his hand hovering over the butt of his pistol. "And now you're going to talk me into coming along peaceable like?"

"No," Tucker said and, in that instant, he *knew* that, even if Trait wanted to come in without a fight, he would not take him peaceably. Looking over his shoulder stopped here. Now. "I don't want you to come in."

Trait's smile faded. "They why are you here?"

"I'm here to see you planted in that cemetery out back."

"You think you can take me?" Trait asked, and for the briefest moment, his voice wavered.

He's not sure if he is faster.

Tucker bladed himself, making a smaller target as he stepped back as far as he was able inside the small room. *Get the other fool talking,* he had always known. If he's talking, he's not shooting. "Too bad about your old man. Would have been up to me, he'd've lived."

"That's sweet."

"Lived long enough to hang."

Trait's face turned crimson, and his jaw muscles clenched and unclenched. "Just for that—"

Tucker drew and dropped to one knee in a single motion. Even taking Trait by surprise, he had drawn and got the first shot off, grazing Tucker's arm before he felt his own gun jump in his hand from the recoil. And jump again as Tucker fired once more. Trait clutched his chest, his second shot kicking up the dirt floor of the saloon. He tried to say something, but he fell face-down, dead.

Tucker had to use both shaking hands to guide his Colt into the holster.

On wobbly legs, he stepped around Trait and walked to the plank bar, looking about.

"I'll buy the best in the house just because that was such good entertainment," Simon said. He walked through the door and shook his head at Trait's body. "Boy should have been drawing instead of talking." He brushed past Tucker and walked behind the planking. He selected a bottle of whisky, pouring two fingers in two shot glasses. He held one up and clinked his glass against Tucker's.

Tucker downed his whisky in one gulp, some of the brown

liquid drooling down his chin, and he wiped it away. "You *knew* it was Trait robbing the stages."

Simon nodded. "Let us say, I suspected, from the descriptions folks have been giving me."

"And you knew there was no back door to this building? You knew you wouldn't be able to help me once I got inside here?"

"Right again," Simon said.

"Put that glass down."

"What?"

"The shot glass. Put it down."

Simon shrugged and had set the glass onto the wooden plank when Tucker threw a hard-right cross that landed flush on Simon's chin. His legs buckled, and he backed up a step. He felt for the plank for support and didn't go down. "What the hell was that for?" Simon said, rubbing his chin.

"For not telling me it was Trait I'd find in here."

Simon filled both shot glasses again and took a chair beside the bar. "If I'd told you it was Trait been robbing the stages, you'd have worked yourself to a frazzle even before you came in to this saloon. And men with a frazzle-on don't think right. And they don't shoot right when they need to."

"If you knew it was Trait, why didn't you take him yourself? You got that ungodly-big buffalo gun good for a half mile."

Simon downed the whisky and motioned for the bottle. Tucker handed him the whisky before taking out his bible. When his hands shook so the tobacco fell out of the paper, Simon reached over and finished rolling the cigarette for him. "You would always wonder—until the day you died—whether or not Trait was the quicker man. If I killed him, you wouldn't ever have known."

"He was," Tucker said. He sat across from Simon, who handed Tucker a snotty bandana for his bleeding arm. He tied it around the grazing wound and looked down at the body.

"Trait was considerably faster than me."

"He might have been the faster," Simon said, "but he wasn't smarter. That was pretty shrewd, getting him to flap his gums like that before you drew." He downed the whisky, and some of the liquid trickled down his white beard. "You're the one standing. Don't make any difference who was actually quicker, now does it?"

Tucker held out his glass, and Simon filled it. "I suppose not."

"*Suppose* not?" Simon laughed and nodded to the body. "That there's the proof lying on the floor." Simon leaned down and rolled Trait over. Even in death, he displayed a look of surprised disbelief. "Only thing that matters is who'll still be on this side of the grass tomorrow." He nudged the corpse with the toe of his moccasin. "Trait, my boy, you are worth five hundred dollars to ol' Simon."

"Not so fast," Tucker said. "You didn't kill him. I did."

"A mere technicality," Simon said. "I found him."

"Then you should have brought him in or killed him yourself. He's mine." Tucker brushed past Simon. "Me and Jack figure on using that reward money to build up the ranch."

"Now wait a minute . . . you never hunted men for bounty before."

"And you never took another man along when you did," Tucker said.

Simon stood and paced the floor. "How's about a compromise?"

"I'm listening."

"How's about we take the body into Cheyenne and split the reward?"

"I got to get back to Jack. I have a ranch to help run. I got no time—"

"Then I'll take this bag of crap to Cheyenne and bring your share?"

Tucker mulled that over and decided it had no down side to it. If Simon went through with his promise to bring Tucker half the reward money, he and Jack *would* be living high, able to buy some more cows. Maybe another horse or mower. But if Simon never showed up with the reward, Tucker would never see the bounty hunter again. And that was all right, too. "You got a deal."

Simon smiled. "Then let me buy another round of this fine whisky."

"Why not?" Tucker held his shot glass. "You haven't actually bought any yet."

EPILOGUE

The following morning Tucker parted company with Simon Cady. He had tied Trait McGinty over a swayback horse—trading Trait's fine roan for the nag the station master had corralled. Plus some money to boot. Tucker thought he ought to have a cut of that blood money as well, but he never pushed Simon for it, was just glad to be rid of him, not knowing if he would ever see the vicious bounty hunter again. Even though a part of Tucker wanted to be rid of the man, a part of him would miss Simon.

As he left the Hat Creek Station, men played horseshoes in the middle of the compound, and a woman gathered eggs in the fold of her skirt. Two boys barely old enough to fiddle with a knife were playing mumbly-peg beside the telegraph office, while a hostler curried Trait's roan gelding the station master had dickered for. Trait McGinty would never see these things again, the deadly outlaw disappearing over the ridge on the back of the nag while Simon whistled as he rode.

Tucker hated to admit it, but Simon had been right about Trait all along—though Tucker resisted giving Simon any credit for it. Tucker *would have* wondered until the day he died if he was as good as Trait McGinty in a stand-up gun fight. Now Tucker knew, and he started shaking as he relived the gunfight. And though he never felt good about killing another man, there had been something satisfying in seeing the killer soaking up the dirt floor in that Hat Creek saloon.

Tucker rode as far as the Camp Collier stage station, but he didn't ride in. He needed to be alone, to think. People coming up to him and congratulating him for killing the stage robber was something he didn't want to endure right now. There had been enough back-slapping at Hat Creek when folks found out Trait was the killer and robber of the stages. One day, perhaps, Tucker would welcome the notoriety. But right now, he wanted the solitude of being with himself and his thoughts.

He killed a fat prairie chicken that evening and roasted it over a small fire. Indians were roaming hereabouts still, he knew, perhaps from the agencies. He wasn't going to help them to kill and scalp one more white man, so he kept the small fire under trees, any smoke dissipating in the low-hanging pine boughs.

The sun set slowly in this part of the hills. As he sipped the last of his coffee for the night, he thought back to the last few months since he'd been paroled from prison. Jack had so many lofty plans for them, dashed when his claim was stolen by the Flynns and McGintys on behalf of Perry Dowd. Right now, Tucker thought, that might be a blessing. Within the last couple of months, he had spoken with miners wandering south from the gold fields. The big mining companies—they said—had taken over Deadwood Gulch when panning for dust was no longer viable, even for men with high ambitions and strong backs. The big companies brought in the equipment and the resources to crush rock, and they used mercury to squeeze the last bit of gold from the granite sediment. Gold dust had died in Deadwood just within the last two months: Tucker and Jack had gotten away from there just in time.

Soreback snorted just as the sun peeked over the horizon, if there ever is a horizon in the Black Hills. The mule stomped his feet, eager to be back on the trail that would lead them to the ranch and lush grass.

Tucker made a hasty breakfast of jerky and weak coffee before swinging into the saddle. Soreback seemed to know the way home, and Tucker let him have his head, taking his time when it fancied him, picking up the pace when he missed home.

They had ridden to that tall ridge overlooking their ranch when Soreback set his feet solid, jarring Tucker's teeth and nearly throwing him from the saddle. "What is it?" Tucker asked, not expecting an answer, but knowing the mule knew something Tucker didn't—something he didn't like.

Tucker grabbed a piece of parsnip he had got from the cook at Hat Creek and coaxed the mule higher up. Even before they topped the ridge line, Tucker smelled what Soreback had balked at—smoke. Tucker reined the mule at the edge of the forest overlooking the ranch below.

The tent he and Jack called home before they got a chance to erect a proper house lay burned in the center of a hundred-foot black scar on the meadow grass where the fire had spread. The bull—their prized possession that would be the basis of their herd, lay bloated beside the tent, a dozen arrows sticking out of him.

A body lay partially buried under the tent. Tucker sucked in a deep breath as he spurred the mule down the slope. He took the Winchester from the saddle scabbard as he rode, expecting the worst.

Expecting Jack.

Tucker pulled up short and sprang off the mule, running to the body. He threw the burned tent aside.

A Lakota warrior lay facedown in the charred grass, the back of his head gone where a bullet had torn into him. Jack had gotten off at least one shot, but where was he?

Tucker stood and circled the camp, walking hunched over, studying the sign. Nine—perhaps ten—Indians had ridden down to the ranch from the east. Agency Indians? Tucker knew they passed through the Black Hills on their way to hunting grounds on the Powder River or the Shining Mountains to the west.

He widened his circle around the camp, avoiding a heifer riddled with arrows, and he spotted a plug of tobacco beside the critter. Tucker pinched the tobacco between his fingers— hard. It had lain here in the sun for a day. Maybe two.

Tucker spotted boot marks furrowing the dirt behind cattle being driven by the Indians.

He stood and looked to the west where the marks of cows and ponies and a man being dragged grew faint. Tucker imagined Jack—rawhide securing his wrists—fighting to keep up with the Indian ponies, fighting to remain erect without being dragged to death, and Tucker could only imagine what fate the Lakota had in store for Jack.

Tucker walked to where Soreback grazed at the edge of the meadow away from the burnt grass. "Sorry, my friend, there's no time to munch on grass right now," Tucker said as he swung into the saddle. "We gotta find Jack."

ABOUT THE AUTHOR

C. M. Wendelboe entered the law enforcement profession when he was discharged from the Marines as the Vietnam war was winding down.

In the 1970s, his career included assisting federal and tribal law enforcement agencies embroiled in conflicts with American Indian movement activists in South Dakota.

He moved to Gillette, Wyoming, and found his niche, where he remained a sheriff's deputy for more than twenty-five years.

During his thirty-eight-year career in law enforcement he had served successful stints as police chief, policy adviser, and other supervisory roles for several agencies. Yet he always has felt most proud of "working the street." He was a patrol supervisor when he retired to pursue his true vocation as a fiction writer.

He writes the Spirit Road Mystery series (Penguin), Bitter Wind Mystery series (Midnight Ink), Nelson Lane Frontier Mystery series (Five Star), and the Tucker Ashley Western Adventure series (Five Star).

The employees of Five Star Publishing hope you have enjoyed this book.

Our Five Star novels explore little-known chapters from America's history, stories told from unique perspectives that will entertain a broad range of readers.

Other Five Star books are available at your local library, bookstore, all major book distributors, and directly from Five Star/Gale.

Connect with Five Star Publishing

Visit us on Facebook:
  https://www.facebook.com/FiveStarCengage

Email:
  FiveStar@cengage.com

For information about titles and placing orders:
  (800) 223-1244
  gale.orders@cengage.com

To share your comments, write to us:
  Five Star Publishing
  Attn: Publisher
  10 Water St., Suite 310
  Waterville, ME 04901